THE
GIRLS IN
THE HIGH-
HEELED
SHOES

THE GIRLS IN THE HIGH-HEELED SHOES

AN ALEXANDER BRASS MYSTERY

MICHAEL KURLAND

TITAN BOOKS

The Girls in the High-Heeled Shoes
Print edition ISBN: 9781783295388
E-book edition ISBN: 9781783295395

Published by Titan Books
A division of Titan Publishing Group Ltd
144 Southwark Street, London SE1 0UP

First Titan edition: February 2016
1 2 3 4 5 6 7 8 9 10

Did you enjoy this book? We love to hear from our readers.
Please email us at: readerfeedback@titanemail.com

To receive advance information, news, competitions, and exclusive
offers online, please sign up for the Titan newsletter on our website:
TITANBOOKS.COM

To Linda...
...because

I am for Broadway when the moon is low
And magic weaves along the fabled street
For I can search for ghosts of long ago
When time was slow and violins were sweet.
And few there are who note the haunted eyes
That hint of dreams too gossamer to last
And few there are when youth and beauty dies
Who bar the benediction of the past...

Phillip Stack

INTRODUCTION

My father was a reader. He read everything from historical novels to detective stories to encyclopedias, even a few science fiction novels and an occasional racing form. And I grew up reading through his library, *Samuel Pepys Diary*, *The Saint Meets the Tiger*, *Adventures in Time and Space* (the Healy & McComas anthology that turned me on to science fiction— still a great book), *The Three Musketeers*, and whole shelves of wonderful fiction and essays from the 1930s. When I decided that I wanted to become a writer, at the age of 10, the people I wanted to emulate were Cole Porter, Samuel Hoffenstein ("the Poet Laureate of Brooklyn"), Noel Coward, Dorothy Sayers, Rex Stout, Dashiell Hammett, and especially Robert Benchley and Dorothy Parker. (And, I must admit, Mark Twain and Gilbert and Sullivan, but I digress.)

In my imaginings I would have an apartment on Central Park South, right across the way from George, or possibly Ira Gershwin, and spend the days in happy banter with Benchley, Thurber, Parker, and the staff of *The New Yorker*. In the evenings, if I wasn't attending the opening of a new Sam and Bella Spewack play, I would sit down at my Underwood Standard and type out deathless prose. If only I had a time machine. And, of course, modern antibiotics.

The Alexander Brass novels are the offspring of my love affair with the 1930s. I have him as a columnist for the *New York World*, a fine newspaper which, in real life, died in 1931 over an inheritance dispute, and which had a sign over the city editor's desk: "Never write down to your readers—anybody stupider than you can't read."

The title of the second book, *The Girls in the High-Heeled Shoes*, comes from a 1930s era toast my mother taught me:

> *Here's to the girls in the high-heeled shoes*
> *That eat our dinners and drink our booze*
> *And hug and kiss us until we smother*
> *And then go home to sleep with mother!*

Perhaps a bit non PC for today, but certainly heartfelt.

In the tales of Alexander Brass I have tried to recreate the feel, the atmosphere, of what it was like to be alive in the 1930s, to be part of a generation that was forced to grow up fast in the middle of a great depression, and who developed that rarest of talents, the ability to laugh at themselves.

MICHAEL KURLAND
12 February 2015

1

Two-Headed Mary had been missing for three days before anyone noticed that she wasn't around. Another day passed before her absence was taken seriously, and Cholly-on-the-Corner was sent to look for her. He checked at her usual pitches in front of some of Broadway's better theaters, and some that were not so better. He talked to the bartenders at the between-the-acts joints in which she was known to imbibe and the waitresses at Schrafft's restaurant on Broadway and 44th, where she was known to lunch. He spoke to some Broadway citizens who were known to be acquainted with the lady. He didn't find her.

Alexander Brass and I were having a late supper at the Knickerbocker Grill on 54th and Sixth and listening to Benny Goodman and his boys make music on the bandstand, which is, after all, Brass's job, and he is my boss, when Cholly came over to the table to tell us about it. "I am on da glim fer Two-Headed Mary," he told us, plopping into the empty seat at our table without bothering to ask. "She ain't been where she's supposed ta be at fer a nummer a' days now, an' some a' her friends ah startin' ta worry so's dey ast me ta put out da woid."

(That's kind of close to Cholly's diction, but I'd need to use the phonetic alphabet to transcribe it accurately, and I don't know the phonetic alphabet, so's youse will have to settle for something closer to standard English since de udder gets tiresome quickly.)

Brass took a bite of steak and chewed it thoughtfully. "That's odd," he said. "I don't think Mary has missed more than five matinee days in the past five years. She certainly never missed two in a row. She hasn't been seen around the Street?"

"She ain't been on the pitch anywhere what anyone's seen her at it. And she's kind of hard to miss."

"And she's not at home?"

"I don't know," Cholly said seriously. "Where does she live?"

Brass looked at Cholly and Cholly looked at Brass. Cholly is a big man, large in all dimensions; but you wouldn't call him fat. Not if you were standing anywhere within reach of his ham-sized fists, you wouldn't. He had been a prizefighter for a while, where he was known as Charles "the Mountain" Finter, and perfected the art of falling down. He fought some of the big names in his day: Dempsey, Tunney, and some others, and mostly he lost; but he quit one day when his head stopped hurting. "Your head's supposed to hurt when you get hit," he explained. "When you can't feel it, it's time to find another racket."

"Are you just passing the time," Brass asked, "or is there something you and yours think I should do about this absence?"

"I thought if you was to mention it in your column—you know, about her being gone—then maybe someone what has seen her might own up to it, her being missing and all."

We paused for a moment to applaud Mr. Goodman as the last exuberant riffs of "Sing, Sing, Sing" died away and he and his boys left the bandstand for a well-deserved break. Ambrose, our waiter, appeared at the table with a teacup and saucer, and handed it to Cholly, who took a careful sip from the cup and put it down.

"Prohibition's been over almost two years now, Cholly," Brass said, grinning. "You don't have to drink it out of a teacup any more."

"It is tea, Mr. Brass," Cholly explained, offering the cup for examination. "I ain't supposed to drink nothing stronger than tea. I got a ulcer, and sometimes I spits blood."

Brass sighed. "Drink your tea," he told Cholly. "I have no objection to putting an item about Mary in my column, but supposing she's gone off somewhere on private business and she doesn't want anyone to know about it?"

"Then she should of left word around the Street that she'd be gone," Cholly said seriously. "She knows she's got friends on the

Street what would worry about her."

My boss is Alexander Brass, and his syndicated column "Brass Tacks" goes out to a couple of hundred papers around the country and a few in Canada. He instructs his readers on the State of the World and reports on strange things occurring in distant places; but mostly he tells about happenings on the Great White Way and comments on the hijinks of the high and mighty; particularly those high in the hierarchy of the show business or mighty in the related fields of politics or crime. Within the past couple of weeks he has written about President Roosevelt, Dutch Schultz, Mussolini, Fanny Brice, Harpo Marx, the Prince of Wales, Billy Rose, and New York's latest phenomenon, Special Prosecutor Thomas A. Dewey (whom he referred to as "that dapper crime fighter," prompting a phone call from one of Dewey's aides wondering whether that was good or bad).

Brass fiddled thoughtfully with his brandy and water. "Who is it that is so upset at her absence?" he asked.

"Some of the chorines in *Dames, Dames, Dames,* which is at the Alhambra, put me on to it," Cholly explained. "You know she helps out the girls when they needs it. When a girl is between shows and hasn't got the rent or what to eat, she's good for a five-spot. Or when a girl has serious boyfriend trouble, like black eyes or a fat lip, Mary will call me and I'll go over and give the boyfriend a reason or two to keep his hands in his pockets."

"I didn't know you were so noble, Cholly," I said. "We ought to do an item on you."

Cholly swung around. "And maybe not," he said, holding his thumb an inch from my nose.

I raised my hands in quick surrender. "Sorry," I said. "It was just an idea. Besides, Mr. Brass does all the deciding around here, I'm just an errand boy."

"So Two-Headed Mary's been money-lender to the theatrical community," Brass mused. "I didn't know panhandling was so lucrative."

"Yeah," Cholly agreed. "Me, too. But that's what the girls tells me."

Cholly-on-the-Corner, now probably in his mid-forties, has become a theatrical hanger-on. But he is more than tolerated by those he hangs about; he is valued. It started when he quit professional boxing and became a carny attraction. He gave exhibition bouts, and offered ten dollars to anyone who could stay in the ring two rounds against him. "It could of been one round," he said, "but I wanted to give the audience their dime's worth." Then he got a job as a walk-on in *The Fighting Maxwells*, to add color to the prizefight scene in the second act. When Simon Wilder, the director, found out that he really had been a fighter, Wilder hired him to show matinee idol Walter Fitzbreen, who played Minton Maxwell, the hero, how to look like he knew what he was doing in the ring. When the show closed, after a six-month run, Cholly was hired by Jack Barrymore to be his personal trainer and keep him sober for a few months until he (Barrymore) went out to Los Angeles to make a movie.

By then he was hooked, and he spent his days in and about those legitimate theaters from 43rd Street to 56th Street, between Sixth and Tenth Avenues, that are collectively known as "Broadway." He did odd jobs, subbed for missing workers, chased away overly amorous stage-door johnnies, behaved with the utmost decorum at all times, and was absolutely trustworthy with whatever a producer or house manager or chorine chose to trust him with. He got his nickname because, when he wasn't in a theater, he hung out at a papaya juice stand on the corner of 54th and Seventh Avenue. There came a time when he was needed at the Belasco Theater regularly, and Eddie Panglitch, the house manager, would turn to someone and say, "Go and get Cholly on the corner and tell him I want him."

We chatted over a range of subjects while Brass finished his steak, and Cholly his tea. We discussed the attempted assassination of "the Kingfish," Senator Huey Long, last night in Baton Rouge. Some doctor had accosted the senator in a hallway in the state capitol and put a couple of bullets in his stomach. The doctor had promptly been blown away by three of the Kingfish's State Police bodyguards. Some people thought it was political; Long's populist Share the Wealth clubs were rising in membership and popularity, making him a powerful contender for the presidency in the next election. It was an open question as to whether the Republicans or the Democrats were more scared of him. The opinion of the local reporters, a cynical lot, was that he had hopped out of the wrong bed.

"I don't know why the guy shot him," Cholly ventured, "but I been reading about how funny it was that he went everywhere with his bodyguard, even into the Senate. But now I guess it ain't so funny no more."

We talked about the Max Baer-James J. Braddock title bout at Madison Square Garden a couple of months ago (Braddock won on a decision after fifteen rounds; Baer was gypped, Cholly asserted. Brass, who had had a ringside seat, agreed. I missed that one, but I agreed on general principles: I had met Max Baer and I liked him) and the Joe Louis-Primo Carnera bout two weeks later in the same arena (Louis K.O.'d the ex-champion in the sixth. He might become the next Negro World Champion, according to Cholly, if Braddock, the bum, agrees to fight him. Brass and I had both been at that one. Brass agreed with Cholly. I am no judge of such things, but from what I saw anyone climbing into the ring against Mr. Louis had better have made out his will and said goodbye to his nearest and dearest). The conversation then switched to the decline of the American theater for a little while, until Benny Goodman and his boys were making their way back to the bandstand. Then Cholly-on-the-Corner got up, solemnly shook hands with Brass and me, and departed.

"Well, what are you going to do?" I asked Brass.

"About what?"

"About Two-Headed Mary. Are you going to do a mention about her being gone?"

"Of course," Brass told me. "'Philanthropist panhandler missing.' My readers will eat it up. If she doesn't reappear soon I can do a paragraph on it once a month for the next year. Then, on the first anniversary of her disappearance, I'll write a full-column 'Mysterious Disappearance' story. Feature writers will add her to the pantheon of perpetual missing persons like Judge Crater and Ambrose Bierce. We can have the whole country out looking for her. Boy scouts in Topeka and volunteer fire departments through Ohio and Indiana will send out search parties to examine deserted quarries and peer down closed mine shafts. I wonder whether anyone has actually ever been found in a deserted quarry or down a closed mine shaft."

Brass sipped his brandy and contemplated the follies of the human race. "But it will probably amount to very little. The odds are that Mary is just sleeping off a binge in some Bowery hotel or smoking the dream pipe in one of those dives off Mott Street, and she'll show up in the next few days on her own."

"Maybe she's been carried off by Indians like Evangeline, or has ran off with her secret lover like Aimie Semple McPherson or stolen a bunch of money like Billie Trask," I suggested. "That should be good for some copy."

"'Evangeline' is a poem by Longfellow," Brass corrected me with the sigh of a long-suffering pedant. "You're probably thinking of Virginia Dare, who was the first English child born in North America. She vanished with the rest of the settlers on Roanoke Island sometime before 1591."

"That must be the lady I meant," I agreed.

Benny Goodman blew a tentative E-flat.

"And the fact that Miss Trask was working in the box office of the Monarch Theater and disappeared at the same time as the box-office receipts doesn't mean she took them. There are several other explanations for her disappearance and the vanishing money that are not being considered by the authorities, or by my fellow journalists."

"They might have information you don't," I suggested.

"I'm sure they do," Brass agreed. "They must know the color of the girl's eyes and hair, her weight, the names of her intimates, and what small town in Indiana, or wherever, she's from. But they don't know, and neither do you nor I, whether she has that money."

This was part of an ongoing discussion between us. We'd been following the case in the papers and speculating on it since the story broke. The consensus was that Trask had taken the money, but Brass has never been a consensus player. "She's been gone two weeks now," I said. "My bet is when they catch up with her, she's got the missing dough in her girdle."

"I doubt if she wears a girdle," Brass said. "Remember, she was a dancer in the *Lucky Lady* company until she hurt her leg."

"Well, at least I was right about Aimee," I said.

"At least," Brass agreed. "Let's hope Two-Headed Mary has a secret lover; I could do something with that. But right now I'm going on to the Stork Club. With luck somebody whose name is known to the common man will be throwing drunken punches at someone even more famous for insulting his wife or girlfriend, or Roosevelt, or the League of Nations, or Gypsy Rose Lee, and I'll have the opener for a think piece about the vagaries of human conduct. I feel like doing a think piece, it requires so little thought. You go on home, if you like."

So here it was a hair before one in the morning and my workday was ending. This is not a complaint. I value my job; and not just because in this month of our Lord September 1935, almost six years since the day immortalized in the *Variety* headline, WALL STREET LAYS AN EGG, an employer still doesn't have to advertise a job. He just has to go into a dark corner, make sure there is nobody in earshot, and whisper quietly up his sleeve: "I need someone to sweep the floor and lift heavy objects. I can pay ten dollars a week." Before he can make it to the front door, four hundred people will be lined up outside, politely, quietly, hopefully.

But I not only have a job, I have the job I wanted: amanuensis and legman for Alexander Brass. My name is Morgan DeWitt and I have worked for Brass since the week I arrived in New York four years ago with my suitcase in one hand and my diploma from Western Reserve College in the other, determined to write the Great American Novel before I was thirty. I am still working on the novel. I have five years to go. Wars have been fought and won, dynasties have fallen, obscure army corporals have risen to lead great countries in less than five years; so I still have a chance with the novel. Besides, would it be so bad if I didn't finish it until I was thirty-five?

Brass has warned me that working for him will ruin my writing style. He has also said that any writer who is conscious of his style as he writes is an inept farceur. I suppose both could be true. But I like my job. The hours are lousy, the working conditions vary from elegant to dangerous, the pay is barely adequate, even for a young single man with an English degree from a small college in Ohio as his only reference, but I have learned more about life— about people—each week I've worked for Brass than I would in ten years of doing anything else. I have dealt with gangsters and their molls, politicians and their molls, stars of stage and screen, con men, kept women, kept men, nightclub owners, nightclub singers, nightclub crawlers, doormen and princes, whores and princesses, and have discovered no universal truth, no rulebook for understanding humanity. But I have learned, faster and more directly than I could have elsewhere, that it is presumptuous for any man to assume that he understands any other man well enough to write about him; and ridiculous for any man to assume that he understands any woman.

Brass and I separated at the door; he grabbed a cab to the Stork Club and a night of listening to stars and starlets and would-be stars and their press agents and sycophants whispering boozy secrets in his ear. I raised the collar of my raincoat and pulled my hat down against the cold drizzle and headed for the 57th Street subway entrance. One of the city's saving graces is that the streetcars, buses, and subways run all night. The other is that, though New Yorkers know that their city is the center of the known universe, they are not at all stuck up about it.

Twenty minutes later I was home, which is a room in a brownstone rooming house on West 74th Street between Amsterdam and Columbus. I share the house with an ever-changing assortment of actors, actresses, dancers, singers, musicians, playwrights, waiters, waitresses, and other recent arrivals who are going to make it big in this city without a heart, or die trying. Sometimes reality is surprisingly trite. There is also a young lady who reads cards and tells fortunes at various restaurants around town, a retired New York cop who works as a guard at the Museum of Natural History, and a small-time bookie who works out of a cigar store on Broadway and 86th. My next-door neighbor is a retired circus clown named Pinky. An ever-changing slice of life, my rooming house.

There is a shared living room where people of the opposite sex can entertain each other, since propriety and Mrs. Bianchi, the landlady, discourage the mixing of the sexes in any of the upstairs rooms; brief visits with the door open are barely permitted. The room has an upright piano (no playing after 10:00 P.M.), a couple of couches, a few overstuffed chairs, some beat-up wooden chairs, a writing desk, and, at the moment I came into the house, a uniformed patrolman in deep conversation with Maureen, our resident card reader, on a couch in the corner. Since they were holding hands and gazing meaningfully into each other's eyes, I didn't think Maureen was in any great danger of getting arrested for fortune-telling, so I tiptoed upstairs and fell into bed.

2

To compensate for the late hours, I usually don't arrive at the office until between ten and ten-thirty. Brass tries to make it by eleven. Normally after I get up and ablute, I make a small pot of coffee and spend the next hour at the old Underwood on the desk under my window, working at my novel—can't be a novelist without writing a novel. But this morning I stared at the last page I had done—thirty-two—and decided to put aside the manuscript and let it age. Perhaps it would improve with age. It was a slice-of-life story called "So Breaks a Heart—A Saga of Broadway." It was about a young man who works for a famous columnist and what he learns about life and women and other things and how he has his heart broken by a girl who loves him but cannot be faithful to any man.

It was autobiographical, but it was sappy and it didn't read true. I think the reason truth is stranger than fiction is that when it is written as fiction, it is not believable.

When a random stranger—say someone you meet at a party—finds out you're a writer, even a would-be novelist like myself, one of the first questions is always "Where do you get your ideas?" My friend Bill Welsch, a regular contributor to *Black Mask*, claims they are mailed to him on postcards from a fellow in New Jersey named Bodo. The truth is that ideas for plots and characters are constantly flung at you by life, and your job is merely to catch them, sort them, and throw back the ones that are undersized. It isn't the ideas that are the problem, it's arranging them in a lifelike and realistic manner within the story. The task is one of selection, organization, and staying far enough removed from the material so that it will read like the truth. Truth in fiction is an artfully contrived facade.

I considered the problems of being a writer as I got dressed, and wondered whether *The Writer* or *Writer's Digest* would be interested in an article by one of America's major unpublished novelists.

I washed, brushed, and dressed in a brown single-breasted suit that said, or at least strongly implied, "man of the world," and had set me back thirty-five dollars, and was headed downstairs, trench coat over my arm, by quarter to nine. I walked along Central Park West, observing the pigeons, sparrows, squirrels, small children and their nannies, and other fauna, and thinking over the state of the world and trying to decide what sort of book to attempt next. Starting a novel is easy. Taking it to completion is, for me so far, a distant goal. Perhaps I should switch to short stories or squib fillers for newspapers. Who knows—I might write the Great American Squib.

My thoughts moved, mercifully, on to the missing Two-Headed Mary. The lady was a true Broadway character of the sort that Damon Runyon might write about. Telling her tale would present certain problems in delicacy and restraint, but Alexander Brass had solved worse. In his coverage of the Hall-Mills case a decade ago, he had managed to convey what the minister and his choir singer were doing in their time alone together with mostly biblical references, and without getting more than a couple of dozen letters from readers whose sensibilities were offended (but who nonetheless had read every word). Theodore Garrett, Brass's man-of-all-work, had done a montage of those letters, and it hung in the entrance hall to Brass's apartment.

Brass had two people working for him in his office on the sixteenth floor of the *New York World* building on Tenth Avenue and 59th Street. There was Gloria Adams, his researcher and copy editor, who doubled as the receptionist when there was any receiving to be done; and there was me. Gloria, whom I privately think of as the Ice Princess, is blond, five-foot-two, beautiful, and of indeterminate age. She can't be as young as she looks, and she looks far too young to be as knowledgeable and self-assured as she is. (If Gloria were to read that last sentence she would red-pencil it heavily and write something about "balance" in the margin. But I think it means what I think I want to say, so I think I'll just leave it alone.)

I got into the office about ten-thirty, nodded hello to Gloria, who was behind her desk in the front room, carefully hung up my tan British trench coat, which gives me that air of elan that I otherwise lack, and tossed my dark brown fedora on the hat tree. Gloria looked over my suit and gave me an approving nod. She thinks that people should always dress as though they are in imminent danger of meeting their maker, and will be judged 20 percent on their good works and 80 percent on their tailor. "Are there any news?" I asked her.

"Not a new," she responded. "But here's the mail." She indicated a wicker basket stuffed with envelopes on one side of her desk. It is part of my job to sort the mail and answer that part of it not destined for other ends. I took the basket and retreated to my little cubbyhole office in the short hall between Gloria's well-appointed reception room and Brass's vast sunlit chamber with a view of the Hudson River, which flowed past some three blocks away for Brass's personal amusement.

Brass came in about an hour later and settled in his office. I brought him the three letters that he had to look at, and placed them carefully on the blotter in front of him. He was staring out the window at the passing scene. A couple of old four-stack destroyers were puffing their way up the Hudson, working their way past two tugs that were pushing a long row of barges the other way. It was very nautical. Inspired, I snapped to attention and saluted. "Good morning, Commodore Brass," I said. "Ensign DeWitt reporting for instructions."

"Good morning, Mr. DeWitt." He turned to look at me. "Go keelhaul the mizzenmast. And don't annoy me until at least twelve bells."

"Aye, aye, sir," I said. I did a smart about-face and went back to my office to begin answering the stack of letters. A little while later I heard the steady clatter of Brass's Underwood typewriter over the intermittent clacking of my own. It was a sweet sound, the sound that paid my salary as well as that of Gloria and Garrett. It also kept Brass well supplied with those toys that made his life worth living. In addition to the cars—he now had six— he had recently developed an interest in science and scientific instruments. A couple of months ago he had purchased a six-inch reflecting telescope from a pawn shop—Brass was fascinated by pawn shops—and had installed it on the terrace of his Central Park South apartment. Last Tuesday night, he showed Gloria and me the moons of Jupiter with paternal pride. He had some old maps of Manhattan, purchased from a Cortlandt Street dealer, and was tracing the island's early streams and water-courses to find out what happened to them as the city spread its concrete around and over the original landscape. What, if anything, he intended to do with the water when he found it I don't know.

About an hour after the typing started, he called me in to pick up the column, triple-spaced just like a real reporter would type it, and bring it to Gloria for copy editing and fact checking. I was expected to read it and comment if I saw anything I didn't like, but usually he just glared at me or shook his head sadly when I did. Gloria's opinion he respected, mine he tolerated.

I paused at Gloria's desk to see if he had included anything about Two-Headed Mary. The opening piece said nice things about Senator Huey Long, who was not expected to live out the day. The piece on Two-Headed Mary was the third item, sandwiched between a favorable mention of Clarence Day's new book, *Life with Father*, and a long think piece on how the world was getting ever smaller, what with the S.S. *Normandie* just crossing the Atlantic in four days, eleven hours and thirty-three minutes, and the *China Clipper* flying boat going into regular service between San Francisco and Manila. The piece on Mary read:

THE GREAT WHITE WAY is missing one of its lights tonight. We know her as Matinee Mary and, in the casual, uncaring way of New Yorkers, know little more about her except that for much of the past decade this earnest matron in the print dresses and flowered hats has stationed herself outside Broadway's theaters during intermissions and dunned the matinee audiences for worthy causes. She learned what shows would open the purses and wallets of the audience and which would not, and stood, rain or shine, where she could do the most good. She has a kind heart, and has been known to help a chorus girl in trouble with advice, friendship, and perhaps a folded-up bill slipped into her hand.

But for the past week Matinee Mary has not been standing under the broad, protective awnings of the Broadway theaters, and no one seems to know where she has gone. Mary, the chorines at the Broadhurst and the Belasco miss you. Forty-sixth Street is a little darker without your smile. We hope you're o.k., Mary, and we want to see you back under the awning of the Majestic or the Alhambra with your collection tube and your sempiternal smile real soon.

"Matinee Mary" was a pretty good invention. Brass couldn't very well call her Two-Headed Mary in print, not without explaining the name, which wouldn't have been nice.

"So," Gloria said, seeing what I was reading, "Two-Headed Mary is missing. Maybe one of the audience members actually read what it says on that collection tube of hers."

"They might have punched her out," I said, "but they wouldn't have kidnapped her."

"You never can tell," Gloria said. That being the unofficial motto of the office, I couldn't argue with her. The joke is that kind, sweet Mary was a con woman. But she gave her marks a fighting chance. If anyone ever stopped to read the legend wrapped around her donation tube they would have known that this was no ordinary charity that Mary was collecting for. "Give," it said, "GIVE—for the Two-Headed War Orphans of Claustrophobia— Give—GIVE."

And thus her nickname.

The column appeared on Wednesday, September 11. By that afternoon we were fielding phone calls from actors, dancers, stage managers, and other people in "the business," as the showbusiness folk call their occupation, as though it were the only business on the planet worth considering. And a few from those denizens of Broadway whose professions couldn't be classified, at least not if they wanted to stay out of jail. None of them had any worthwhile information regarding Two-Headed Mary's whereabouts, but they all wanted us to know that they thought well of her. By the next morning, we had several letters from chorus girls, and one from a chorus boy, detailing how Two-Headed Mary had helped them with money, advice, or a place to stay when they were in need. I gave the letters to Brass with a note clipped to them that read: "St. Mary of the Grift. Maybe we should pass the story on to Damon Runyon." He walked by my cubical later and glowered at me and muttered "Runyon indeed," under his breath.

The next day, which would make it Thursday, at noon I was in the outer office discussing with Gloria the sensitive question of the acquisition of office supplies when the slender, well-groomed scion of the aristocracy, K. Jeffrey Welton, appeared in the doorway. He sported a red and blue striped tie and a red carnation boutonniere in the lapel of his gray cashmere suit jacket. His shoes were glossy black patent leather. His was the sort of elegance that makes we mere mortal men identify with toads; and we envy him but we do not like him. Women, I believe, feel differently—although how a woman can like a man who is habitually prettier than she is, I do not understand.

There are those who claim that the United States of America has no aristocracy; they are misguided. The Weltons and the Vanderbilts and the Astors and the Rockefellers and one particular set of Adamses and some Dutch families whose ancestors were burghers in Nieuw Amsterdam, and some others whose families have been here so long that their names no longer reverberate in casual conversation, are the American aristocracy. Some of these families are social, and are high up in the society Four Hundred, some irrepressible souls make up a part of café society, some pay lawyers and other servants large retainers to see that their names do not come before the public at all.

The Weltons made their money manufacturing shoes in Massachusetts. Welton boots covered the feet of both Union and Confederate soldiers during the Civil War, and American, British, and, it has been alleged, German soldiers during the World War. There was a congressional investigation about the latter incident, but it came to naught.

"Ta, all," K. Jeffrey said in his clipped, slightly nasal, aristocratic voice. He leaned on his walking stick and smiled into the room. "What's the good word?" Welton's father still made shoes, but K. Jeffrey had taken his pittance of the family fortune and shifted it from the shoe business to the show business. You can imagine how his family must have felt about that. But whatever they felt about his choice of profession, they couldn't argue with his success. He had come straight from Yale to Broadway and started in the esoteric field of play production about the same time I came to New York and began working on the Great American Novel. I had never gotten past page sixty in any of my attempts. K. Jeffrey had already produced four plays: one flop, two that just eked out their nut before closing, and a reasonable success. The success, the musical *Lucky Lady,* was even now in its sixth month at the Monarch Theater.

"Mr. Welton," Gloria said, smiling sweetly up at him as he approached her desk. "Mr. Brass supplies the words, we just work here. What can we do for you?"

"This bloody Mary business," he said, leaning on the desk and smiling down at Gloria. "Has she turned up yet?"

"Two-Headed Mary?" I asked.

"That's her," he agreed. "Very clever calling her 'Matinee Mary,'" he said judiciously, "but then your boss is a clever man."

"If she has reappeared we have not been told," Gloria said. "Would you like to speak to Mr. Brass?"

"Sure thing," Welton agreed. "If the old man is in, I'd like to chew the fat with him."

"I'll see," I said, rising from the chair I had deposited myself in upon Welton's entry.

"Are you in?" I asked Brass, who was staring out his window at something in New Jersey. "K. Jeffrey Welton would speak with you."

"What does he want?" He asked, swiveling around in his chair.

"He didn't say," I said. "Just that he wants to chew the fat with the old man. By which, of course, I knew immediately that he meant you. Sir."

Brass grimaced thoughtfully. "I'll come out," he said. "It will be easier to get rid of him."

Welton was leaning against Gloria's desk when we emerged,

watching her. His pose was artfully casual, but there was something about his look that suggested that Gloria was a piece of cheesecake and he had just realized he was hungry. Gloria, who was used to being a piece of cheesecake in men's eyes, was smiling up at him with a smile of devastating innocence.

Brass took in the pose at a glance. "Welton," he said. "There's a biblical injunction against coveting thy neighbor's employee."

"He wants me to star in his next show," Gloria said, batting her eyelids theatrically. "Little me! Imagine!"

"Get it in writing," Brass advised. "I'll have Syd negotiate the deal for you." Syd Lautman was Brass's attorney, and a very good and thorough one he was.

K. Jeffrey grinned. "You people don't let any grass grow under your palms," he said. "A little friendly proposition between a man and a woman, and all of a sudden it's a business deal."

"Predatory, we are," Brass said. "Ready to take advantage of the innocent Broadway producer. What can I do for you, Welton?"

"Mary," Welton said. "I understand she hasn't turned up yet."

"True," Brass agreed.

"The girls in my show are worried about her. They suggested I put up a reward for finding her. The idea being if I can do it for someone who's a thief, I can do it for someone who's a good Samaritan. And from the stories the girls tell me, Mary is an angel in disguise."

"A thief?" Brass paused. "Oh, that's right. *Lucky Lady* is your show. You mean the Trask girl."

"That's right. Billie Trask. Nice kid—I thought. Stole a weekend's worth of box-office receipts, among other things, and disappeared. I have posted—I guess that's the word, although I didn't actually post anything anywhere—a thousand-dollar reward for finding her and my money."

"Were the receipts that much?" I asked.

"A little less," he said. "Which means, if they find her with all the money, I won't quite break even."

Brass frowned. "Didn't you have insurance?"

"Sure. It covers the theater rental and utilities for two days. Paying the cast and crew and the investors, I'm on my own."

"Do you really think she did it?" I asked.

K. Jeffrey thought that over for a moment. "I certainly hope she didn't," he said. "As I say, I liked her. But the police think she did it. Apparently she had a secret boyfriend, and they think she ran off with him."

"Do you want me to put that in my column?" Brass asked. "About the reward for Mary?"

"What do you think?" Welton asked.

"Why don't you wait a few days? Perhaps she'll return on her own."

"All right," Welton agreed. "If you think so. We'll give her the weekend to show up. Listen, keep me informed, will you?"

"And you," Brass said. "If you hear anything about either of our two mysteries, let me know."

Welton nodded. "Turnabout, and all that," he said. "If it isn't one thing, it's another. Well, must be going. Ave atque vale, old amicus." And with that, and a wave of his hand, he was out the door.

"It shows," Brass said, "the advantages of a Yale education. One can say goodbye almost entirely in Latin."

3

Two hours later, Sandra Lelane came to the office. Gloria was off researching something about the Spanish navy for Brass, so I was sitting at the reception desk at the time. Miss Lelane was demurely dressed in a green frock that went well with her shoulder-length light brown hair and soft hazel eyes, and she was wearing what to my untrained eye looked like the minimum of makeup. If I hadn't recognized her I might have guessed her to have been a shop girl or a princess, and she would have done either very well. I stood up when she walked in. I would have taken off my hat if I were wearing a hat.

She approached the desk and the slight odor of lily of the valley came along with her. "I would like to see Mr. Brass," she said. Her voice was soft and pleasant, and lower than I remembered.

"You're Sandra Lelane," I said.

She smiled and the room got warmer. "You know me," she said.

"I have seen you," I said. "In *A ll the King's Horses* and in *The Good Word*. And you were at Ira Gershwin's birthday party last year. You sat on the piano and sang 'A Wonderful Party' and 'The Half of It Dearie Blues' and a couple of other of the Gershwins' stranger songs. I sat in a corner and worshiped you from afar."

"Good God," she said. "Next time come closer. A girl likes to be worshiped from close-up." She looked me up and down. "What's your name?"

"Morgan DeWitt."

"Well, Morgan DeWitt, now that you're close-up, I hope you like what you see."

"Even better," I said. "Excuse me for a second, I'll tell Mr. Brass you're here."

I tore myself away from the desk and went back to Brass's office. Brass was leaning back in his chair, his hands laced behind his head, staring at the large Pearson landscape on the far wall with a woods and a river in the foreground and a medieval castle sitting on a hill in the distance. As a fellow writer, I recognized that he was hard at work. "I hate to interrupt you in the throes of creation," I told him, "but you've got company."

"Have you ever considered," he asked me without looking away from the painting, "what a pointless and frivolous exercise we conduct daily from this office."

"No," I said, "not really."

"Well, consider," he said. "If you work on an assembly line making cars, it might be boring, repetitive, manual labor, but when it's done you have something: a car. You can point to it as it goes down the street and say 'Peer under that car and you can see the very bolt that I tightened.' If you write a book, as you keep threatening to do, someone centuries from now could crack it open and read of your ecstasies and sorrows. If you paint an oil painting, good or bad, people a thousand years from now could look at it and recapture some of the emotion that went into creating the canvas."

"Not if I painted it," I said.

"But we," he said, ignoring me, "we who write ephemera in the dailies for the masses, we see our thoughts converted to fish-wrapping or used for paper-training puppies within the week."

"Sitting in your penthouse all alone among your meaningless possessions, holding back the tears," I said. "Why it's enough to make a fellow drive his La Salle, or his Packard, or his Bugatti right into the Hudson River. Say at the City Island Boat Dock, where this fellow has been eyeing that forty-two-foot schooner."

"Sloop," Brass said.

"Certainly," I agreed.

Brass eyed me. "Sarcasm is a dangerous weapon in the hands of those unskilled in its use," he said mildly. "Why some are even foolish enough to aim it at the man who signs their paycheck."

"No!" I said. "What a thought!"

He shook his head sadly at my lack of respect. "Who?" he asked.

It took me a second, but I retrieved the answer to the question with the grace and finesse of Gehrig fielding an infield fly. "Sandra Lelane."

"The actress? What does she want?"

"Shall I ask her?"

He sighed. Forced to engage in conversation with a beautiful woman. "No, bring her in."

I marveled at the power of a verb as I went out to retrieve Miss Lelane. If Brass had said, "*Send* her in," I would have had to think of some excuse to come back in with her, but "*bring* her in" made it mandatory. I brought her in.

Brass rose. "Miss Lelane," he said.

She came forward and extended her hand. "Mr. Brass. You must call me Sandra."

While they shook hands I pushed a chair up to the desk for Sandra, but she remained standing.

"Thank you," Brass said. He didn't add "You may call me Alexander"; he doesn't like people calling him Alexander. (We won't even discuss "Alex" or "Al.") I retreated to a corner of the couch.

"Please do sit down," Brass said. He sat down himself to encourage her. "What can I do for you?"

She sat and crossed her legs carefully and smoothed out her skirt. "Help me find my mother."

Brass considered this for a moment. "Where did you lose her?"

She pushed herself halfway to her feet and then thought better of it and sat back down. "I'm sorry," she said, leaning forward, "but this is not a joke to me!"

Brass moved his arm in a pushing motion. "Sit back," he said. "I apologize for what must have sounded like a frivolous comment, but your request is not one that I was expecting. Losing one's mother is indeed serious, but why on earth did you come to me? The police have a missing persons department. If you don't trust in their perspicacity, I can recommend an excellent private investigation service. I am not a policeman, I am a columnist."

"I came to you because I can't go to the police, because I daren't trust a private detective, and because if it wasn't for you, I wouldn't know my mother was missing. You wrote about her in your column yesterday."

Brass allowed himself to look surprised. "Your mother? Two-Headed Mary?"

She leaned back. "That's right," she said.

"Well!" Brass said.

"I asked about you on the Street," Sandra said. "I was told that you were a straight joe; that you could keep a secret. Is that right?"

"That's a large part of my job," Brass told her. "If my friends and contacts didn't think they could trust me, they wouldn't tell me anything."

"That piece you did about Mom. You didn't blow her grift, and it must have been quite a temptation."

"It would be a good story," Brass agreed. "But everyone on Broadway knows she's called 'Two-Headed Mary,' and why, and none of them have told."

"Contrariwise," Sandra Lelane told him. "They tell everyone they know. I must have heard it a couple of dozen times, and nobody in the business knows she's my mom. But who are they going to tell that matters? The marks don't hear it. But you must have a million readers."

"Two and a half million," Brass corrected. He couldn't help it.

"Well. And most of them marks. I'm not saying they'd ride her out of town on a rail. But they'd come to look. In every audience there'd be someone who knew, and when they came out at intermission and saw her, the whisper would go around, and they'd all look, and no one would bite. Not another dime would go toward war orphan relief."

"I wouldn't go that far," Brass said.

Sandra leaned back in her chair, the fingers of her right hand drumming steadily on the arm of the chair, and stared at Brass. "So I'm going to tell you a few other things that I'd just as soon didn't come out," she said. "And you'll see why I want your help. And I don't want something for nothing. I hear a lot around the Street, and I'll trade you stuff you shouldn't tell for stuff you can use. Tit for tat. Can we do that, tit for tat?"

"A lot of my business is conducted that way," Brass allowed, smiling. "But we don't have to make it a formal arrangement. I will keep your confidences anyway, and if there's anything you think I might like to know at any time, I would like to hear from you."

"Okeydokey," she said. "But I pay my debts. Here's the pitch." She shifted in her chair and started drumming with the fingers of her left hand. "Mom and me, we haven't been what you'd call close for a while now, like maybe ten years. I left home when I was fourteen."

"What did you do?"

"I came to live in the city. Mom lives out in Brooklyn, would you believe. On Eastern Parkway. I stayed with a friend on the East Side and waited tables and studied voice and dance. I was in the business when I was sixteen, in the back row of the chorus of Ted White's Scandals."

"So you were working inside the theaters while your mom was working outside."

"Yes. You could say that, but she wasn't at the war orphan stand that much then. Mom and I didn't have a big blow-out or anything. I guess you could say we had a disagreement in the way each of us wanted to live her life."

"Your mother didn't approve of you going into the show business?"

"She was all for it. It was me who didn't approve of my mother staying in the grift. I refused to take money that had been earned in such an immoral manner, would you believe. I suppose I was a horrible prig at fourteen. Teenagers can be awfully moral."

"I supposed that's so," Brass agreed. "Those who aren't busy being awfully immoral."

"If you'll excuse me," I said, "bilking nickels and dimes from Broadway theatergoers doesn't seem to me to be a major crime." Sandra turned to look at me. "Back then, that was a sideline," she said. "She grew up on the grift, and by fourteen I wasn't so innocent myself." She switched her attention back to Brass. "When I was a kid Mom was one of the Professor's crew—you know the Professor?—and I was part of the background at a big store con for the first time when I was six or seven. By the time I was eleven, I was a capper. When the Professor didn't have a big store operating, there were dozens of short cons we would run, just to keep in practice. We did the badger game for a while. You'd be surprised how fast a mark will fork over his poke when he finds out that the jill he took up to his room is only thirteen."

Brass nodded. "I can well believe that," he said. He apparently was following all this, but I admit I was lost.

"Mom quit the heavy grifting a few years ago, and became Two-Headed Mary full-time. She'd been doing it as an occasional moneymaker for a long time; she got a kick out of dressing like a Scarsdale matron, and she worked the theaters between the big scores. But now, it was Christmas three years ago, she swore to me that she was done with all the big cons."

"And you're afraid that she's back at it?"

"It's not that. I'd be furious if she was running a big store or a golden wire, but what I'm afraid is that she isn't—that she has really disappeared—that something's happened to her. But I can't go to the police, or even the private cops, because suppose she has gotten herself involved in some major grift? I can't blow the gaff on my own mother."

"Why did she quit?" Brass asked. "Your moral influence?"

Sandra shook her head. "She let it be known around that she was afraid she'd lost her touch. But the truth was she was clearing too much money as Two-Headed Mary."

A silence followed this assertion. I was about to blurt out something like "Come off it!" or "Who ya kidding?" or "So's your old man," when Brass saved me from this social error by doing it for me.

"What kind of money are we talking about? Exactly how much does Mary clear in the average week?" he asked.

"Her name's not Mary, you know," Sandra said. "Her name is Amber—Amber Bain. My real name is Lucille Bain, would you believe."

"So." Brass leaned back in his chair. "What is Amber's kick on this two-shoes off-the-wall flim-flam?"

Sandra's eyes widened with approval. "You know the lingo pretty good," she said. "You ever been on the game?"

Brass grinned. "Bad boys led me astray in my youth," he said. "But I swear, Your Honor, that I'll never do it again."

"Would somebody like to tell me what you two are talking about?" I asked.

She turned to me. "Get your boss to tell you," she said. "He shows signs of having led a very interesting life."

"It gets more interesting with every passing day," I said.

"I'm not dead yet," Brass said, looking annoyed. "Back this conversation up a little and tell me what kind of money we're talking about here."

"I'd say Mom averaged a hundred and fifty to two hundred a week," Sandra said.

My jaw didn't actually drop with astonishment, but I'm sure that it wanted to. "I'd say I'm in the wrong business," I said. "Where can I get myself one of those collecting cans?"

Sandra turned around and considered me seriously. "Well, you're dressed well enough, and you look sincere enough, but I don't think you'd do that well. You could probably clear twenty or thirty a week, though, and a citizen can live pretty good on that."

"It's nice to know I have something to fall back on," I said. "How does your mother do so well?"

"I don't know for sure. I think it's the sincerity pitch. She looks like a society matron who doesn't need the money, so if she's willing to give up her afternoon bridge game and come downtown to stand out there collecting, it must be a worthy cause. So most people give her at least a dime, many give her a quarter, and some plutocrats have been known to stuff dollar bills into the collection tube. The people who go to the Broadway theaters are the people who still have jobs. Figure a hundred to two hundred people coming out at each intermission, and if she times it right, she can hit three or four intermissions a day, since they don't all let out at the same time. Then she can hit another two or three as the theaters let out after the show, although she doesn't do as well then; the people are in a hurry to go elsewhere."

"So she can clear, maybe, thirty bucks a day," Brass said. "You're right, that's a hundred and fifty a week, easy."

"That's my mom!" Sandra said. "Brave little woman out there, helping the orphans."

"Everybody is scamming somebody on Broadway," Brass said. "That's part of the romance that is this city; just ask Damon Runyon."

"Mom takes a wider view," Sandra said. "She says that everyone in the world is trying to con you or fight you, and that what separates us from the barbarians is that we've mostly taken up conning instead of fighting." She stood up. "I have to get to my matinee. Will you help me?"

"What is it that you'd like me to do?" Brass asked.

"I've been trying to call Mom's apartment for the past two days, and I keep getting a busy signal. The operator says the phone's off the hook. I'm worried. Come with me to Mom's apartment after the matinee. Maybe we can find some hint about where she's gone. I'd go by myself, but in case something, you know, has happened to her, I'd rather not be alone. And there's no one else I can ask."

"I'll go that far," Brass agreed. "I'll pick you up after the performance and we'll head over. Brooklyn, you say?"

"We can take the subway," Sandra suggested. "I go everywhere by subway."

"I don't," Brass said. "I have a perfectly good car. We'll use it."

"Whatever you say," she agreed. "I'll see you then."

She departed, leaving behind her an odor of lily of the valley and a puzzled Morgan DeWitt. "Will you explain that conversation to me?" I asked Brass, "and don't say, 'What conversation?'"

Brass gazed at me mildly. "Of course," he said. "Let's see now: a 'big store' is a con game invented at the end of the last century by the Gondorf brothers. It involves setting up an establishment, appropriate to the con, that looks so real and uses so many people that the sucker—excuse me, the 'mark'—can't even begin to think that the whole thing is a phony put-on just for his benefit. If the gang is trying to peddle paper-that is sell phony stock certificates—then the 'big store' will be a stockbroker's office, complete with ticker tapes, a tote board, ringing telephones, brokers, clerks, customers, messengers, and a security guard or two. If the con is a 'golden wire,' which is a sort of race-track scam, then the store will be a bookmaker's parlor, with the races being called on a loudspeaker, racing results being written on great big blackboards, customers eagerly betting, and so on."

"I get the idea," I said. "What about 'two shoes' and 'off-the-wall'? I can guess 'flim-flam.'"

"A 'two-shoes' is a phony charity, probably from 'Goody Two-

Shoes.' An 'off-the-wall' or 'stand-up' con is one that is done by one or two people ex tempore, as it were, with few props and no advance preparation. A flim-flam is a con game."

"That's what I thought. My mother would sure be proud, the things I'm learning."

"The badger game—"

"I know about the badger game," I told Brass. "Man, woman, hotel room, woman's 'husband' bursts in—man pays off."

"A classic," Brass said.

"Who's the Professor?" I asked.

Brass leaned back in his chair and stared at the ceiling. "The Professor is the master of the big store con," he told me. "He's a small, dapper man with, last time I saw him, a neat spade beard. He can look like a college professor, a diplomat, a bank president, a scientist, or whatever he wishes, and do it well enough to fool other bank presidents or diplomats or whatever. He's been around for at least thirty years, so he must be getting old and I don't know whether he's still in business. Legend has it that he has taken a couple of senators, an ex-governor of Ohio, J.P. Morgan and lesser tycoons of every description, at least one king Leopold of Belgium is mentioned—and several chiefs of police."

"What's his name?" I asked.

Brass shrugged. "The police believe his birth name to be Arthur Vincent Leidenburg, but he denies it and seems rather amused when the subject is brought up. Whatever his real name is, I doubt if he has used it in decades."

"You met him?" I asked.

"He was selling a friend of mine some stock," Brass explained. "I suggested that he find another mark. He was very nice about it. He said he was just bilking my friend as a sort of finger exercise, to keep in practice and keep his troupe busy while the heavy mark came back from Saint Louis or Sioux Falls or some such place."

"You didn't turn him in—have him arrested?"

"No," Brass said. He gave me a look that suggested that I should not follow that line of questioning any further.

Gloria came in, a stack of books under her arm. "I just passed Sandra Lelane in the hall," she said.

"She wants us to help find her mother," Brass told her.

"Oh," Gloria said. "Of course." She put the books on the desk in front of Brass. "The pages are marked." She nodded to me and went back to her office.

I stared after her. "Isn't she even curious?"

"The Swiss psychologist Carl Jung has a theory about something he calls the 'collective unconscious.'" Brass said, meditatively playing with the small ivory Chinese god he keeps on a corner of his desk. "Gloria seems to be tapped into that, or something very much like it. She regularly knows things that she has no way of knowing. Haven't you noticed?"

"I think she's just too stubborn to ask questions when she doesn't know something," I said.

"There's that possibility," Brass admitted.

4

Garrett was downstairs with the La Salle sedan at three. A large, ebullient man with a convoluted mind and a fondness for elaborate rhymes, bad puns, the Plantagenet dynasty, and things alcoholic, Theodore Garrett could have been a success at anything he put his mind to, but he refused to put his mind to anything more complex than the *Times* crossword puzzle or a few pages of doggerel verse. He worked for Brass as butler, chauffeur, bodyguard, and general factotum; a relationship based on a friendship that went back many years. Someday I would have to ask Brass how they had met. I had asked Garrett several times, each time getting a different and more fantastic answer. Once he claimed to have been sergeant-major of the relief column sent out to rescue General Gordon at Khartoum. They arrived too late to help Gordon, but Sergeant-Major Garrett personally saved a young street urchin who was about to be killed by the Mahdi's troops. "And, would you believe, that lad grew up to be Alexander Brass." Although the story was told with much verisimilitude, the fact that the massacre of the garrison at Khartoum took place in January 1885—I looked it up—would have put Garrett in his mid-seventies, and he looked to be no more than half that. Of course he had an explanation for that, too: "In my researches in the Himalayas I came across several strange and exotic herbs, which…"

Garrett threw himself into each of his roles with enthusiasm and an eye for detail. Today he was wearing a well-pressed chauffeur's uniform, well-polished black shoes, and his chauffeur's demeanor. He saluted us, two fingers to the brim of his gray cap, as we came out the door of the *New York World* building, and ran around to open the door. When we were seated, he ran back to the driver's seat, brought us smoothly into traffic, and headed down Eighth Avenue. At about 48th Street, we were slowed by the onslaught of cabs heading in to pick up the matinee theater crowd as they headed home. So it was a full fifteen minutes before we pulled up in front of the Royal Theater just as the last of the matinee audience staggered out the row of doors.

Among the things that mark the true New Yorker, as those of us who have lived here for more than two years are called, is the way certain place-names are pronounced. Houston Street in Greenwich Village, which is not named after Sam Houston, but Custis Houston, a gentleman of color who was a Revolutionary War hero, is pronounced "How-stun." The Royal Theater, named after Lillian Royal because her husband thought she should have a theater named after her, is pronounced "Roy-Al" with the emphasis on the "Al."

A four-by-six billboard to the right of the doors spread the title: FINE AND DANDY over a John Held Jr. drawing of a flapper and her beau energetically dancing what was certainly the Charleston. Over the title was MUSIC & LYRICS BY MAX OGDEN, under it STARRING JOHN HARTMAN & SANDRA LELANE. Below the dancing couple a blue banner said: SUCH SONGS! SUCH DANCING! THE TWENTIES ROAR AGAIN!!!! For almost two hours the show would take you back a decade to when everyone had money, or the hope of money, and the most pressing social issue was the length of the flappers' skirts. It was doing very well.

Garrett set the brake and turned to us in the backseat. "Queen Elizabeth," he announced, taking his cap off and running his fingers through his thinning hair, "was twice as good as Joan of Arc."

Brass chuckled. "I know you're an Anglophile, Mr. Garrett," he said, "but that seems a bit arbitrary and extreme."

"Oh, I'll grant you that Joan of Arc was a wonder, Mr. Brass," Garrett announced, "but Queen Elizabeth"—he raised two fingers in the air—"Queen Elizabeth was a Tudor!"

It hung there for a second. Brass leaned back in his seat and stared at Garrett, who had turned to face the front, his shoulders shaking with silent laughter. I snorted, feeling that peculiar mixture of admiration and disgust brought on by an outrageous pun. Why this should be, I do not know. Brass took a deep breath. "You are either a very troubled man, Mr. Garrett," he said, "or the most untroubled man I've ever known."

A couple of minutes later Sandra Lelane came from the alley leading to the stage entrance. She wore a brown knit dress and a large red head scarf or shawl, tied under her chin, and she looked as unassuming and unpretentious as only a truly talented actress can. The matinee crowd had disappeared by then, but by some strange mesmeric process, as she emerged from the alley a group of fans appeared and surrounded her, waving various objects for her to autograph. Most of her fans were young and female, and they had the energy and eagerness, as well as the simple wool skirt and sweater uniform, of would-be actresses. The few men—boys—in the throng had a similar, although gender-modified, appearance of apprentice thespians. Sandra chatted with them, laughed with them, nodded sympathetically with them, and signed whatever they thrust in front of her. It was about ten minutes before she made it into the backseat of the car. I moved to the front seat to give her more room.

"Hello, all,' she said. "I must be back at the theater by six-thirty. Will that be a problem?"

"No, mum," Garrett said, turning to smile a wide smile at her. "I'll see to it, mum, I will." He faced front and moved the car away from the curb.

Sandra stared at him for a moment then leaned back in her seat. "Can you find Eastern Parkway?" she asked. "The Brooklyn Botanical Gardens?"

"Yes, mum," Garrett said.

Two-Headed Mary lived in an apartment building across the parkway from the Botanical Gardens, which is cheek-and-jowl with the Brooklyn Museum; a fine institution of which most New Yorkers—that is Manhattanites—are unaware. Garrett pulled up to the awning and a doorman in the full-dress uniform of a captain in the Ruritanian Guard leaped out from the building to greet us. The wind tugged at his fancy dress-coat and almost blew off his buskin or taskit or whatever those high, fancy hats are called, but he clutched at it with his left hand while he held the door open for us. We decarred and staggered through the wind into the building. A small placard on a stand right inside the entrance informed us that this was OLMSTEAD TOWERS; 2, 3 AND 4 BEDROOM APTS and that there was NO VACANCY.

"I brought my key," Sandra said. "I think it's the right key. I haven't been here in two or three years."

I paused to stare in wonder about me. The lobby, a combination of rich, dark wood and gleaming white tile, with little niches along the wall for plaster busts of ancient Romans, stretched off a good distance to the left and right, uncertain as to whether it belonged in an English country home or Caracalla's baths. Four rococo-gilded chandeliers, each with a cluster of small round lightbulbs, distributed light and shadow along its length. Approaching us was a portly man with a walrus mustache who, by the coils of gold braid on his uniform, was at least a field marshal in that same Ruritanian Guard. His normal post, from which he presumably directed his troops, was behind an ornate Gothic gilt-filigreed lectern to one side of the door. A palatial lobby with attendants out of a Rudolf Friml operetta; we did not have such things in Manhattan apartment houses. "The glory that was Greece," I muttered to Brass, "the grandeur that was Brooklyn."

"May I assist you, madam?" the field marshal asked. "To whom do you wish to see?"

"Mrs. Bain, apartment seven-E" Sandra told him.

"I'm sorry, Mrs. Bain is not at home."

"That's all right," Sandra said. "I'm her daughter. I have a key."

A look of surprise crossed the field marshal's face, and was immediately suppressed. "Your name, please," he said.

"Sandra Lelane. The super knows me. That is if Norman is still the super. Is he around?"

The field marshal's expression now could have been either indignation or indigestion. "Madam, is this a jest?"

"Jest?" Sandra did her best not to look alarmed. "What do you mean?"

He took a step back and a deep breath. "Never mind. Mr.

Schreiber is somewhere about the building. If you will wait here, please." He left in a scurry for the distant left side of the lobby where they kept one bank of elevators.

"What do you suppose—," I said.

"I don't suppose," Brass replied.

Sandra clutched Brass's arm. "You don't think something has happened to Mother and they don't want to tell me?" she asked.

Brass freed his arm and put it around her. I wish I'd thought of that first, but then he outranks me. "Let's wait and see," he said.

About ten minutes later the field marshal reappeared with a small man in a wrinkled brown suit. "Normy!" Sandra said.

The brown-suited man held out both hands, which Sandra took in hers and squeezed. "Miss Lelane," he said. "It's truly nice to see you again."

"Normy, what's going on? Is my mother all right?"

"Yes. It's not that. Well, I don't know, I haven't seen Mrs. Bain in a couple of weeks. But—you see—well—"

Sandra tightened her grip on his hands. "A couple of weeks?"

"Well, something like that. But, I mean, she's been away a lot recently, so we didn't worry about it."

"What do you mean 'a lot'?" Sandra demanded.

"She told me she was staying with her sister who was sick," Schreiber explained. "Which is why I wasn't surprised."

"Surprised at what?"

"When you came by yesterday—but it wasn't you. Was it?"

"What are you talking about?"

The field marshal interrupted. "It's my fault, Miss Lelane. This young lady came by yesterday and said she was you. She said Mrs. Bain had asked her to drop by and pick up some belongings."

"And you let her go up?" Sandra asked Schreiber. "Normy, really!"

Schreiber gestured with his shoulder, his hands being occupied. "Ponce, here, Ponce the brilliant, passed her through."

Field Marshal Ponce lowered his head. "I'm real sorry, Miss Lelane. Mr. Schreiber wasn't around, and I'd never met you, and she seemed right. I mean, I knew you were a glamorous Broadway star, Mr. Schreiber talks about you all the time, and this lady was certainly glamorous. And she said she had a key."

"Let's go upstairs," Brass interrupted, "and see what this glamorous star was up to."

Schreiber led the way to the elevator, leaving Ponce to return to his gilded lectern. The elevator operator, a short, thin elderly man with big ears, stared intently at the front of the cage while he manipulated his gilded levers. The discreet elevator man is the employed elevator man.

"Could your mother be staying with her sister?" Brass asked Sandra.

"She doesn't have a sister," Sandra said, glaring at Schreiber's ear as the super studiously avoided her gaze.

Brass examined the outside of the door to Two-Headed Mary's apartment carefully before he let Sandra put her key in the lock. Then she opened the door and stepped into the small entrance hall, the three of us close behind her.

Sandra paused in the doorway and sniffed the air. "Perfume," she said. "Cheap perfume. Eau de tart. And that comic-operetta Falstaff downstairs thought the dame was me!" She clicked on the light switch by the door, took two steps forward and stopped. "What the hell?"

The clothes closet in the entrance hall had been emptied, and coats, hats, galoshes, and umbrellas had been strewn about the hall floor, along with a darts set, a Shirley Temple doll, and a croquet mallet. Past the entrance hall was the living room, which would require some work before it could be lived in again. Books had been pulled off the bookshelves that took up the wall to our left, cabinets had been opened and emptied onto the floor, cushions had been removed from the oversized couch along the back wall and tossed in a corner, closets had been dumped. The telephone, one of those ornate instruments called a "French phone," was on the floor in front of its little table inside the living room door; the body sprawled to the left and the handpiece to the right. Brass picked up the phone, united its two halves, and replaced it on the table. "I take it this is not an example of your mother's housekeeping," he said.

"Mom is fanatically tidy," Sandra told him. She crossed the living room to another door and disappeared down a hallway. After a moment she reappeared in the doorway. "They're all like this," she said, "all the rooms. Why the hell would anyone…" She disappeared back down the hallway again.

Schreiber stood in the living room doorway and was staring angrily down at the mess in front of him. "This is an outrage!" he said firmly. He raised his voice. "An outrage!" He bellowed into the other room, "Don't worry, Miss Lelane, I'll call the police. Then I'll send a crew up to clean this mess. Don't worry about a thing."

"Not just yet, please, Mr. Schreiber," Brass said, coming over and putting a hand on Schreiber's shoulder. "No police yet. We'll tell you when. And please, as a favor to Miss Lelane and her mother, don't tell anyone about this. We'll keep it our secret for now."

Schreiber glared pugnaciously at Brass. "Will we?" He asked. "And just who are you?"

"My name is Alexander Brass, and this is Mr. DeWitt. We're friends of Miss Lelane."

"It's all right, Normy," Sandra said, appearing in the doorway. "Mr. Brass is right. Let's not make a fuss about this."

"If you say so," Schreiber said, but he clearly was not convinced. He stared about him indecisively for a moment and then made up his mind. "I'll be downstairs," he said. "I'll see you again before you leave." He tiptoed around the debris and left.

"I think Field Marshal Ponce is in for a hard time," I opined.

Brass crossed the room and squatted amid the pile of books that had been pulled from the bookcase. "Mary—you don't mind if I keep calling her Mary, do you?—had quite an eclectic taste in her reading," he said, picking up some of the books at random and looking at them. "Jane Austen, Dos Passos, Shaw, Cervantes, Mark Twain, Edgar Wallace, Dorothy Sayers, Dawn Powell…" He cleared a space and sat on the floor. He was lost in the world of books, and it would be some time before he emerged. Brass treated books with the same reverence with which he treated women; and if there was anything he held in higher regard than books or women, I had not noticed it in the four years I had worked for him.

I followed Sandra back into the interior of the apartment as she stalked from room to room surveying the damage. There were eight or nine rooms, including a dining room, two bedrooms, a butler's pantry, and a maid's room with its own bath off the kitchen. I was gaining more respect for Brooklyn. "Swell digs," I told Sandra.

She glanced at me. "Not at the moment," she said.

Sandra went through the rooms slowly, touching this and that, straightening an occasional object, checking some of the things to see if they were broken, and cursing under her breath when one of them, an oversized cup that, for some reason was in her mother's bedroom, proved to be cracked. None of the rooms had been spared the vandal's touch, and no object was too small to have been dumped onto the floor.

The door to the other bedroom was closed, and I had a momentary queasy feeling opening it, remembering that the last time I had viewed a ransacked apartment there had been a corpse behind one of the closed doors. But this one was merely a continuation of the established theme, two dressers with drawers pulled out and piled by the bed, and a tangle of sheets, pillowcases, clothing, and cosmetics on the bed. "Your room?" I asked Sandra.

"A long time ago," she said. She went over to the bed and stared down at the jumble. After a moment she reached down and retrieved a much-worn stuffed animal of indeterminate species, and clutched it to her chest. "Binny," she said defensively, eyeing me as though she thought I was going to protest at a grown woman clutching a stuffed toy. "It's my Binny."

"Your Binny?"

"That's a good sign," Sandra said.

"Of course it is," I agreed. We continued our perusal of the wreckage.

"She was looking for something," Sandra said as we rounded back to the living room. "But she didn't find it."

Brass was still on the floor, leafing through the pile of books. "Something small," he said. "Whoever did this looked through all the books, and you can't hide anything large in a book."

"You could cut out the inside and glue what's left of the pages together," I suggested. "I've seen that."

Brass looked pained. "But still," he said, "some of the books that have been examined are quite slender."

"Perhaps she merely looked at the shelf behind them," Sandra suggested.

"No," Brass said. "Watch." He got up and stuck some books back on the shelf. "If she, or, I rather suspect, they, were merely vandals or had just wanted to search behind the books"—he brushed the books aside, and they scattered to the floor, several landing facedown and open and one losing its dust jacket.

Brass quickly retrieved the books and gently closed them. "Oh pardon me thou crumpled piece of print," he said.

"Mr. Brass feels about books the way mother eagles feel about their eggs," I told Sandra.

"But these books were not scattered,' Brass said, carefully returning the books in his hand to a shelf, "they are in a pile, where each was dropped after it was gone through." He demonstrated, leafing through a copy of *The Maltese Falcon* and dropping it on the pile by his side. "Our vandals were searching for something that could be hidden in a book."

"Like what?" I asked, "the deed to the silver mine?"

"Knowing my mom," Sandra said, "it could be exactly that. The greatest silver mine in all the land, hitherto kept secret and out of production by the big silver interests. But now the Colonel is determined to give the little guy an even break."

"What colonel?" I asked.

"It doesn't matter. And the stock will be printed on thick, creamy paper. And the company will have an evocative name."

"Evoking what?" Brass asked.

"Trust," Sandra said. "Trust and great wealth. Like 'The Prince of Wales Mine,' with his portrait on the certificates—after all, he does have an American girlfriend, or 'The Four Kings and an Ace Mine'—names suggesting that the property was won in a card game are very effective or 'The Silver Bullion Mine.'"

"What makes you think they didn't find what they were looking for—whatever it is?" I asked.

"Simple," Brass answered for Sandra. "Our searchers have torn the whole apartment apart. If they had found whatever they sought, they would have stopped there."

"Right," Sandra said.

"Of course," I agreed.

"But they didn't get Binny!" Sandra hugged her well-worn stuffed animal with the innocent, all-encompassing pleasure of an eight-year-old.

Brass shelved a few more books and turned to look at Sandra.

"Is that a bear?" he asked politely.

"Binny's a raccoon," she told him.

"Binny?"

"As in bindle," she told him, holding up the beast for his examination.

"Ah!" he said. "A bindle. And is it?"

I dropped into a clear spot on the sofa. "A what?" I asked.

"It's been my mom's bindle for twenty years," Sandra said.

"And they went right by it."

"As they were supposed to," Brass said. He turned to me and lectured—his favorite sport: "'Bindle' is a Carny term for a container holding your most precious possessions. It's the bag of stuff you grab when your hotel room catches on fire. Hobos use the word for the sack holding all their worldly goods, since they have so few of them. If the sack is tied to the end of a staff, so they can carry it over their shoulder, the staff is called a 'bindle stiff.' In the grift a bindle is where you hide your poke, which makes it the repository for your secrets. I've always been fascinated by the way in which words take on divergent meanings according to the users' needs."

"Me, too," I said.

"When I was a little kid Mom figured that one of my stuffed animals was a great hiding place. Let's see if Mom has any secrets worth hiding these days." Sandra parted the fur over the fuzzy beast's stomach and unzipped a very thin zipper about four inches long, which had been cleverly concealed by the joint where the right leg joined the body. Reaching in to the body cavity, she removed four bankbooks and a small piece of yellow lined paper folded into quarters. We waited with well-concealed impatience while she examined her find.

She riffled through the bank books one by one and whistled sharply through her teeth. "Either the Orphans of Claustrophobia are doing even better than I thought, or Mom has taken up another hobby," she said, passing the books to Brass. "There's something over twenty thousand dollars in these."

"A healthy nest egg," Brass agreed. "What's on the sheet of paper?"

She unfolded it. "It looks like an address."

"Could it be where she is?" I asked.

"I don't know," Sandra said.

Brass took the paper and looked at it. "Four-sixty-four Fenton. Does it mean anything to you?"

"No. I don't even know where that is."

"It conveys nothing to me either, but since she kept it carefully hidden, it must mean something," he said, handing it back. "I assume this means that your mother wasn't planning to stay away, or she would have taken Binny—or his contents—with her."

Sandra Lelane stuck it and the bankbooks back into the raccoon, zipped it closed, and stuffed it into her oversized handbag. "I hope nothing's happened to her, damn her!"

Brass took her hands in his and searched her face. "Are you all right?"

"I'll be okay. It's just—"

"We'll find her," Brass said. "At least we'll give it a damn good try. This, here, proves nothing except that someone who knew Mary wasn't home thought she had something she wanted."

"But whoever it was had a key."

"I don't think so. What she had was a lock pick. There were slight scratch marks around the keyhole."

"Oh. What does that mean?"

Brass shook his head. "Presumably that whoever entered here didn't have your mother's keys, but beyond that I have no idea. Incidently, do you have a recent photograph of your mother?"

"There's probably one in her bedroom," Sandra said. "Give me a moment." She disappeared back into the interior of the apartment. A couple of minutes later she was back with an 8 x 10 photograph in stiff cardboard folder with the emblem of the Stork Club embossed on the cover. "This must be a recent one," she said.

Most of the big nightclubs have house photographers; girls in brief costumes who come around and take your picture while you eat or dance or gaze soulfully into the eyes of your date. It's a way of proving to the crowd back home that you were a big sport while visiting the big city. It costs five bucks a snap, and we blasé Gothamites usually don't want to pay the tariff for a picture of us looking soused with a woman who is probably not our wife.

This photograph was a close shot of a man and woman sitting

at a table against the wall. The man was wearing a tux, and had his face turned to whisper into the woman's ear, so I couldn't really tell what he looked like. The woman had on a low-cut evening gown with puffy shoulders and was very attractive. She might have been as old as forty, but I would have bet on a good five years younger. She was laughing in the photo, presumably at whatever the man had just said. She looked like she had a great laugh. "Is that your mom?" I asked.

"Yes."

"A very good-looking lady."

"Yes."

"She doesn't look like the same woman I've seen outside the theaters."

"That's her matron disguise," Sandra said, handing the photo to Brass. "This is her glamour girl. She has a different look for all occasions, my mother."

"Who's the gentleman with her?" Brass asked.

"I have no idea."

We went back downstairs to find Schreiber by the gilded lectern, engaged in discussing Field Marshal Ponce's sins with him in a fierce murmur. Ponce's ears were red and as we approached he suppressed a sniffle.

Brass stopped at the lectern. "A word with Mr. Ponce, if you don't mind," he said.

"Why not?" Schreiber said. "I've had a few words with him myself."

Brass turned to Ponce and smiled reassuringly. Ponce didn't look reassured. "Could you describe the young lady who impersonated Miss Lelane?" Brass asked.

Ponce raised a hand in front of him, palm down, as high as his collar, and squeaked an unintelligible squeak.

"Take a deep breath," Brass said. "Take two. Then speak."

Ponce breathed. "Blond, she was," he said. "Very blond. About this high." He wiggled the fingers of his extended hand.

Brass estimated. "About five-foot-four."

"I guess. A red dress, not too long, you know what I mean, and a fur wrap. Like a lady. With a lot of makeup, but, you know, tastefully applied. Like the girls at Leon's Tip-Toe Inn."

Sandra snorted. "A blond bimbo with a painted face, and he thinks it's glamorous."

Ponce tried to find a place in his shoulder to hide his head.

"Was she alone?" Brass asked.

"There was a gentleman with her."

"Ponce!" Schreiber uttered. "You didn't say—"

Ponce shifted uncomfortably. "Well, I forgot, what with everything."

Brass said, "Describe the man."

"Short. Very short. Shorter than the lady. Thin. With a nose." He indicated a nose with his fingers. "Well dressed, in a dark suit and tie and everything."

"Everything presumably means he was wearing shoes," Sandra said.

"Black shoes," Ponce agreed.

Sandra snorted again. "I have to get back to the theater," she said.

Brass turned to Schneider. "Could you change the locks on the apartment?" he asked. "Don't clean up inside yet."

"I'll do that," Schreiber agreed.

"Thank you Normy," Sandra said.

"I hope your mother's okay," he said.

"So do I," she said.

5

We dropped Sandra off and returned to the office; Brass to his great oaken desk to stare out at the Hudson and seek inspiration for his next column, and I to my tiny cubicle with its large but ancient Underwood to resume answering letters, one of the more important and occasionally more interesting parts of my job. Brass believes that all mail from his readers that can be answered should be answered, and that the answers should be concise, honest, courteous, and grammatically correct.

We keep a log of what subjects the letters are on and what column they are in response to, if it's possible to tell. In today's mail there was a letter from a man named Pruex in Iowa who had read that "they" were going to saw Manhattan Island loose from its moorings, tow it into the harbor, and then turn it around and bring it back so that the Battery would be at the north end of the island and Washington Heights at the south. He claimed to be "apprised and acquainted with the use of the two-man cross-cut saw," and could supply his own partner, and wanted to know to whom he would have to apply to get a job. He did not say where he had read this information or who "they" were. I wrote him back that Mr. Brass would certainly look into it and that any information concerning the renovation of Manhattan Island would appear in his column, which Pruex should keep reading regularly.

There was also a missive from a gentlemen named Dochsmann, given name at the moment 279894, who was a guest of the state of New York's resort facility at Sing Sing for the next eight to twenty years. In three neatly typewritten pages, he claimed a complete lack of connection with the actions for which the state had awarded him his rent-free home on the Hudson and asked Brass to look into it. We averaged two or three letters a week much like this, except that most of them were not typewritten but were laboriously printed in pencil on lined paper, and Brass took them seriously. He and five companions, including another journalist, a retired judge, a police inspector, a detective-novel writer, and one of New York's leading defense attorneys, made up the Second Chance Club, which gave some few people convicted of serious crimes one last shot at proving their innocence. It also gave Brass enough material for four or five columns a year, but he might well have done it anyway.

All the Second Chance letters were looked at by all the members of the club. If four of the six agreed, then the case was looked in to by a private detective or a reporter paid for by the Club. If there was something to it, it came before the group again, and if all six agreed, they took up the case. Of the fourteen cases they had handled so far, six men had been retried and freed, two had been pardoned by the governors of their states, two had been determined by the Club to actually be guilty, one had been found guilty at his second trial—although the Club collectively still believed him to be innocent—and three were still pending.

I had a personal letter in the stack, from a young lady named Elizabeth who was now in Switzerland at a very expensive clinic becoming cured of some very personal problems, one of which, according to her father, the senior senator from New Jersey, was me. I didn't much care for the senator either.

Elizabeth had been gone a couple of months and was probably not coming back, at least not to me, but I was not yet over her or our relationship. When I thought of her, I still felt as though a healthy, energetic mule had just kicked me in the stomach, but luckily I didn't think of her more than about twice a minute. We had both agreed before she left, even without her father's prodding, that separation was the wisest course. Unless I had jumped on the next boat to Switzerland, where I don't speak any of the languages and would be unemployed, separation was unavoidable; but it did feel slightly better to have been consulted. Along about six-thirty, when I was beginning to consider calling it a day and wondering what to do with the evening, Gloria the Ice Princess came to the doorway of the little cubicle I like to call an office. "How would you like to take me out tonight?" she asked. "To the theater?"

"Be still my heart," I said, making a vague gesture toward the appropriate area of my chest.

She smiled a chill smile. "Mr. Brass wants us to talk to the gypsies in a couple of shows and see if we can get a line on Two-Headed Mary; find out what she's been doing, who she's been talking to. He'd like us to see if we can pin down the last time anyone actually spoke with her."

"Gypsies," for the benefit of you who are not denizens of the Great White Way, are the boys and girls in the chorus lines of Broadway musicals.

"Are we to be permitted to actually see a show?" I asked.

"Sandra Lelane sent Mr. Brass house seats for tonight's performance of *Fine and Dandy*," Gloria told me. "He can't go since he and Winchell and Bob Benchley and Dorothy Parker and a couple of dozen other journalists and magazine types are dining with the Honorable Fiorello LaGuardia tonight, and Hizonner might say something notable or quotable, so he has passed them along to us. We are to start our research after the show."

Gloria had a dinner date with a girlfriend and then had to run home and change clothes. I couldn't see why; the blue frock she was wearing looked sufficiently elegant to me, but then men never understand these things. I would have to change clothes myself anyway. For most men, a plain dark suit would do for the theater, unless it was opening night, but Brass believed in the old virtues like wearing evening garb to evening events: dinner jacket, boiled shirt, black bow tie and all. And I, as his amanuensis and dogsbody, could do no less. We arranged to meet at the theater.

I addressed an envelope for my last letter, added it to the stack, took a sheet of three-cent stamps out of the drawer, and spent a minute licking and pasting. Then I draped a cover over the Underwood, donned my coat and hat, thrust my afternoon's work down the mail chute, and allowed Mel the elevator boy to take me down to the lobby. I crossed Tenth Avenue to Danny's

Waterfront Café on the corner of Fifty-ninth right across from the *World* building, where I sat down to the roast beef dinner with mashed potatoes and gravy and okra and a couple of Danny's fresh-baked rolls.

After the main course, I had a slab of apple pie and chatted with the boss. Danny is about a one-third owner of Danny's, and is gradually buying the other two-thirds from her father, Manny, who claims that he is retired. He comes in two or three times a week to be helpful, which consists of telling Danny what she's doing wrong and how she could do it better, and every night she prays to God that he'll get himself a hobby or a new girlfriend, or be struck dumb. Occasionally, when he's being very helpful, she prays that he'll get hit by a truck.

We traded gripes for a while, then I got up and put a couple of quarters on the table. "Keep the change," I said.

I went home to put on my monkey suit.

Pinky, my next-door neighbor, followed me into my room. A retired circus clown in his mid-seventies with a story for every occasion, most of them involving circus people and their tenuous relationship with the mundane world outside, he had become a close friend in the two years I had been living in the rooming house. "So how're you doing, already?" he asked, perching on the edge of my bed.

"Not bad," I said. "You?"

"Can't complain. Can't complain." He held both hands up, palms toward me. "Look at this," he said. "Maple syrup and vinegar. Wonders, it does. Two tablespoons three times a day."

"For what?"

"The rheumatism." He waggled his fingers at me. "Just a touch, but it was slowing me down. A clown needs his fingers. Can't make balloon animals without your fingers. But this stuff— maple syrup and vinegar, with just a touch of cod-liver oil for the emulsification—does the trick. Fellow at Clown Hall told me about it. Syd Lester. Great walkabout clown. Been using the stuff for years. Swears by it. He's ninety-two. Says he's only eighty-four, but he's ninety-two."

"Clown Hall?"

"The Automat over on Seventy-ninth off Broadway. Lot of

circus folk hang out there. We call it Clown Hall. You ought to come by some afternoon while we're chewing the fat. Lot of stories there. Lot of material for that column your boss writes. 'Course if you ask questions, they clam up; it's the way they are. A fellow could learn a lot if he keeps his ears open and his mouth closed. Come on over with me sometime, I'll introduce you around."

"Thanks," I said. "I'll do that." I adjusted the knot on my bow tie and stood back to admire the result in the mirror over the dresser.

"You going somewhere?" Pinky asked.

"Going to see a play. *Fine and Dandy* at the Royal."

"Seen it," Pinky said with feeling. "Many young girls running around in skimpy costumes. Yaketta yaketta. Dancing. Step-kick, step-kick, like that. The Charleston. Skirts flying. Showing a lot of leg clear up to the pupik."

"That sounds right," I agreed cautiously, deciding not to ask him where one kept his or her pupik.

"I liked it." He nodded. "Gets the blood moving. When you're my age it's not a bad thing to get the blood moving every once in a while."

"It's good at any age," I said.

"As I remember, the girls in the side-show in the Hays Traveling Circus and Carnival showed a lot more than that," Pinky said. Many of his best stories started with "As I remember." And he remembered everything.

"'Course most of them wasn't that good-looking. But when they're young and pretty near naked, a fellow don't notice their looks in any kind of detail. I remember there was this one girl—Flossie, we called her—who joined the show in Cleveland back in 'sixteen or 'seventeen. She—"

"I've got to go," I said, grabbing my black Homburg—Homburgs were in this year, toppers were passé—and heading for the door. "Finish your story when I get back."

"I will," Pinky promised. He smiled. "I think I'll just spend some time thinking about Flossie, now that I've got her on my mind."

I got off the subway at Forty-second Street and, after performing my usual obeisance to Times Square, walked up Broadway to Forty-fourth. The sights, sounds, and smells of the Great White Way fill me with a sense of wonder no matter how many times I experience them. This great outdoor cathedral to Mammon and the arts is vibrant and alive twenty-four hours a day, and the bright lights drive away the night. When I first arrived in Gotham fresh from Ohio, the hayseeds still scattered through my hair, I could stand for an hour at a time in front of the *Times* Building and stare uptown, past the giant billboards, past the brilliantly lit marquees for the Paramount, the Loews Criterion, the Loews State, and feel a part of the great, vibrant living organism that is Broadway.

Now that I am a native New Yorker—having been here four years—I still stop and stare, and I am still awed. As I walk past the Rialto and the Nora Bayes and the Schubert and Broadhurst Theaters, I remember all the clichés and feel all the trite emotions that playwrights are always putting into plays about the theater. Kids from all over America do come to New York every year trying, hoping to make it in the theater. Most of them find other jobs or go home in a few years, crushed or strengthened by the experience according to what they brought to it and just what hand was dealt them. Some of them make it big, some make it just enough to keep trying, and some keep trying regardless. Broadway is a lure and a trap and a soul destroyer, and yet it is a myth-maker and a spirit-lifter and a magical land and the greatest place in the world for those with enough talent—or luck—to make their mark. But enough about me.

It was about quarter past eight when I got to the Royal Theater. The audience was just beginning to drift in to take their seats. Gloria was already there, having an earnest discussion with the man behind the will-call window in the corner of the lobby. She was wearing a dark blue evening dress that looked prim and proper at first glance, but managed to suggest several improprieties at second or third view. She turned around as I walked over to her and nodded to me.

"You look swell," I told her.

She eyed me from hat to shoes. "You'll do," she said. "Let's go in." We passed into the theater and were ushered to our seats.

"Nobody out front has any clear memory of the last time they saw Two-Headed Mary," Gloria told me in an undertone, sounding annoyed. Gloria has an elephantine memory, and small respect for the failings of others. *She* would have remembered.

The curtain went up on *Fine and Dandy,* and we were thrust a decade back, to a fantasy vision of the carefree days of yore, when every office boy could become a king and every shop girl a queen; when life was a glorious cycle of song, to crib a line from Miss Dorothy Parker, and we didn't yet have even fear itself to fear. The songs were sprightly and the dances exuberant. The beautiful carefree flappers sang and danced with their ardent beaux and had no troubles that a kiss wouldn't cure, and, for an hour and a half, neither had we. The show was an unabashed pastiche of Twenties musicals; a romantic fantasy with overtones of early Cole Porter and the Gershwins and a hint of George Cohan, and a patter song that owed a debt to Gilbert and Sullivan. What plot there was, was subordinate to the joy of the moment, and the audience reveled in a yesterday that never was.

John Hartman, the male lead, was better than good, he worked hard, moved well, and sweated charm. But the audience made it clear that it was Sandra Lelane that they had come to see. Sandra danced until she couldn't possibly have had any breath left, and stopped and sang, her clear soprano easily reaching to the back of the house. And the audience gave freely of its applause. Once or twice she sang and danced at the same time and she did both with the grace and presence of a born star. She was alternately ethereal and earthy, and always infinitely desirable.

Any of the chorus girls and boys backing up the two leads would have been a star him or herself anyplace but Broadway. But the world knows that a star in Dallas is only a chorus girl on Broadway; and those who were serious about their craft would prefer the chorus of a Broadway show to a star turn in the sticks.

At intermission Gloria and I discussed how best to talk to the chorines. "Just talking to one girl is likely to take ten or fifteen minutes, if she has anything to say," I pointed out, "and the others aren't going to want to stand around waiting for their chance."

"True," Gloria said.

"Why don't we run around to as many theaters as we can get to in the first half hour after the shows let out," I suggested, "and invite anyone who knows Two-Headed Mary well or who spoke with her during the week before she disappeared to join us at a table at Sardi's for a drink or even a bit of food—on Mr. Brass."

Gloria patted my hand. "Very clever," she said.

"No chorus girl, in my experience, has ever turned down a free meal," I added, "particularly when there are no strings attached."

Gloria smiled the sweet smile of the tiger as it is about to pounce. "Of course not," she purred. "The pay is lousy, the hours are long, and the work is difficult and demanding, not to mention exhausting. And most of the dinner invitations they get have definite strings attached—with hooks on the end. If you think being a chorus girl is a piece of cake—"

"Of course not," I assured her. "I have nothing but the greatest respect for those who toil in the vineyards of the theater."

"And how do you come to know so much about chorus girls anyway?" she demanded.

"Years of research and self-denial," I told her, "and I feel that I am the better man for it."

"Better than whom?" she inquired sweetly, "and in what way?"

The rising of the third-act curtain spared me from revealing that I had no clever answer.

Gloria and I split up as the show ended. I went backstage there at the Royal, and she headed out to the Winter Garden, where *At Home Abroad* should be letting out, and then, she thought probably, to the Alvin and Cole Porter's long-running *Anything Goes*.

The magic name of Alexander Brass got me past the stage doorman without having to appeal to Miss Lelane. The dressing rooms were one flight up an ancient wrought-iron circular staircase. I paused by the star's dressing room to tell Sandra how wonderful I thought she had been, but the room was already crowded with men doing just that, so I just waved at her from the doorway and slowly and silently faded away farther down the hall to the chorus girls' dressing room.

Two counters ran the length of the dressing room, one against each wall. There were four or five half-height mirrors distributed along each counter, each framed in light bulbs. The thirty or so chorines in the crowded dressing room were seated before the mirrors, or with their own small makeup mirrors, busily slathering cold cream on their faces or rubbing makeup off when I opened the door. They were in various stages of dishabille, some wearing dressing gowns but most just in what a popular song describes as their scanties. Pinky would have enjoyed the view. I know I did. Loud staccato conversation criss-crossed the room, punctuated by occasional peals of girlish laughter. The girl nearest the door shouted, "Man aboard!" when she spotted me, and several of them hastily grabbed dressing gowns to cover themselves. Most of them didn't bother: what's one man in the dressing room, more or less? One of the girls about three seats down on my right, a particularly blond girl amid this bevy of blond beauties, eyed me inquisitively. "You're cute," she said, "in a penguin sort of way. Who do you want to see?"

I smiled at her and climbed up onto a convenient, but wobbly, chair, "Ladies, may I have your attention for a moment?" I yelled. The noise level dropped ever so slightly. "My name is Morgan DeWitt; I work for Alexander Brass," I yelled. The noise level dropped sharply. Brass was an important columnist. There were worse things for a girl's career than getting her name in a nationally syndicated newspaper column. A chorus of "shush"es ran around the room, stifling the remaining chatter.

"Many of you might have seen the paragraph Mr. Brass did a few days ago on Two-Headed Mary. Well, she's still missing, and we want to do a follow-up. We'd like to talk to anyone who has seen or spoken with her in the past, say, two weeks."

"Will it get my name in Brass's column?" a blond five or six chairs down on the left asked.

"When did you see her?"

"When would you like me to have seen her? The name is Jeanette Winters." She spelled "Jeanette" for me.

I took a deep breath. "The idea," I said loudly, "is for those of you who have actually had any dealings with Two-Headed Mary recently to join me at Sardi's in about half an hour, where you can tell me about it over a hamburger or one of Sardi's famous chicken salad sandwiches and the beverage of your choice."

"A sandwich?" came a mezzo-soprano voice from the far side of the room, "is that the best he can do?"

"I was concerned about your girlish figures," I said. "If you wish something more substantial, by all means; Mr. Brass is nothing if not generous. That is, if you know something worth being generous for."

"How do we know you work for Alexander Brass?" a short brunette with a pug nose demanded.

"How do you know I don't?" I retorted. "If I'm lying, it's a pointless lie, since I'm offering to feed you en masse, as it were, and you will all share in that safety that is said to be in numbers. Besides, Brass's other assistant, the lovely lady who's known as Gloria, will be joining us."

"Will Mr. Brass be there?" the nearby blond wanted to know.

"Probably not," I admitted. "But if you have anything interesting to say, you'll get a chance to tell him about it."

It took me another ten minutes to get out of there, with three of the ladies of the chorus thinking that maybe they knew something that would be a reasonable trade for a free meal and a girl named Viola getting my promise that she could come along if she could locate a fellow chorine named Liddy and bring her, since, said Viola, Liddy and Two-Headed Mary had been special friends. Liddy had run out to see someone right after the show, but Viola thought she could find her. I scribbled "Sardi's ASAP" on the back of one of my cards and gave it to her to pass on to Liddy.

6

After leaving the Royal, I went to the New Amsterdam Theater where the twelfth edition of *George White's Scandals* had just opened. George White's audiences have enjoyed being scandalized since 1920, when the first *Scandals* was produced, and this latest version of the show had opened last week to rave reviews and SRO box office. The chorus of beautiful girls—can't have scandals without beautiful girls—would not have to seek other employment for some time. I spoke to the girls from the dressing room doorway and got their sympathetic attention; Two-Headed Mary was well liked. Three of the chorines were going out for a late dinner with Rudy Vallee, the show's star, which I thought was an unfair monopoly in restraint of trade, but they claimed to have nothing for us anyway, so that was okay. Two others thought they had some information that might be worth a sandwich, or at least a drink. Then I scurried over to the Alhambra and *Dames, Dames, Dames* just in time to catch most of the chorus girls at the stage door as they were leaving.

Between us, Gloria and I garnered an even dozen ladies of the chorus who claimed recent acquaintanceship with, or knowledge of, Two-Headed Mary. It was a hair before midnight by the time we got our troupe assembled, what with the removal of stage makeup and the donning of civilian makeup and street clothes. Sardi's was crowded, as one might expect on a Thursday night. The crowd was "one-half street, one-half straight, and one-half out of state," as Tiny Benny once put it. Benny, a man of enormous girth who sat in and around a booth against the back wall of Sardi's front room, said things that other people quoted. What he meant by that particular crack was that the late-evening Sardi's crowd was made up of theater people, would-be theater people, and midwestern tourists who thought that the theater was evil, but maybe it wouldn't hurt to look if you didn't touch. If you tried explaining to Benny that one can't have three halves of anything, he had a ready answer: "Who asked you?"

I went in first to see if we could get a table in a somewhat sequestered location while Gloria gathered our cluster of chorines by the door. Adele Sardi, who ran the place with her husband, Vincent, the original Sardi, nodded to me when I came in. A short, quick woman who had been a noted beauty in her youth, and that not so long ago, Adele ruled the restaurant with a sure hand and an unfailing sense of humor. "Morgan," she said, "you look tired. Too many late nights and not enough sleep. Mr. Brass works you too hard. Let me get you a strong cup of coffee and a piece of cheesecake."

"What I need is a place to seat a dozen or so people and a little privacy," I told her. "Gloria and I have to interview some young ladies of the theater."

"For Mr. Brass?"

"Of course. That is my life. Am I not Mr. Brass's good right arm?"

"I don't know. Last week you were his nose and ears." Mrs. Sardi paused to consider. "The large table in the back room is a possibility. The Waiter's Union Steering Committee, Local Nineteen, was meeting back there, but they were done an hour ago. Most of them have already left. A few of them are still sitting there, drinking white wine and cursing management. They can do that in the kitchen. Give me a minute." She darted off.

Ten minutes later we were gathered around the big table in the back room. Florian, our waiter, he of the long face and sad eyes, took the drink orders, and ambled off to get the assorted martinis, gimlets, Rob Roys, champagne cocktails, ambrosias, gin and tonics, and soda waters while the girls studied their menus. When drinks are on their way, can food be far behind? We decided to hold off any meaningful discussion until the drinks were on the table and the food ordered. I did the preliminaries: getting out my little pocket notebook—can't be a reporter without a pocket notebook—and taking names. They all more or less knew each other; the gypsy community is small and tight.

Terri, Maxine, and Aud ("it's short for Audrey") were joining us from the Royal. Dossie and Vera came from the New Amsterdam; Yvette and Gilly from the Alhambra. From the chorus of *At Home Abroad* at the Winter Garden came Trixie and Suze. Honey, Jane, and Didi ("but everyone calls me 'Knees'") were the crew from *Anything Goes* at the Alvin. (There, I hold nothing back. I didn't collect last names.) Their voices ranged from high and giggly to low and sultry. Their ages ranged from nineteen to somewhere around thirty. This is Gloria's estimation, we didn't ask and they all looked to be a very healthy nineteen to me. They were all of about the same height—rather shorter in person than they seemed on the stage, I noted—and mostly different shades of blond. Whether natural or suicide, I couldn't tell. (A suicide blonde, as *Joe Miller's Joke Book* would have it, is one that's dyed by her own hand.) Seeing so much youth and beauty en masse it was kind of hard to tell them apart, although any red-blooded American boy would have been glad to spend a year or two trying.

Junior Skulley wandered unsteadily into the room behind Florian as he returned with the tray of drinks. Junior's eyes were red and bleary from booze and lack of sleep, and his hands were pushed deep into the pockets of his dinner jacket, which bore the spoor of a recent dinner. He spotted our collection of chorines and froze like a bird dog. "Heigh-ho, Morgan," he said when he regained the power of speech. "Where'd you get the bevy of beautiful dolls? You and Brass putting on a show?"

"This is a private party," I told him.

"Of course it is," he agreed, taking two precarious steps forward. "Ah, the beauteous Miss Adams," he said, his eyes lighting on Gloria. "I find her enchanting and she finds me funny. But one lives in hope."

"Hello, Junior," Gloria said. "It's a free country; you have a right to hope."

Junior pulled his right hand from his pocket and seemed surprised to find a half-full glass of scotch still firmly in his fist. He sipped at the scotch as he stared soulfully at the girls around the table. Son, heir, and namesake of city contractor Edwin James Skulley Sr., Junior was in his mid-thirties, but looked a boyish fifty. He had no interest in his father's business; his two vocations were drinking and chorus girls. As these took up most of his time, he had no hobbies.

"A toast!" he said, advancing to behind my chair as Florian passed out the last of the booze order.

"One toast, and then go away," I told him. "This is business."

"Of course it is," he agreed. "Who said it wasn't?" He extended his glass. "Ladies? A toast to you; visions of beauty all."

To a woman they all leaned forward and raised their glasses, except for Yvette, who made a show of turning to face the other way, her glass tabled but her chin raised high. Perhaps she just didn't like his face.

"Yvette, my love, you are even more beautiful than I remember," he said, raising his glass to salute the back of her head. Perhaps she had good reason to dislike his face. He saluted the rest of the table with his glass, from left to right. "As are you all," he added. "And, to you all, a toast!" He raised the glass.

> "Here's to the girls in the high-heeled shoes
> Who eat our dinners and drink our booze
> And hug and kiss us until we smother—
> And then go home to sleep with Mother!"

With that he bowed to the girls. "Thank you all for your attention," he said. "Perhaps I will see you again sometime. Now I have to get back to... to..." He turned and staggered back out the door, still going "to... to..." like a lost and bewildered toy train.

As Junior disappeared out the door there was a brief colloquy among the girls regarding his manners, morals, and general desirability as a dinner companion. Three of the girls admitted to having been out with him and, to the accompaniment of assorted giggles and sighs, they dissected him quickly, cruelly, and, as far as I could tell, accurately. He was a drunk, a wastrel, and had a one-track mind; but he was good for a dinner or two as long it was in a public place and a girl didn't mind getting slightly pawed over. Essentially, the consensus was, poor Junior was harmless. Yvette flushed red at several of the more intimate comments, particularly regarding how a girl would have to be a fool herself to take a fool like Junior seriously, but she maintained a dignified silence.

As Florian finished taking food orders Gloria stood up and I opened my notebook to a clean page. Gloria *pinged* on a water glass with her fork in the time-honored way of making noise at a dinner table. "On behalf of Mr. Alexander Brass, I thank you all for coming and sharing what you know about Two-Headed Mary with us," she said as the chatter died away. "As you must know, she has been missing for over a week. Let me start with the big question: Do any of you think you know where Mary might have gone?"

They looked at one another.

"Did you try her apartment?" Gilly asked. "She lives somewhere on the Upper West Side. Maybe around Ninety-second and Riverside."

"Did she tell you that?" Gloria asked.

"I, well, I think so."

"I thought she came in every day from Connecticut," Aud said. "You know, New Haven or Bridgeport or someplace." They kicked that around for a while, Suze (rhymes with booze) swore that Mary had told her that she had a penthouse apartment in the east 70s, but she couldn't remember just where. No one mentioned Eastern Parkway, or anywhere else in Brooklyn. Evidently Mary liked to keep her home life well separated from her professional appearances.

The discussion segued into other aspects of the secret life of Two-Headed Mary. Apparently she really did help the girls out with a five-spot or occasionally even a ten if one of them needed it, and she was a good listener and she gave good advice when asked.

"She got Billie Trask her job," Honey added, "after Billie hurt her leg. She talked Welton into giving her a job at the box office."

"Yes, yes," Didi "Knees" said. "But look where that got her."

A mixed chorus of "boo," "hush," and "shame on you," sounded from around the table. "Billie didn't take that money," Trixie said positively. "I used to room with her before she moved in with Liddy.

If Billie had accidentally left this restaurant with this spoon"—she held up the long spoon she was eating her parfait with—"she'd worry about it all night, tossing and turning, and then come back and confess the next morning. Honest she would!"

Didi frowned. "But I heard her boyfriend made her do it."

"And I heard," Maxine said, leaning forward and whispering in a stage whisper that could be heard in Cincinnati, "that that wasn't what her boyfriend made her do at all—and it wasn't because she hurt her leg that's he had to quit the chorus!"

"Why Maxine, you little bitch!" Trixie said. "She might have been in trouble—that kind of trouble—or she might not, but if she was, it could have happened to more than one of us at this table—and don't say it couldn't!"

"If the girl was pregnant," Honey asked, "then who took the money?"

"There is nothing that says that you can't be pregnant and a thief," Jane said, "if you're going to be a thief."

"She was no thief!" Trixie insisted.

I decided that I'd better bring the conversation back to the subject before it got away from us entirely. "So Mary helped her with her problem," I suggested, "whatever it was?"

"She liked helping chorus girls," Maxine offered, "because she had a daughter who was in the chorus."

"That's right," Didi agreed. "Such a sad story."

"Sad?" I asked.

"The kid died," Didi explained. "Right after she got offered a principal spot in the *Vanities*."

"Name was Ruby," Maxine said. "She was hit by a Fifth Avenue bus. Mary didn't show it much—she was a real trouper—but she was terrible broken up. Wouldn't ride buses any more."

"I thought the kid got TB and died," Dossie offered, "like Camille."

"The kid's name is Lenore and she's not dead. She married a drummer and moved to San Francisco," Terri contributed. "Mary was real mad about it. She said she wouldn't have minded so much if the guy was a violinist or even a piano player. But drummers aren't dependable."

None of the girls seemed particularly bothered by the constantly changing stories of their benefactor. They ate, drank, and were merry until almost two in the morning, and I filled up sixteen pages of my notebook with what I like to call my shorthand. None of them was sure just when she'd seen Two-Headed Mary last, although we pretty much pinned it down to a couple of days before she disappeared—or at least before her disappearance was noticed. They all agreed that she had not seemed worried or upset, had not behaved noticeably different, and had not indicated that she was going anywhere.

I went home and hung my suit up, washed my face, and dropped into bed. I slept soundly until about nine, an hour later than usual, and spent an hour at my aging Underwood to begin my new novel. I had decided to let the old one mature, or possibly rot, with the other dozen or so partials I had done over the past couple of years. The new one was to be a historical fantasy in the mode of James Branch Cabell, Talbot Mundy, or Edgar Rice Burroughs— take your pick. Since my imitations of life read like fantasy, I'd see what I could do with the genuine article. My working title was either "The God King" or "Dancing in Babylon," I hadn't decided which. At the end of an hour I had a beginning:

> It came to pass that in the sixteenth year of the Stewardship of Khassam the Observant there was born to the merchant Lufar in the city of Bazra the Eternal a boy child, which was named Sindbad.
>
> Some there are who teach that the measure of a man's life is taken from his first breath; and all the good or evil, pain or joy, triumph or woe, that shall befall him is already cast in immutable lines upon the tablet of his existence, as the words of a play are written for the actors. If this were so, and if the actor could read his part before the play commenced, which of us would choose to see the curtain rise?
>
> But this is mere conjecture.

And conjecture it would remain, at least until tomorrow morning. I pulled the page from my patient Underwood and put it in the manuscript box, covered the machine, shrugged into my jacket and topcoat, donned my hat, and trotted off to the office.

After the usual badinage with Gloria, I dropped into the chair in front of my office typewriter, reflected on how life was just one damn typewriter after another, and typed up my notes from last night. I left them on Brass's desk along with a chit for $37.40 in expenses. Maybe he could find something useful in them.

I was clipping items of interest from last week's *Variety* and *Billboard* magazines and arranging them artistically by subject for pasting into our scrapbook, when Brass came in at ten-thirty. Don't be misled, Brass's interests are broader than showbiz and glamour; we also clip the *New York Times* and the *Daily News* and the *Wall Street Journal*, and save two years' worth of back copies of the *American Mercury*, the *Nation*, the *New Republic*, *Harper's*, the *Partisan Review*, and random issues of various other magazines that catch Brass's eye from time to time.

At 10:45 the intercom buzzed three times, the signal for Gloria and me to go into the inner sanctum.

Brass was standing behind his desk and glaring at the door as we entered, a sign of annoyance. Legend has it that when he was truly peeved he stood *on* the desk, but that may be apocryphal; at least I had not seen it in my four years with the firm. He waited as we approached. When we reached the edge of our side of the desk, he sat down and smiled up at us.

"Thirty-seven dollars and forty cents," he said, indicating a small pile of money on a corner of the desk.

"Ah!" I said.

It had been the final sign of Brass's trust in me when, after I worked for him for two years, he had given me fifty dollars in expense money to keep in my wallet, to be used to pay for useful information and renewed by chit whenever it was depleted. The trust in question did not involve the money as such, I handled much larger sums for Brass almost from the day of my employment. It was trust in my judgment as to what constituted useful information. Gloria, I believe, kept a hundred, which she seldom needed to use: men told her things just to see if they could make her smile or frown—laugh or cry was out of the question.

"Go on, take the money," Brass directed. "Just remember in the future, if I'm going to entertain a dozen chorus girls, I'd like to be there to enjoy it. Unless, of course, you got something I can use out of the discussion. But I don't see anything of even passing interest in these notes."

I picked up the bills and stuffed them into my wallet. "It seemed like a good idea at the time."

"You spent thirty-seven dollars of my money, and discovered that Two-Headed Mary is indeed kind to chorus girls, sympathetic to their problems, and willing to help them out when they are in need. Good. But we knew that. You found out that Two-Headed Mary might have been responsible for getting Billie Trask the job from which she either stole or didn't steal a large sum of money. Someone in the police department would probably like to know that, but it's nothing I can use."

He paused to take a breath. "Further, you've found that Mary claims to live in four different places, none of them the right one; has five different daughters, two of them dead, none of them the one we know; has a boyfriend on the police force, a husband in the navy, and a dog which is, at different times, a schnauzer, a dachshund and a St. Bernard." He riffled through my notes. "And then there's her past. She told one of your young ladies that she used to be in the chorus herself; Florenz Ziegfeld having personally picked her out for the 1916 *Follies* when she was just a girl. That was, of course, between or among her careers as a nurse, a high-wire performer, and one of the girl riders in the *Buffalo Bill Wild West Show*."

"She does seem to have a dislike for telling a story the same way twice," Gloria offered. "Maybe it has something to do with her years involved in the big con. Maybe she likes to keep in practice."

Brass shook his head. "When you're on the grift you're prepared to lie," he said, "but you don't make a fetish of it. It's too hard remembering what you said to whom. The idea is to make up a believable story and stick to it."

"Maybe she's practicing for the Olympics," I suggested. "Freestyle prevarication, skeet-shooting, and leaping to conclusions."

Brass eyed me speculatively before transferring his gaze to the Pearson landscape on the wall behind me. "This does add an interesting new dimension to the problem of finding out what happened to her," he said.

"And then, of course, there's the sister that she has been

visiting—the one her daughter claims doesn't exist," I added.

Gloria and I maintained a discreet silence while Brass pondered further.

"I take it back," Brass said. "This information is possibly useful. It establishes a pattern that we might not have realized. It may be of great importance in finding her, or finding out what happened to her."

"A pattern of prevarication," Gloria said. "Where does that get us?"

"Before we can find Two-Headed Mary," Brass explained, "it may be necessary to discover just which Two-Headed Mary has turned up missing."

Brass has a knack for saying things like that: they seem to make sense, but when you try to work them around in your mind the sense tends to stay just beyond your grasp. I thought that one over. "I think I get it," I said, "but didn't they all go missing at the same time, since they're all in the same body?"

"Consider the possibilities," Brass said. "She may have had to suddenly leave the country, or at least the New York area. She may be hiding out from someone. She may have been kidnapped. She may be using a different persona in the furtherance of some goal or scheme, possibly connected to her having been on the grift. Or she may have been—or appeared to be—so dangerous to someone that she's been eliminated."

"You think she's been taken for a ride?" I asked.

"It's a possibility."

"I thought gangsters avoided killing women."

"That's because so few women are threats or business rivals. But I don't insist that it was gangsters. There is no class of society that is exempt from committing murder."

"It might not be anything as serious as you're thinking," Gloria offered. "Maybe she just went on vacation without realizing that anyone would miss her."

Brass shook his head. "In that case, she would have read my column, or someone would have pointed it out to her, and she would certainly have called her daughter or someone on the Street, or possibly called me directly at the newspaper."

I refrained from pointing out that there are cities where "Brass

Tacks" is not available, people who choose to read papers that don't carry "Brass Tacks," and people who wouldn't read "Brass Tacks" if it were thrust before their eyes. Brass would not have thought that to be constructive criticism and at the moment, jobs are not that easy to get, even for people with my wit and tact.

"If what happened to her was the result of actions or threats by a second party: abduction, mayhem, concealment, voluntary or involuntary incarceration, then it becomes relevant to discover just which Two-Headed Mary her adversary believed he was acting on. Consider the possibility that one of Two-Headed Mary's blithely told fantasies resulted in her disappearance," Brass said.

"Like what?" I asked.

"There are many possibilities. Suppose Mary told someone that she was really the daughter of John D. Rockefeller. And suppose that person kidnapped her and is now sending ransom notes to a very puzzled Rockefeller household. Or suppose she professed to know the location of some fabulous treasure, and someone took her at her word and won't believe her protestations of prevarication."

"Suppose she told someone she was Anastasia, the Tsar's daughter," Gloria suggested, getting into the spirit of the game, "and she's been abducted by Bolsheviks."

"Suppose she's been arrested on Tenth Avenue for being drunk and disorderly, and she's serving two weeks on Rikers Island," I said.

Gloria glared at me.

"Unlikely," Brass said.

I tried again. "Suppose the rapture came, and she's been wafted off to heaven."

Brass rested his heaviest gaze on me. "We live in an unfortunate age," he said.

I nodded my agreement. "An age of fast cars, fast music, and fast women," I said, quoting some magazine article I had read.

"An age of banter," he said. "An age of forced witticism when people strive to come out with a bon mot when they can't even find the mot juste."

He had me there.

"You know what banter is, don't you?" he asked me.

"Yes, boss," I said.

"Banter is what the mouth does when the brain is not in gear. And don't call me boss."

We could have gone on like that for a while, but we were interrupted by an arrival. Suddenly there came a rapping as of someone sharply tapping, tapping on the frosted glass panel in the reception room door. We used to keep it open all day, but we once had a bad experience with unwelcome visitors and now it was kept closed and locked unless someone—Gloria or myself usually—was at the reception desk to look over visitors.

I scurried out to the door and opened it. The man in the hall was a little taller than my five-foot-ten, wide, rock-solid and craggy, with a carefully clipped, graying mustache and an expensive light brown store-bought suit. I'd say he was in his early fifties. He was standing in a pair of well-shined cowboy boots with scenes from what was probably the battle of the Alamo tooled around the sides, wearing a heavy silver belt buckle engraved with a picture of a cowboy roping a steer, and topped by a ten-gallon Stetson.

"Howdy," he said. "You Alexander Brass?"

"I'm his amanuensis," I said, stepping aside to let him in. "What can we do for you?"

"Name's Gates," he said. "I'd like to speak to this Mr. Brass. I want to ask him what's being done to find that Matinee Mary he wrote about."

I closed the door behind him. "And what's your interest?"

"Did you know her name's not really Mary?" he asked.

"Really?" I said.

"That's right. Her name's Phillippa.

"Phillippa? That's a new one."

"I'm not rightly sure what you mean. Her name's Phillippa, sure enough. Phillippa Stern, but now it's Phillippa Gates, and she's my wife!"

"You're right; we didn't know that," I agreed.

7

Gates took his Stetson off and clutched it in his left hand while extending a firm, callused right hand across the desk. "Howdy, Mr. Brass," he said. "Gates is my name, Casper W. Gates. I've come right up here to see you without hardly pausing to unpack my bags or nothing because my little Filly's missing, and these here New York policemen that I spoke to don't seem to give a good goddamn."

Brass shook the hand gingerly. "Your little filly?"

"My Phillippa. Cute as a button and smart as a whip. The sweetest little woman this side of the Rockies. I exclude the other side of the Rockies 'cause I ain't never been there." He smiled a slight reminiscent smile. "That's kind of our private joke."

Brass gave me an inquiring glare. "We know her as Mary," I explained.

"Ah!" Brass said. He turned back to his guest. "Do continue, Mr. Gates." Gloria got up and moved into the corner behind Gates so she could take a few unobtrusive notes.

"I ain't seen her since the day after the wedding," Gates said. "We spent the night at her place and was fixin' to go on our honeymoon when I had to leave for a few days. I felt awful, but there wasn't nothing I could do about it. Some real important business came up concerning one of my properties and I had to high-tail it back to Mariposa, which is where I hail from. That's Mariposa, Texas; a little old town a few dozen miles south of Dallas. My spread, the

CeeGee Ranch, is right outside—well, actually it kind of surrounds Mariposa. Filly wanted to come but there weren't no room for her in my plane—I fly my own plane; a two-seat De Haviland biplane with a four hundred and fifty horsepower Wright-Curtis rotary engine. That bird can sure move like a scared mustang! Anyway, I couldn't take Filly 'cause of course I had to take Bobby Lee. He's my co-pilot, radio man, and mechanic. He takes care of the plane. I'll be getting a bigger bird now that I've got my Filly to take with me." He paused for breath, and then slumped into the chair that I had thrust behind him. "Where is she, Mr. Brass?"

"Well, Mr. Gates…"

Gates smiled a tired smile. "Ain't nobody calls me 'Mr. Gates' but my enemies," he said. "Call me Pearly. Everybody in Texas does, from Jimmy Allred, who at present is the governor of our great state, to the hands at my ranch. Even their young'uns call me Uncle Pearly. I believe a man should be sociable. Even when he's not in Texas."

I grinned. I couldn't help it. "Pearly Gates?"

"That's me," he agreed. "Just call me Pearly."

Brass grimaced. Pearly probably thought it was a smile. "Texas Bonhomie," he said. "Just one of the things we Easterners love about Texas; that and sagebrush and rattlesnakes."

"No kidding?" Pearly asked. "I'm not overly fond of rattlesnakes myself, although I do believe that there are some folks as collect them. Mostly we just shoot them."

Brass sighed. "I'd like to help you find your wife. Tell me about her, Mr. Gates. How long have you known Phillippa, where'd you meet; what you know about her family, her habits, her hobbies, her interests; what you two did together; everything you can think of about her."

Gates frowned. I thought he was reacting to Brass's churlish refusal to call him "Pearly," but that wasn't it. "Everything I know about my Filly? Sir, there has been a misunderstanding. I have come here to discover what it is that *you* know, not to disclose the intimate details of my life to a newspaper reporter."

Brass leaned back in his chair with his hands behind his head and stared at the Texan. "You misunderstand me, Mr. Gates," he said mildly. "You have my word that I have no desire to print anything you may tell me here. I am neither a gossip columnist nor a reporter. I am a chronicler of this era we live in, but I can do my job without interfering in people's private affairs. I will respect the privacy of anything you choose to confide in me."

Gates thought this over, trying to decide what, if anything, was the difference between a chronicler and a gossip columnist, but he was too well brought up to ask. Finally he stuck his hand out to be shook. "I do believe you, sir," he said firmly. "I apologize for doubting you."

Brass gingerly took the hand and shook it. "If you want me to help you find your missing spouse," he went on, "then you must help me. I have talked to several other people who knew Mary— Phillippa—but none of them knew her well enough to predict where she might have gone."

"Then you're already looking for her?"

"That's so."

"I thought... When I landed at Floyd Bennett Field and Jimmy Danton—he's my broker here in New York City—showed me the clipping of your story, at first I thought it was some kind of joke or hoax or something. Or maybe some kind of publicity stunt, and you'd end up revealing the marriage. 'New York Society Matron Weds Texas Millionaire.' Or something. But then Danton said he'd been trying to get ahold of Mrs. Gates since he read the clipping, and she hasn't been at her apartment or at my suite at the Waldorf. I spoke to a policeman at that little police station a couple of blocks away from the Waldorf and he said there wasn't anything they could do on account of she is a grown woman and all. And maybe we'd had a fight or something and she left of her own accord. We hadn't had no fight. Hell, I hadn't even been around." He leaned forward and fixed a steely gaze on Brass's nose. "It couldn't be that this is some kind of stunt, could it? Because if it is I would suggest that somebody end it mighty quickly before I get riled."

"If so, it's not of my making," Brass assured him. "As far as I know the woman we know as Mary has been missing for over a week now, and none of her acquaintances have any idea where she went or why."

Pearly leaned back in his chair. "She always was a mysterious little lady," he said, "long as I've known her."

"And how long is that?" Brass asked.

Pearly reflected. "About six weeks. That is, about six weeks before I left for the CeeGee last week. We met, I remember, at the Longacre Theater during intermission. I try to see some of this New York theater every time I get to town. These were doing a couple of short plays that Jimmy told me I ought to go see. I don't know why, they weren't much good except for one: *Waiting for Lefty*. About taxicab drivers here in New York City. Full of social consciousness and that there sort of stuff. 'Course I don't take cabs much, since Bobby Lee drives me just about everywhere in the Duesenberg."

"How do you like that," Gloria said from her corner. "I wouldn't have thought that *Waiting for Lefty* was the sort of play that would be good for trade."

Pearly twisted around to look at her. "Trade?" he asked.

Gloria gestured. "Standing outside the theater with her collecting tube," she explained.

"Oh, you mean her charity work? No, she wasn't doing that that evening. Ain't it wonderful, the volunteer work she does? Anyway, she had just come to see that play. *Waiting for Lefty*. She just loved it. She understands all about workers' rights and unions and that stuff. She's taught me a lot already."

"And I have no doubt that she will teach you a good deal more," Brass commented.

I suppressed a smile. Gloria had a small coughing fit.

Pearly shook his head. "I sure hope so," he said. "But what could it mean, what could have happened, her disappearing like this?"

"Just how did you meet during that intermission, do you remember?"

Now that Pearly was convinced that we weren't going to spread his private affairs all over the front page, he was willing, eager to talk about his missing beloved.

"Say, it was the strangest thing. I was in the lobby, getting ready to light my cigar, when I turned around and plum banged into her. She almost fell over, and she spilled this glass of orange soda or whatever it is they sell at that stand in the lobby and it got all over her dress."

"And?"

"And she said, 'Damn!,' which is kinda what you might expect to hear a lady say under those circumstances."

"Granted."

"And I said, 'Sorry about that, little filly.' And she gave me the strangest look and said, 'How'd you know my name?'"

"And that was it?"

"Isn't that the strangest thing? I just happened to say, 'little filly,' like one might, you know, and it turns out to be her name."

"Strange," Brass agreed.

"Almost like as if fate had stepped in to take a hand," Pearly said, a sense of the wonder of things in his voice.

"Almost," Brass agreed. "And then?"

"And then we talked and we talked. She told me about how I reminded her of her first husband who was a flier in the American Eagle Squadron in the Great War and died in combat. And I told her how that was very strange because I was a flier in the Great War, in the One-Fifty-Fifth Recon, and I might have met her husband. She told me how her husband had left her all this money and how she decided to use it to do good things, and about the charity work she did, collecting for worthwhile causes. I told her about my ranch in Mariposa and she told me about how she had always loved horses since she was a little girl." He paused for breath.

"Ah!" Brass said.

"But what has any of this to do with her disappearing like that?"

"We don't know. But unless she banged her head and has amnesia, whatever happened to her is probably rooted in her past, so discovering her past will aid us in finding her."

Pearly considered this. "Did you know that she's called 'Two-Headed Mary' along Broadway?" he asked.

"I'd heard something like that," Brass admitted.

"It's cause she wears two hats, kinda. One the society lady going to all these plays—she loves to see plays cause she used to do some acting herself—and the other the charity lady collecting for the orphans and suchlike."

"That must be it," Brass agreed. "You spent the night in her apartment?"

Pearly blushed. Honest. "We was married," he said defensively. "Just where is her apartment?"

"It's on the corner of Park Avenue and Eightieth Street. The address is 910 Park Avenue, I think."

"Is it? That's interesting," Brass said.

"It's a right nice place, full of all this antique furniture. Very pretty, but it makes me a mite uncomfortable. A lot of it ain't all that solid-looking. I told Filly as how it makes me afraid that I'll break something just by looking at it too hard. I go for Bauhaus modern myself."

"Have you been up there since you got back?"

"Not yet. I ain't been anywhere yet but the hotel, the police station, and here. But I called on the telephone, and she's not there."

"Maybe she has a reason not to pick up the phone."

"The phone goes through a central switchboard, and the operator lady told me she ain't been in for some days."

"Ah!" Brass said.

The conversation went on for another twenty minutes or so, and we learned that Two-Headed Mary, or "Filly," if you prefer, had a liking for opera, for long walks through Central Park early in the morning, for rides on the Staten Island Ferry, for Marx Brothers movies, and for Italian food.

Brass promised to keep looking for Mary and to keep Pearly informed if we discovered anything. Pearly, in turn, promised the same. Pearly asked if Brass could recommend a good private detective, and Brass said he could, but that Pearly should wait a few days before taking any such action. After that, Pearly left.

"Why," I asked Brass, after escorting Pearly to the elevator, "did you discourage him from hiring a shamus?"

Brass eyed me. "Shamus? You've been reading detective novels," he said. "I didn't think it would be a good idea for Mr. Gates to hire a private detective right now because if the detective was any good he would soon discover the truth about Two-Headed Mary, which is not what Mr. Gates needs to hear at the moment." He turned to Gloria and raised an instructional finger. "Send a telegram to one of our contacts in Texas," he told her. "Consult a map and figure out which one is closest to Mariposa. Get some background on Mr. 'Pearly' Gates."

Gloria nodded and made a note on her steno pad.

"And you," he said, wiggling the finger at me, "I have a task for you, too. The only Fenton I can find in any of the local city or county directories is a Fenton Road in Quogue, Long Island. It's a small town on the Long Island Railroad. Take a trip out there tomorrow and see what sort of establishment it is. Do not alert the natives if you can help it."

It took me a second to recall the reference. "464 Fenton" was the address, if it was an address, that was on the scrap of paper in Mary's bindle. "I know Quogue," I told him. "It's near Southampton. I have friends in Southampton."

"Good," Brass said. "Tomorrow is Saturday. Take the rest of the day off and visit them."

"I had this Saturday off anyway," I told him.

"And you still do," he said. "Most of it."

Brass swiveled his chair around to stare pensively out at the Hudson River. It was Friday, time to write "After Dark," his syndicated column for forty-six Sunday papers around the country chronicling Gotham's nightlife for the envious auslanders, and he was already hard at work. We tiptoed out of the room.

That evening I took the Eighth Avenue subway down to West Fourth Street, mingling with the hoi and the polloi. Associating with the common folk is what gives a writer that depth of understanding that makes for great prose. As the car rattled back and forth along the tunnel I listened for examples of the wisdom of the proletariat from my fellow passengers. I leaned forward to overhear two young ladies in the seat next to mine, and heard, "So then I decided we needed a chaperone…" I leaned closer to discover when "then" was, but they glared at me until I leaned back. On the platform at West Fourth, an older lady was earnestly telling her friend, "…and then he threw a teakettle at me—which I think is basically a hostile act!" I silently agreed with her and went on my way.

I headed for the Blind Harlequin, a coffeehouse on MacDougal Street in the heart of Greenwich Village; a hangout for local writers of varying degrees of success and fame. I was having dinner with a couple of friends of mine, real fiction writers who sold regularly and did their best not to rub it in. Bill Welsch was somewhere around forty, and was making a decent living writing stories for *Black Mask* and a variety of pulps; mostly hard-boiled detective, with a few war stories thrown in. He had done most of the things he wrote about: flew a Spad in the big war, been an expatriate writer in Paris, a private detective in Chicago, and a few other things that he hadn't gotten around to writing about yet. He had a clean, lean prose style that looked easy and wasn't.

Agnes Silverson, a handsome woman in her late thirties, wrote the "Dagger Dell, Private Eye" series for *All-Detective Story* magazine and a couple of other pulps under the pen name Charles D. Epp. Stories that were that hard-boiled should have a man's byline, her editors felt. Not that any of them cared personally, they assured her, but they thought that their readers wanted to picture the writers as cynical, tough he-men with their shirtsleeves rolled up and a cigarette dangling from the corner of their mouth as they punched out the story with two fingers on some old, beat-up portable on the table of their cheap hotel room between slugs of bourbon.

"And the thing is," she told us, "I live at the Paris on West Twelfth, which is the cheapest hotel in the city that isn't a flop. I type with two fingers on an old, beat-up portable. And I am no stranger to either the cigarettes or the bourbon. If I only had a cock, I could be the next Paul Cain."

We discussed the State of the Novel and how it had been going steadily downhill since Dickens and Twain. We tried to decide whether Kipling was an important writer. We made disparaging remarks about Hemingway, Fitzgerald, and Franz Werfel. We drank coffee.

Toward the end of the evening I told them about the disappearance of Two-Headed Mary and her penchant for elaborate stories. They were interested: writers are always interested in material they can adapt to their own stories; if it is real, so much the better, it will add that unmistakable air of verisimilitude.

"She got married just before she disappeared," I told them. "It wasn't under her own name, at least I think it wasn't, but I guess it's still legal. A rich Texan named—I swear—Pearly Gates. They met at the theater. *Waiting for Lefty.*"

"A good play," Agnes said.

"I haven't seen it," I admitted.

"You must. It is a play of the people."

"The people," I said.

SCENE: *The Blind Harlequin, a Greenwich Village coffeehouse.*

> *It looks like all other coffeehouses in the Village; old wooden tables, battered wooden chairs, earnest people speaking intently about this and that.*

TIME: *The Present (September 1935)*
The air is thick with cigarette smoke and the honest sweat of the masses. Bill, Agnes, *and* Morgan *are sitting at one of the small tables drinking black coffee, except for* Morgan, *who has put cream in his, and talking the honest talk of the working class.*

BILL: *(pounding on the table with his hard, callused hand)* ...one hell of a playwright. Not more of this pseudo-intellectual Marxist drivel that passes for proletarian theater, but a clean, sharp glimpse into the soul of the working man. We'll hear more from him. Odets is his name. Clifton...

Agnes stares intently across the table, concern for the urban proletariat written on her face, a face wreathed in the smoke of the cheap cigarettes she is chain-smoking.

AGNES: *(correcting Bill, but without animus)* Clifford. Clifford Odets.

BILL: Clifford. Wrote *Waiting for Lefty.* It's about hack drivers. Real hack drivers. They sweat, they curse, they bleed. It's about the cab driver strike last year, sort of.

AGNES: I saw it a couple of months ago at the Longacre. It's
            a hell of a play.

*Impressed by his companions' earnestness, the fire of Socialist
realism burns in Morgan's eyes.*

MORGAN: So I'll go see it. If it's as good as you say it is, I'll go
            see it.
AGNES: You'll experience it.
BILL: And this guy playing the lead… Kazan…
AGNES: Elia Kazan.
BILL: Yeah. I think he must *be* a hack driver.
AGNES: A hell of an actor. One hell of a play. Socially
            conscious, but good.
BILL: A hell of a play.

They stare at each other, their faces mirroring the futility of life.

I may have exaggerated the scene a little for dramatic emphasis.
They went on like that for a while. I was at home and in bed at
about one-thirty, with "A hell of a play" ringing in my ears.

8

At 9:04 Saturday morning I was on a Long Island Railroad local that pulled in to Quogue right on time at 12:23. The Quogue station was a platform with a small shed surrounded by woods, and no sign of a station master or attendant. A narrow two-lane blacktop road wended up to it from the north and away from it to the south, and there were no houses in sight. The three other people who got off dispersed rapidly, and shortly I was standing alone.

I headed off in what I fondly hoped was the direction of stores and civilization, or at least a man mowing his lawn, and was rewarded after walking for five minutes with the Lennon General Store—Hardware, Dry Goods & Sundries, with a gas pump around to the side. The woman who ran the place was in the back pumping kerosene out of a fifty-five-gallon drum into a bunch of one-gallon tin cans. "Afternoon. What do you need?" she said as I came into view.

"I need to find Fenton Road," I told her.

"Go left," she told me, without pausing in her pumping. "In about a mile you'll reach the Montauk Highway. Cross it and keep going. You'll be on Quogue Street. Shortly you'll reach the center of town. Right outside of town, where the road forks, with Quogue Street on the right, you go left, up the hill. That'll be Hale. The second road to the left is Fenton."

"Thanks," I told her. "I'd like to get a bottle of pop."

She paused to wipe her forehead. "Cooler's by the front door. Leave the nickel on the counter."

"Thanks," I said again. I took a Dr. Brown's from the cooler, dropped my nickel, and trudged off to the left.

The town had a strong New England feel, with good-sized Colonial houses, many actually dating back to before the Revolution. Most of them now belonged to the "summer people," who came with their kids, dogs, and servants on or about Memorial Day and departed en masse on Labor Day, leaving the big houses empty, and the seven hundred or so permanent residents to fend for themselves.

Four-sixty-four Fenton Road was a two-story Victorian in a row of Victorians, each on a sizable lot with a white picket fence separating it from its neighbors and from the street. When I reached the house there was a station wagon parked in front of it, and a man in gray flannels and a tweed jacket was pounding a FOR SALE sign into the lawn by the front gate. My deduction that the man was a real estate agent was fortified by the words JAMAN & CO. REAL ESTATE on a side panel of the station wagon.

"For sale, huh?" I said brightly.

The man gave the post one last whack with his mallet and turned to me and smiled. "That's right," he said. "Interested?"

"Maybe," I told him. "Who lives here?"

"Nobody. That's why it's for sale."

I grinned to show I could take a joke. "Okay," I said. "Who did live here, why is he moving, and how much does he want for the property?"

"I'm having it appraised this afternoon," the agent told me. "The doctor may take a few dollars under the market price to move it quickly."

"Why is he moving?" I asked suspiciously. "Well dried up? Termites walking away with the porch?"

The agent rose in defense of his property and told all. Kindly old—well, middle aged—Dr. Pangell was retiring and moving back home to somewhere in the Midwest. It had been a sudden decision, but with the end of the season all of his patients who could afford to pay for his services had moved back to the city anyway.

"What sort of doctor is he?" I asked.

"The usual sort," he said. "He's not a horse doctor, if that's what you mean."

"Where could I find him?" I asked. "I'd like to talk to him."

The real estate man gave me a look. "Why?"

"Why not?"

He stepped a step toward me. "Just to tell you, not that I'm thinking you might, but just to let you know: I have a contract with Dr. Pangell. You can't get the house any cheaper than what I'll offer it for, and you can't do me out of my commission."

"I wouldn't think of it," I assured him.

"Well, just to tell you. But you can't talk to the doctor anyhow. I don't know where he is. He's left town already. He's going to call me when he gets settled."

"I see," I said. "Thanks."

"Here's my card," he said, pushing the pasteboard into my hand.

I walked back down to Quogue Street and managed to verify the real estate man's story in the drugstore. The doctor had, indeed, left town last week, and it was a real shame because now the nearest doctor was twenty miles away, and he was a retired GP from Brooklyn who didn't like to make house calls.

I thought of walking back to the station, but rejected it in favor of taking a cab to the summer home of my friends Max and Florence Bosworth in Southampton. Max is a doctor specializing in diseases of people who live within a half mile of his Madison Avenue office, and Florence teaches a fourth-grade class at P.S. 6, on East 85th Street. I spent the rest of the weekend lying in the sun, walking along unspoiled sandy beaches, and admiring the somber traces of yellow, red, and orange beginning to color the leaves of the oak, birch, and occasional maple trees in the half-pint forest behind the cottage. Once it occurred to me to ask Max if he knew of Dr. Pangell over in Quogue, but he said no, and that was that. I helped the Bosworths prepare the place for its long winter's nap and was rewarded for my labors with sets of tennis, home-cooked meals, and a ride back to the city in their aging Pontiac station wagon late Sunday night.

* * *

Monday morning dawned bright, clear and cool. Birds were singing and, as I took my usual long-cut through Central Park on my way to the office, the horses on the bridle path were prancing and snorting, glad to be alive. It was the sort of weather to put human troubles in perspective; insignificant and callow placed next to the wonders of nature. Which shows how much the weather knows about it.

When I arrived at the office, Gloria was at her desk sorting mail, and Inspector Willem Raab of the New York City Police Department sat gingerly in one of the cane-bottom Louis the Whatever chairs against the reception-room wall, chewing on a pencil stub and reading the September *American Mercury* magazine, which is one of the bits of ephemera we keep in a rack for our guests' amusement. I tossed my hat over the peg and cocked an inquisitive eyebrow at Gloria. She smiled sweetly back at me. "We have a visitor," she said.

"So we do," I agreed, taking off my overcoat and hanging it carefully on its hanger in the little clothes closet. "Good morning, Inspector. Are you going to enter the essay contest?"

Raab focused his eyes on me. "What essay contest?"

"Somewhere near the back of the magazine. Twenty-five hundred words or less on, if I remember correctly, 'The Present Troubles of the Country.' H. L. Mencken is one of the judges, and I forget who the others are. Decision of the judges is final. In case of a tie, bribes will be solicited."

Raab looked at me doubtfully. "You could hardly get out of the gate in twenty-five hundred words. Hell, I could give you a quick ten thousand words on Manhattan, north of Fifty-seventh Street." He closed the magazine and tossed it back into the rack. Pushing himself to his feet, he sorrowfully examined the pencil stub he had been chewing and thrust it into his vest pocket. "This isn't morning," he groused, "it's mid-afternoon."

Inspector Willem Raab is a large, heavy, solid man. At first glance he appears to be somewhere between portly and fat. But the look is deceiving. Raab is, as the mayor put it at a dinner given for the inspector a couple of months ago, "as big as a mountain, as strong as an ox, and as brave and faithful as a bulldog." And if Mayor LaGuardia says it, it must be so. Raab has been in charge of Homicide North since before I arrived in New York, and during that time it has become clear, and a thing of wonder to those used to Tammany hacks even in the police department, that he is also as smart and capable as he has to be and as apolitical as he is allowed to be. He and Brass are old friends. Even when circumstances cause them to be adversaries, each tries to keep the underlying friendship in mind.

"I guess the boss isn't here yet," I said to Raab, "but I'll find you a more comfortable chair if you like."

"Of course Brass isn't here yet," Raab said. "It's only a quarter past ten. Couldn't expect a man to be at his desk working at only a quarter past ten, now, could we?"

"Your sarcasm is wasted on me," I said. "As long as Mr. Brass pays my salary on time, he can come in whenever he likes."

Raab pushed himself to his feet. "It don't matter," he said. "I can see Brass later. First I need to talk to you; ask you a few questions. Maybe you can help clear up something."

"Me? No kidding?" I was nonplussed, a condition I'd seldom achieved. I mentally reviewed my recent transgressions, but could think of none that would interest an inspector of detectives. "Let's go into my—no, we'd better go into Mr. Brass's office, mine is hardly big enough for me." I turned and led the way.

The inspector settled himself on the black leather couch, his favorite seat in the office, and leaned back, his arms outstretched flat across the back of the couch. I pulled one of the office chairs over to a respectful distance and sat. Raab eyed me thoughtfully. "Let's start with this: how well do you know Lydia Laurent?" he asked.

I thought about it for a second, considering several wise answers, and decided that it would be better to play this one straight. "I don't," I said. "Not by that name, anyway."

Inspector Raab leaned even farther back, sliding his legs forward stiff-legged in front of him, and smiled a friendly, reassuring smile. I felt a twinge of apprehension at the back of my neck. In the four years I had known him, Raab had never smiled at me before. "What makes you think she had another name?" he asked.

"I'm just being scrupulous," I told him. "I have no reason to think anything about this person I don't know."

"If the other name was Maureen Yency—would that refresh your memory?"

I shook my head. "As far as I know, I have no memory to refresh."

The inspector stared at the ceiling. "A young, blond dancer, maybe five-two, hair bobbed, blue eyes, pretty face, well constructed. Ring any bells?"

"Nary a tinkle," I told him. "Except that, not counting hair or eye color, those are my minimum standards for a date. Unfortunately, girls who look like that usually have minimum standards of their own, so I seldom date. Dating is highly overrated anyway. I'd much rather spend a quiet evening at home darning socks. Why do you ask? Does she say I know her? What has she done? If she's as good-looking as you say, I might be willing to provide her with an alibi, but of course I'd have to meet her first to judge for myself."

If that sounds glib, I was talking to fill the time with my words while I considered one of Raab's words. *Had.* Verb, transitive, past tense. *Had.* Not *has.* The young lady, whoever she was, was not around anymore, and an inspector of homicide was asking me questions about her. And Raab was being carefully casual, not a good sign.

Your average citizen believes that if he has nothing to hide, he should talk freely to the police to aid them in their pursuit of criminals. There is little truth to this belief. To the police, loquacity is not a sign of innocence; they may regard it as nervous chattering to hide the consciousness of guilt. When an investigator does not have a pretty good idea of who committed a crime, you're just as good a suspect as the next man. And when a detective does have a pretty good idea of who committed the crime, he may be wrong, and the who may be you. There are many innocent men behind bars; the Second Chance Club has already proven this eight times.

Inspector Raab gazed at me thoughtfully and let the shoe drop. "The girl is dead," he said.

"Ah," I said, wondering what was in the other shoe—the one with my name on it. "And you want to know where I was on the night of January thirty-fourth, nineteen hundred-aught-twelve?"

Raab sighed. "If you could only tap dance, you could take it on the road."

I shrugged. "I don't mean to sound heartless, but a lot of people die every day. A couple of hundred Ethiopians may be being machine-gunned by Mussolini's Praetorian Guard right now and there's nothing I can do about it."

Brass stalked into the room and tossed his overcoat on a chair. Since he usually fastidiously hangs it in the closet in the front room, Gloria must have signaled him to hurry on through. It was nice to know she cared.

"Morgan is right, you know," Brass said. "I hope I'm not interrupting."

"Good morning," Raab said. "I was going to get to you."

Brass went behind his desk and sat down, swiveling left and right to make sure the chair still swiveled, and then leaned back. "We mortals are not provided with an endless supply of sympathy," he said. "If we tried to feel sorry for every bad or evil thing that happened, even just those we hear about in normal intercourse, we'd be swamped by emotion from moment to moment. Of necessity we must save our sympathy for those we know."

Raab scowled at my boss. "We are discussing a dead girl," he said. "Name of Lydia Laurent. Mean anything to you?"

Brass thought for a moment and then shook his head. "Not that I can remember," he said. "How did she die?"

"You and your apprentice here are so scrupulous with your language it's hard not to think you have something to hide," Raab said. "Him with his, 'not by that name,' and now you with, 'not that I can remember.' Can't either of you give me a simple yes or no?"

"No," Brass said.

"Phooey," Raab said. He took a cigar out of his jacket pocket, turned it over speculatively a few times, and then shoved it back into his pocket and turned to me. "Come on, where do you know the girl from? How long had you been intimate with her? Nobody's accusing you of anything, we just need to know her background, who she talked to; that sort of stuff."

"Intimate?" I took a deep breath. "As far as I know, I do not know, and have certainly not been intimate with anyone named Lydia anything," I told Raab. "I'd like to help, but there you have it."

"How did this girl die?" Brass asked, "and what makes you think she and DeWitt were, as you say, 'intimate'?"

"I don't insist on the 'intimate,'" Raab said. "But he knew her all right."

Brass looked at me. "Did you?"

I shook my head. "Like I said, I don't think so."

"That ain't what you said," Raab said.

"Let's hear it," Brass told Raab. "What have you got, and why are you harassing my assistant?"

"Is that higher or lower than an apprentice?" I asked Brass.

"No," he said.

"This don't qualify as harassing," Raab said. "If I want to do any harassing you could tell the difference. Easy."

"Well then, put your cards on the table," Brass said. "We're at an impasse here. You say DeWitt was intimate with this girl and DeWitt says he doesn't even know her. My bet would be that he doesn't know her. You want to raise me?"

"We'll see." Raab turned to Gloria, who was standing silently in the doorway. "You got something to write on?"

Gloria disappeared for a second and reappeared with a steno pad. "Will this do?"

"Yeah. Give it to DeWitt. You got a pencil?" he asked me.

I fished one out of my pocket. "Sure thing," I said. "We apprentice assistants always carry writing implements about with us. What's the game?"

Raab got up and stuffed his hands into his pockets. "I'll dictate, you write."

"My shorthand isn't very good."

"I'll speak slowly. You write it out."

"Ah!" I said. "Stylomancy."

"Stylo-what?" Raab demanded.

"Handwriting divination. Stylomancy. You're going to tell me that I'm going to marry a tall blond girl who's four-foot-nine with dark brown hair and have three children, one of each."

Raab snorted.

"Not a bad construction, stylomancy," Brass said. "From 'stylus.' Is it yours?"

"I don't think so," I told him. "I think I heard it somewhere. Isn't that the word?"

"There are several words for the analysis of personality or the telling of fortunes by studying handwriting," Brass told me. "I like *steganomancy*, from a Greek root meaning 'secret writing.'"

He swiveled around to look at Raab. "Did you know you were practicing steganomancy?"

"I'll stegano the pair of you down to the precinct house if you don't shut up and let me get on with this," Raab rumbled.

"Sorry," Brass said.

"Words are his passion," Gloria told the inspector.

Raab glared at Gloria, shifted his glare over to Brass, and then fixed his gaze on me. "Write this," he said. "'My favorite joints in New York are the Stork Club, Sardi's, and the Copa.'"

I scribbled on the pad. "Is that it?" I asked.

"You got that? Under that print the alphabet," Raab said.

Brass and Gloria were watching this operation quizzically, but they were not half as puzzled as I. I did as directed and handed the steno pad to Raab. "What now?"

Raab stared at the writing for a moment, comparing it with something in a small manila evidence envelope he was holding concealed in his hand. After a minute he looked at me almost benignly and ripped out the page and stuffed it and the envelope into his vest pocket. "Now I'll tell you a story," he said, lowering his bulk back down onto the couch. He pulled the cigar out of his jacket pocket and ran it over and under his fingers like my Uncle Jake used to do with a fifty-cent piece before he made it disappear or turned it into an egg.

"I thought you gave up smoking, Inspector," Gloria said.

"I'm not smoking," Raab replied. "I'm holding a cigar. It's very soothing to hold a cigar. When I get upset, I can chew on it. When I get really upset I can crush it between my fingers." He studied the cigar for a moment, ran it around his fingers one more time, and then put it back in his pocket.

"An elderly gentleman name of Defevre went to sail his model boat in Central Park Sunday morning. You know the sailboat lake?"

"There's a rowboat lake," I said.

"This one is small," he made a gesture with his hands as though he were holding a basketball. "Maybe a hundred feet across. Around Seventy-fourth Street on the east side of the park. A concrete-lined oval; sort of like a giant bathtub. There's a club that sails model sailboats there."

"I know the place," Gloria said. "There's this little sort of clubhouse where they store their boats right by the lake. Elegant miniatures of sloops, schooners, even some square-riggers. Most of them are handmade by the club members. I went to watch them sailing when Mr. Brass mentioned the club in a column about three years ago."

"Why so I did," Brass agreed.

Raab nodded and plowed on. "Defevre was out there at first light. To catch the morning breeze, he said. He arrived at the park somewhere between five-thirty and five-forty. Sunrise was at five-thirty-eight. Sometime later—he estimates it was around six-fifteen—he doesn't carry a watch, only a stopwatch to time his boat—his dog, Marat, started barking at something in a nearby clump of bushes. Defevre thought the dog had lost his toy, so he got his boat pole—this sort of long pole with a hook on the end that they use to push the boats around—and poked under the bushes. He pulled out a shoe; a woman's shoe. The dog kept barking. Defevre pushed his way between the bushes and found a clear space in the middle. The other shoe was there, lying atop a neat pile of clothing. Next to the clothing, supine on the ground, was the naked body of a young woman. Defevre and Marat ran to the nearest park entrance, where Defevre flagged down a passing patrol car. The officers in the car called it in on a police phone box and followed Defevre back into the park. The body was right where he said it would be."

Inspector Raab took the cigar back out of his jacket pocket and stared at it wistfully for a moment, and then stuck it back. "Now here's where it gets interesting," he said.

I shifted uncomfortably. "Where do I come into it?" I asked.

Raab eyed me with the benevolent gaze of a bear eyeing a ham sandwich. "Patience," he said. "By one of those coincidences by which the Almighty makes it difficult for transgressors, the officers in the patrol car had just questioned and released a member of the army of the unemployed, whom they had seen flat-footing it down the street with a suspicious bundle. The bundle contained what seemed to be a complete set of women's clothes, from top to bottom, inside to out, and the bum in question was not a woman. The bum, name of, ah"—he paused to consult his notebook—"Lupoff claimed to have found them in a garbage can on Seventy-third Street. But the clothing was fairly new and fairly expensive; not the sort of thing that anyone tosses out these days. Even someone well-off enough to buy new clothes every year has a relation or a charity to pass the old ones on to."

Raab paused and turned to me. "You want to change your story?" he asked.

"I haven't told you a story," I said, giving him my best look of bewildered innocence. Which was surprisingly difficult, considering that I truly was both bewildered and innocent.

"So," Raab continued, "when the detectives from Homicide North arrived—a pair of bright lads named Bracken and Yarrow—they examined the clothing by the body and determined that the garments probably belonged to a larger woman. Which of them is such an expert on women's clothing I refrained from asking, although I would hope it is Bracken, who is a married man. At which point the precinct officers told them of the second set of clothes, and they went to speak with the bum—Lupoff—who was awaiting his fate in the backseat of the patrol car. After protesting his innocence and making several comments on the state of the economy and the habits and customs of the police, Lupoff agreed to lead the detectives back to where he had found the garments.

"The detectives went to the garbage can in question and examined it. They discovered a few items that Lupoff had missed; among them a small purse containing two dollars and twenty-three cents and a calling card, but no identification.

"So," Raab continued, "the homicide boys were in the odd position of having one dead, naked female body and two sets of female clothing. It occurred to them that the murderer might have placed the wrong clothes next to the body to mislead the investigation, so they tried a shoe from each pair on the dead girl's foot. They had something of a problem as the body was in full rigor, but it did seem as though the shoes from the garbage can"—he consulted his notes—"a pair of black pumps, fit better than the brown open-toe flats found by the body. This seemed to confirm their earlier observation about the clothing."

"Two sets of clothing," Brass commented. "That's a new one."

"We assume," Raab told him, "that the killer meant for the girl's real clothes to be on a garbage scow headed out to sea by now, and supplied the alternate wardrobe so we wouldn't hunt around. But just why he went to the trouble, that we don't know yet. The clothing doesn't seem to tell us much."

"How do you know the girl's name?" Brass asked.

"It was printed in indelible ink on the back of the dress label."

"The garbage-can dress?"

"Yeah. I guess it told us that much anyway. The other name—Yency—was written on an identification card in a wallet in the pile of clothing by the body. We don't know whether it means anything or not. But Lydia Laurent is this girl's real name." He turned to me. "She was a hoofer in *Fine and Dandy* at the Royal Theater. Is that where you met her?"

"I didn't meet her," I said. And then it hit me. "Wait a minute! We talked to some dancers from several of the musicals the other day, but I don't think any of them were named Lydia. I can tell you in a second." I fished in my jacket pocket for my little notebook and flipped the pages. "Here it is. No-none of them were named Lydia."

Raab took the notebook and stared at the page. "'Terri, Maxine, Aud, Dossie, Vera, Yvette,'—what were you planning to do, set up a harem?"

"It was all very moral and approved by the Legion of Decency," I told him. "Miss Adams was chaperoning."

"They were there at my instructions," Brass said, which was nice of him, considering. "We were trying to get some background on Two-Headed Mary."

"Two-Headed—oh yeah, the old-lady scam artist who has come up missing."

"She wasn't so old," I told him.

Raab looked at me blankly.

"I did a mention of her in my column," Brass said.

"Yeah, I saw it. Did you find anything?"

"Enough about her past to write a book," Brass said. "But much of it was contradictory, and most of it, apparently, would be fiction. Nothing as yet that would give us a lead as to her present location."

"She'll turn up," Raab predicted. "One way or another."

Gloria walked across the room and sat on the wooden chair we keep on the side of the desk next to the wall. "You know, we must have seen her," she said quietly.

"Two-Headed Mary?" Brass asked.

"No. This girl—Lydia. When we went to the show on Thursday, she must have been in the chorus." She turned to Raab. "Lydia was alive on Thursday?"

"She was killed a few hours before she was found—say late Saturday night," Raab said. "Strangled. Manually. By somebody with average-size hands, but powerful." Raab eyed my hands thoughtfully. "From the front," he added. "The killer was watching the girl's face as she died. And his face was the last thing she saw."

I pictured the girls I had seen in that long room and wondered which she was. Lydia. Something clicked in my memory. "Liddy!" I said, slapping the side of the chair.

"What's that?" Raab demanded.

"A girl named—something out of Shakespeare—Ophelia, no, Viola. That's it."

"Another name? Is that the name you knew her as?"

"No, no. I didn't know her. But I remember a girl named Viola—I'm pretty sure it was Viola—came up to me backstage and said that her friend Liddy might know something useful, but Liddy had already left, so Viola was going to find her. I gave Viola my card and wrote something on the back. 'Sardi's,' I think, because that's where we were meeting the other girls."

"You think 'Liddy' is Lydia?" Brass asked.

"If the inspector has my card in that envelope, and it says 'Sardi's' on it, I do."

"She might know something useful about what?" Raab asked.

"Two-Headed Mary."

"Damn!" he said. "What's Two-Headed Mary got to do with this?"

"She's missing," Brass said. "We're looking for her."

"A lot of people are missing," Raab said. "There are a couple of hundred missing persons reports filled out every week in Manhattan."

"Is DeWitt right?" Brass asked. "Is it his calling card you have in that envelope? Does it have 'Sardi's' written on it?"

Raab took the envelope from his pocket and slid the card into his hand. "That's it," he said, holding it up. "With 'Sardi's ASAP' written on the back."

"I forgot the ASAP," I said.

"You damn near forgot the whole thing," he said. "Will this Viola remember you?"

"Probably," I told him. "If not, the girls on that list will."

"Well," Brass said, "are you satisfied?"

Inspector Raab leaned back and stared at the far wall. "No," he said. "The person who killed Lydia Laurent is still walking around and I don't know who he is. No, I'm not satisfied."

"Was the girl raped?" Brass asked.

"The medical examiner thinks not. There were compression marks on her wrists and ankles, so she was probably tied up before she was killed. But she was not raped and not battered." Raab grimaced. "Merely strangled."

"Tell me," Brass asked. "Aside from your moral outrage, this isn't the sort of case that would usually get the head of Homicide North questioning suspects. Just what are you doing here?"

"Trying to spare your amanuensis here the embarrassment of having to come down to the squad room," Raab said.

"Bull," Brass said. "Try again."

Raab sighed. "You won't use this until I tell you it's okay?"

"My word. I will probably never use whatever you tell me at all, at least not directly. I am a columnist, not a reporter."

"Yeah," Raab said. "The master of indirection. Well anyway, Lydia Laurent was the roommate of Billie Trask."

"The girl that disappeared with all the money," Gloria said.

"That one," Raab agreed.

"A missing persons case?" Brass raised an eyebrow, a gesture he must have practiced in front of a mirror to get just that level of disdain in it. "As you just said, there are a couple of hundred every week."

Raab took his cigar out of his pocket and jammed it into his mouth. "It's political," he said. He took a wooden match from another pocket and struck it against the sole of his shoe. He stared at the flame for a moment and then took the cigar from his mouth and carefully blew out the match. He looked around for an ashtray.

"Here," Gloria said. "Let me take that for you." She removed the match to the wastebasket under Brass's desk.

Raab jammed the cigar back in his pocket. "Thanks," he said.

He leaned forward and regarded Brass thoughtfully. "There's more to this case, this Trask business, than is out there in the papers."

"You mean the *Daily Mirror* doesn't know more than the police department about this?" Brass asked. "Won't Winchell be surprised!"

"Yeah, well… there was some other stuff missing from the box-office safe."

"What sort of stuff?"

"That's not clear, at least not to me. But pressure's being put on the commissioner to find the girl, and he is pushing it down the line. So when the Trask girl's roommate turns up dead, it is of more than usual interest." Raab pushed himself heavily to his feet.

"Will you keep us informed, Inspector?" Brass asked.

"About what?"

"Your progress on this case. And if we find anything helpful, I'll let you know."

"Yeah, I'd appreciate that," Raab said. "If you want to go on looking for Two-Headed Mary, that's your business and good luck to you. But my assumption is that the Lydia Laurent killing had to do with the Billie Trask disappearance. And you'd do better to keep away from this Billie Trask case. Hell, I'd like to keep away from it myself."

"What if they're connected?" Brass asked.

"Connected? Now wouldn't that be something." Raab eyed Brass speculatively. "Do you know something, or are you just talking?"

Brass shrugged. "Two women disappear. The same girl knows both of them, and she turns up dead. Don't you think there's a connection?"

"Damn!" Raab said. "I hope not!"

9

Inspector Raab stopped in the outer office long enough to jam his hat on his head and throw his overcoat over his arm, and then strode down the hall to the elevator. As he got on, K. Jeffrey Welton, boy producer, got off.

"Say," K. Jeffrey said in the sort of stage whisper that can be heard from the topmost balcony, "wasn't that Inspector What's-his-name?"

"Raab," I said.

"That's the one. Homicide. What was he doing here?"

"He and Mr. Brass have a regular Monday morning Parcheesi game." I opened the office door wide to let him pass through. "Then they sit around drinking Ovaltine and decoding secret messages with their Little Orphan Annie decoder rings."

K. Jeffrey squinted at me. "Very funny, you are. I want to see Brass. Tell him I'm here, would you, old man?" He stripped his overcoat off and draped it and his hat over a chair.

"Sure thing, old man," I said.

I left Walton contemplating the framed pencil sketch of Aaron Burr on the wall behind Gloria's desk and went through to Brass's office. Brass was in the midst of expounding on trite phrases to Gloria. He was against them. He paused when I came in and looked expectantly at me. "If it isn't one thing it's another," I told him. "The other just came in and wants to see you. His name is Welton." Brass took a deep breath and made a beckoning gesture, which I interpreted to mean "bring him in," and so I did.

Welton smiled at Brass, grinned at Gloria, and slouched into one of the chairs opposite the desk. "That inspector that was just here," he said to Brass. "Did he tell you about the girl they found? The dead one in the park?"

"Yes," Brass said.

Welton nodded. "So I think it's time, and I think I'd like you to be the one to do it."

"Time for what?" Brass asked.

"I'd like you to announce it in 'Brass Tacks,' because everyone on the Street reads your column, especially the Thursday one. So you should probably put it in Thursday."

There was a common myth on the Street, as the guys and dolls of Broadway call their home; one that Brass neither denied nor encouraged, although it was not strictly true. The belief was that all the really important stories about Broadway, all the straight dope about who was doing what to whom and with what and for how long, appeared in the Thursday "Brass Tacks." The truth was that stories appeared when they appeared; Brass wouldn't dare hold up a hot item for fear that fellow scribes Winchell, Runyon, or E.P. Adams would beat him to it. He might make a point of doing a Thursday follow-up on one of the big stories or adding a smattering of Broadway color pieces under the catchall heading "Heard on the Street" to the Thursday column, but that was all. Nonetheless the sale of the *World* went up an extra two or three thousand copies in Manhattan on Thursdays.

Brass stared steadily at Welton and, when no further words were forthcoming, sighed and said, "What am I announcing in 'Brass Tacks'? And why?"

K. Jeffrey bounced to his feet, impatient with we lesser mortals who lacked his rapid and incisive grasp of the flow of events. "My reward," he explained. "I think, with all this happening, it's time. First, you know, the Trask girl flees, then Two-Headed Mary disappears, and now this dead girl."

"You think there's a connection?" Brass asked.

"I don't know," K. Jeffrey said seriously. "But Broadway is a small community and everybody in it knows everything about it, or thinks he does. Since you did the piece on Mary, the rumors have been flying. The people on the Street are connecting Mary's disappearance and the flight of Billie Trask. I hear things."

"That's interesting," Brass said. "What sort of things?"

"I hear around that Mary was married recently, to a big spender from the Great Plains, and she left town to get away from her husband. I hear around that Mary was involved in some sort of confidence scheme in Kansas City, and one of the victims has come looking for her with fire in his eyes and a big fist. I hear that Billie Trask didn't flee with her boyfriend, as the police think, but fled with Two-Headed Mary to get away from the aforementioned boyfriend. These are the sort of things I've been hearing, but you know how gossip goes in this town. The stories seem to be mutually exclusive, and the truth very well might lie in an entirely different direction. I don't know. I know that Two-Headed Mary was friends with Billie Trask, and the dead girl, Lydia, was Billie's roommate, so it does rather seem that the disappearances and the murder may be interconnected in some twisted fashion."

"I take it that the police are no closer to catching up with Miss Trask and your money?" Brass asked.

"So it would seem," Welton said, grinning. "Which has seriously annoyed my brother, Edward. The pride of the family has come down here from Fall River just to stir up the police."

"Edward?"

"Yes. It seems that when the wench took off with the money she also removed from the safe some papers that Edward had secreted there and was particularly anxious not to lose."

"Ah!" Brass said. "You didn't mention that last time you visited us."

"It isn't my, ah, secret, don't you know. But now that Edward has seen fit to inform the police, and thence the public, I see no reason to keep the information clutched to my metaphorical bosom."

"Is your brother in the show business?" I asked.

This was the funniest thing K. Jeffrey had ever heard. He pounded on his thigh with his right hand, bobbed his head up and down, and broke into a sustained chuckle, snort, and wheeze. When he was able to calm down, he pulled an oversized handkerchief from the pocket of his cashmere jacket—he was wearing a deep maroon one today—and mopped his face.

"Is Edward in...," he said. "Oh, really, that is too much," he said. "Edward in the show business! When pigs have wings, and not a moment before!"

"Sorry," I said.

"Oh, don't be. I haven't had such a laugh since we brought the cow up to the top floor of the Sigma Alpha frat house."

"What," I asked, "is funny about that?"

"Well, you see, cows will go *up*stairs, easily enough but they won't go *down*stairs."

"Ah!" I said.

"They had to rent a crane and take the poor, terrified animal through a window. It was a wondrous sight."

"I'll bet," I said.

Gloria shrugged and rolled her eyes in her "boys will be boys" gesture.

"What was in those missing papers?" Brass asked.

"Ah! There you have me. I was not privileged to gaze upon their inky contents." He paused and stared at the ceiling for a moment in deep concentration. "Perhaps 'gaze into their inky depths' would be a better construction—what do you think?" he asked.

Brass shrugged a slight shrug. "It's a matter of personal style," he said.

K. Jeffrey nodded thoughtfully. "At any rate, Edward wants his papers back and is willing to pay a reasonable reward. Edward is a parsimonious man. So are all my family. Parsimonious and abstemious. If Edward were bargaining with the Devil for his soul, he would decide on a reasonable figure and go not a jot higher. But he wants his name kept out of it. Since my name is already muddied by being associated with the show business, he's letting me do it. Good of him, don't you think?"

"Is Edward afraid of having the contents of the papers made public?" Brass asked. "Are they that sort of papers?"

"The fact of it is," K. Jeffrey said slowly, the spaces between his words showing that he was picking them with care, "that there is information in the documents that could be harmful to the family. But the information is in such a form that the naive reader would have no way of knowing what he—or she—has."

"So it's not blackmail?"

"Not yet at any rate."

Brass picked up the little ivory figurine from a corner of his desk and jiggled it from hand to hand, usually a sign of deep thought. He stared speculatively at Welton for a minute. "Just what do you want me to say?" he asked. "What sort of reward are you offering?"

K. Jeffrey pulled a sheet of lined yellow paper from his pocket and unfolded it. "I have it written down," he said, smoothing the paper out on the desk. "I'm going to place this as a quarter-page advertisement in the drama or entertainment section of every paper in town, and with you mentioning it in your column, everybody that means anything will see it."

Brass smiled. It was nice to be appreciated. "Let me look at it," he said.

I peered over Brass's shoulder. The copy was hand-printed in ink. "REWARD," said the headline at the top. And below that:

The *Lucky Lady* Theatrical Company is offering a $2,000 REWARD for information concerning or leading to the discovery of the present whereabouts of Miss Billie Trask, formerly employed by the *Lucky Lady* Theatrical Co., or for similar information concerning the woman popularly known as Matinee Mary.

And below that, in smaller printing:

A total of no more than $2,000 will be paid out to and divided among any persons bringing useful information as to the location of either of these women, or of certain objects believed to be in the possession of one or both of them, within a week of the publication of this notice. Application must be made at the box office of the Monarch Theater. The decision of the producers of *Lucky Lady* as to the division of the reward money among qualified applicants will be final.

"Very professional," Brass commented.

"Very parsimonious," K. Jeffrey said, refolding the document and sticking it back in his pocket. "My brother, Edward, devised the wording. On behalf of the family he will pay up to but no more than half the reward. Up to but no more than half. His exact words."

"A precise man," Brass said.

"You could look at it that way," K. Jeffrey agreed. "Will you say something about the advertisement in your Thursday column?"

"Better not wait till Thursday," Brass said. "If you put the ad in this afternoon, it will appear tomorrow. I'll do a piece on it for tomorrow's paper."

K. Jeffrey pondered. "I suppose you're right," he said. "The sooner the soonest, and all of that. Well then, I'd better make some copies of the advertisement and get them to a messenger for distribution." He pushed himself out of the chair and headed for the office door. In the doorway he paused and turned around. "You haven't heard anything, have you? About Two-Headed Mary or the Trask girl?"

Brass smiled. "Am I eligible for the award?" he asked.

"You'll have to argue that one with my brother," Welton said. He gave a half-bow. "Bye, all. Don't see me out."

I saw him out anyway, and then went back to my minuscule cubicle to type up the results of my Quogue visit for Brass.

10

On Mondays, an important part of Broadway turns itself off. The legitimate theaters and most of the burlesque houses are dark—even chorus girls deserve one night to themselves— and many of the restaurants that service the theater crowd are closed in sympathy. This dormant section of the Great White Way only slightly lessens the glamour, or the glimmer, of the street. As Brass and I sauntered across Times Square this Monday evening, Bing Crosby and Joan Bennett were amusing audiences at the Paramount, thanks to the magic of talking pictures. At 45th and Broadway, the Loew's State had George Raft and Alice Faye in *Every Night at Eight* on the big screen, plus an hour of vaudeville acts on stage. The night, as the Broadway bards put it, was being turned into day by the myriad of lights on billboards, signs and the marquees of the Roxy, the Palace, the Strand, and a dozen other movie palaces within a dozen blocks of Broadway and 42nd Street.

But there was another side of Gotham nightlife that knew not what day of the week it was, nor cared. Joints of all sizes and types that were splattered along the side streets in the 40s and 50s, East and West, in the old brownstone and sandstone buildings, upstairs and down. These establishments, with names like the Hotsy Totsy Club, the Club Venus, Club 46, the Kit Kat Club, the Planet Mars, were described, or at least mentioned, in the "For Men Only" sections of the more daring guides to New York's nightlife. Those with less distinguished names or without names, just addresses, did not make it into any guidebooks and were not on the recommended lists of the Better Business Bureau. These were the small nightclubs and bars that had been speakeasies, and still maintained the aura of doing something that was not strictly legal. In many cases, with gambling parlors in the back rooms or bordellos upstairs, the aura was accurate. These clubs catered to the type of out-of-town fireman who tells the cab driver that he's "looking for some action." In some of the more predatory, known to the trade as "clip joints," a well-heeled customer would get a funny-tasting drink and wake up some hours later sprawled in an alley and relieved of his cash.

The reviews that passed for entertainment at the Hotsy Totsy Club, the Planet Mars, the Club Venus, or the lesser known joints, were small but active. The music was loud, the comics were raunchy, and the costumes on the showgirls were brief. The girls who danced in the revues were streetwise and cynical, and waiting and hoping for better days. Many of them aspired to careers in more legitimate areas of the show business, or wealthy sugar daddies to take them away from all this, or to get far enough ahead of the rent so they could afford the bus ticket back to Iowa and have enough left to show the folks how well they'd done in the big city. For some of them, it was just a job, a way to pay the rent and feed the face; no worse than any other job, and a lot better than being unemployed. Others fed on the excitement and liked the fast life of their fast boyfriends, until the boyfriend traded them in for a newer model, or left for parts unknown, or wound up facedown in the gutter on Tenth Avenue.

And that, my friends, is what passes for a sermon among us wised-up denizens of what has been described as "the longest street in the world."

Brass liked to move anonymously through the Broadway joints that provided so much material for his columns, watered down from the truth, but still strong drink for his midwestern readers who reveled in the cautionary tales he told of the sins of Gotham. He enjoyed mingling with the common folk without being recognized. But these days the anonymity was, at best, partial. Every maître d' and bouncer and hat-check girl in Manhattan, every bartender from Harlem to the Village, and many of the beat cops and quite a few cab drivers recognized Alexander Brass on sight. He had interviewed most of the greats, the near-greats, and the would-be-greats who had passed through New York City in the past decade, and could claim many of them as his friends. But he could still walk down a street or enter a restaurant without creating the sort of fuss stirred up by the stars of stage and screen, notable politicians, and several of his columnist confreres who courted personal publicity.

Tonight we were hitting the joints. Brass likes to consort with the characters that gave Broadway much of its color and flavor, and quite a bit of its crime. He calls it research. We headed west on 46th, passed the Gaiety, the Fulton, and the Forty-Sixth Street Theater, and stopped in at Sid's place between Eighth and Ninth Avenues—the sign on the blacked-over window said in ancient gilt: BALMORAL LOUNGE & GRILL; but it had no grill, lounging was discouraged, and few of the regulars would have known what you were talking about if you called it anything but Sid's place. The sign had been blacked out during the Prohibition years, with no noticeable change in the clientele.

We stopped briefly at the bar to say hi to Sid, a small man of indeterminate age—an age he had been holding for the last two decades—with a large nose that bent ever so slightly to the left, and large ears that stuck out dramatically from his bald head, and to wave to Bessie, his very thin and exceptionally blond bartender, and were buzzed through to the inner room.

The craps game on the felt-covered table in that small, dimly lit chamber was continuous, only the cast of characters gradually changed. Some of the players looked up briefly as we entered, one of them muttered "fresh blood," and the game went on.

Brass plays indifferent poker and fairly good bridge, and these are his games of choice. I quote him for both of these assessments; I don't play bridge and I can't afford the stakes in the twice a month poker game he occasionally sits in on with other masters of the bon mot like Cornell Woolrich, Robert BencWey, Dorothy Parker, Damon Runyon, and whatever editors or publishers can be cajoled into playing. But when we enter a gambling joint, he gambles a little to establish his credentials as one of the boys. I just watch, to establish my credentials as the kid who just watches.

Brass put some money down for a while as the dice went around the table, won a couple and lost a couple. He shot a seven when the dice passed to him, and then an eight, made his point, rolled a three, made it, rolled a nine, sevened out, and passed the dice. I watched. After he dropped from the game, about forty dollars to the good, we went out to the bar and sat in a corner booth and talked to Sid.

Before he acquired the bar from its previous owner in payment of a debt of honor, Sid, who dresses as somberly as a small-town undertaker in a suit that always looks at least one full size too big for him, had been what Broadway calls a "character": a small-time con man, gambler, and hustler. Bessie, his bartender, had been what Brass occasionally referred to in "Brass Tacks" as a "lady of the night." (Brass had used "whore" in a piece once, and thirty-seven papers had dropped the column that day, and two had canceled for good.) She got off her back for good a few years ago when Charlie "Lucky" Luciano decided to organize the industry.

Sid still kept in touch with his old friends in the hoodlum business; many of them were customers and others used him as a mailbox. He knew who had done what and to whom, and who was where and for how long. Brass dropped in every few weeks to talk to Sid and exchange news and views on the happenings in the world of the Broadway characters and their comings and goings.

"Have you heard, Mr. B.," Sid said, putting a shot of Armagnac and a glass of water in front of Brass, "Valentine is cracking down on the local gentry."

"I heard something about it," Brass said. "Sort of a general roundup, wasn't it?"

The Valentine they were speaking of was Lewis J. Valentine, Police Commissioner of the City of New York, who had his own colorful ways of combating crime. Under a new law, which was being called the "Public Enemy Act," anyone who had a criminal record could be locked up for so much as speaking to anyone else who shared the same distinction. Over the past couple of weeks, beginning with Labor Day, Valentine had begun enforcing the law. The police had been making surprise sweeps of Midtown, to take the undesirable elements off the street before they could frighten away the tourists.

"They incarcerate a guy for conversing with another guy who has been in the slammer," Sid said. "Who else would a guy talk to, I ask you? A guy would have to travel many a block to accost a guy who ain't been in the slammer, and then it would be a guy whom the first guy don't even know so much as to talk to anyhow."

"It's not safe on the streets no longer," Bessie said dolefully, setting a draft of beer on a coaster in front of me. "Some fly cop will jump out of a doorway and finger you for associating with known criminals, even though there ain't nobody in sight but you and the cop, and drag you off to the precinct. My Joe just got back this morning after a night of incarceration in a cell with a couple of dozen truly undesirable citizens. There was no room to lie down and he couldn't even perform his bodily functions with privacy. It's disgraceful, what this city is coming to."

Bessie's boyfriend, Joe, was often spoken of by her, but was never around when we came by. His profession, it seemed, had the same hours as her own: late evening to early morning. She never discussed just what he did, but we had the impression that it involved entering business establishments in the absence of their owners in an effort to make them realize the value of burglary insurance.

"The commissioner is being a bit overenthusiastic," Brass agreed.

"Where'd he get a moniker like 'Valentine' anyway?" Bessie complained. "They want to name him after a saint it should have been Dismus, who went around telling people how they was supposed to behave until he was called early to Heaven."

The conversation gently twisted around to Two-Headed Mary. Bessie had seen the mention in "Brass Tacks," and wanted to know whether she had turned up.

"Not yet," Brass said. "And her disappearance gets more mysterious daily."

Sid grunted. "Not surprising," he said. "Mary's never practiced doing anything the easy way. She's a story-teller, only she don't warn you that it's a story you're getting."

"You know the lady?" Brass asked.

"Sure," Sid said. "Known her for years. Called herself a variety of names, then more or less settled on Mary. Her real name's Bain, Amber Bain. Only, for some reason, she don't like nobody knowing that. Got a daughter in the show business. I used to do some rough work for the Professor—you know the Professor? Back in the old days."

"Rough work?" I asked. "I didn't know you did that sort of thing."

Sid looked a question at me.

"Well," I said, "I mean, you're sort of light, and you don't look that tough or imposing, which I would have thought was a requirement. No offense."

Bessie broke out laughing. Sid chuckled. Brass looked amused. "Carpentry, a little electrical wiring, painting, rough work like that," Sid explained. "When the Professor had a big store con going on, I'd help him set the stage. I also took photographs. If we wanted it to look like a stockbroker's office, I'd go take photographs of a real one so we'd have something to copy—or a commercial bank, or a bookmaking joint, or a faro parlor or some such. Then, when the show started I'd take a part, usually something like the cash teller or the tote board operator."

"Responsible positions," Brass commented.

"Yeah. Anyway, the Professor used Mary to class up the act. She always looked and acted like a duchess. The mark couldn't believe there was anything phony going on when Mary was in the room."

"Back then did she ever take a few weeks off and depart for places unknown?"

"I ain't never heard of her doing that."

The conversation then switched around to the State of the Union, and then baseball. When we got up to leave, Sid put out his hand. "Listen," he said. "I'll ask around the Street for word of Mary. If there's anything else I can do, let me know."

"Of course," Brass said.

Sid cocked his head sideways and stared at the ceiling, but he was seeing something else. "You know, them were the good old days," he said. "Working with the Professor and Mary and the crew. There was like a, I don't know, a sense of companionship."

"Nothing encourages solidarity as when you're gathered together to swindle some unsuspecting yahoo," Brass said.

"Yeah," Sid agreed. "That's it."

Brass tapped on the table with a finger. "Tell me, Sid," he said, "do you know a character who's short and thin, with a prominent nose, probably dresses flash, and who's good with locks? Can you put a name to that picture?"

Sid pondered. "Nothing comes to mind," he said. "But I'll ask around. No heat?"

"Not from me. I just want to ask a gentleman of that description a few questions."

"Right," Sid said. "Like I said, I'll ask around."

We went to a couple of more joints before calling it a night. Gashouse Flo and Jennie the Factory, a couple of local ladies of the late evening, cornered Brass in a joint called the Club Boomalay and told him their woes, which sounded much like the complaints of unorganized labor everywhere. Except that in their case management came in the guise of Lucky Luciano and Dutch Schultz. I wondered whether Clifford Odets would like to do a play called "Waiting for the Dutchman." The ladies' stories were fascinating, but nothing that Brass could sanitize enough to use in his column.

At the Kit Kat Club the floor man asked about Two-Headed Mary, but the query was merely friendly and he only knew her from her occasional visits to the club, usually with one gentleman or another.

It was a little after two in the A.M. when Brass decided to call it a night. I should correct the impression you may have that Brass demands sixteen-hour days from his employees. I accompany Brass on these late-night meanderings because I am as fascinated as he is with the characters he talks to and the tales they tell. Brass likes to end the evening with a brisk walk, so we walked briskly uptown.

"I almost forgot," Brass said as we separated at Columbus Circle, he to head east to his Central Park South penthouse apartment, I farther north to my humble room. "No need to come to the office tomorrow morning. I have another assignment for you."

He explained.

By two-thirty I had brushed my teeth and was in bed, staring at the ceiling and considering the possibilities of tomorrow's assignment. By two-thirty-two I was asleep.

11

In his youth it was clear that Sindbad, son of Lufar, was not favored of the gods. He grew thin and tall, but with a sickly cast; and he was cursed with an insatiable curiosity that always put him where he should not be. In his sixth year he fell into the Taleth in flood and traveled several leagues in the foaming torrent before being cast upon a passing rock, and thence to the shore. That he was not killed was regarded by those who knew him, not as a miracle, but as an accident which the gods would remedy as time passed.

Those of you who pick at such things, not recognizing the high caste and immense learning of even the mildest teller of tales, are even now saying: "surely you mean Basra, not Bazra; surely it was the Euphrates into which the child Sindbad was cast, not the Taleth, a river of which the geographers have no knowledge."

And yet I tell you that it was in Bazra, a city already ancient when the Turkic Basra was founded in the seventh century as you count such things, that this tale took place, and over a thousand years before. And the Taleth still flows, although today a meeker river and bearing a different name.

In his ninth year…

The reason that I have never gotten past page sixty in any of my earnest attempts to write the Great American Novel is not that the writing or plotting was bad. It may have been bad, but this was not the reason. I have learned from those who know such things that it is well nigh impossible for a writer to judge his own works. Conan Doyle tried to kill off Sherlock Holmes so he could get on with his more serious writing. Shakespeare probably thought that *Timon of Athens* or *Troilus and Cressida* was his greatest work, and *Hamlet* and *Macbeth* merely potboilers that gave his actors jobs, but wouldn't last.

The reason that I have never gotten past page sixty in any of my attempts so far is that I keep trying to follow my muse, and my muse can't seem to make up her mind. There was the small-town novel; I'd tried one of those, "Colonel Sebastian and the Gazebo," but even though I grew up in a small town I couldn't think of that much worth saying about one. I'd gotten pretty far into "Fools and Comrades," my war novel, before I realized that I was avoiding the war scenes because I knew nothing whatever about war beyond what I've read in the pulps. "The Supplicant," my realistic novel, was mystical; and "Heavy Hangs the Head," my story of the common man, had somehow turned into a Marxist, or at least Fabian Socialist, polemic. And I am neither.

So I've decided to switch to fantasy. It should be easier, right? I mean, you just make up the stuff, right? You get to use this great-sounding language, and sneak in all sorts of references to contemporary problems without having to solve them or even fully understand them; and you sound knowledgeable if not wise. A piece of cake.

So what happened to Sindbad in his ninth year that you or I or anybody else should care about?

Maybe I should try science fiction. "Zed Blox and his Galactic Rangers" or "The Princes of Earth" or "The Stars Like Popcorn"; E. E. "Doc" Smith and John W Campbell Jr. make it look easy. But then all writing looks easy until you roll that blank sheet of paper into the typewriter.

I rolled the sheet of paper out of the typewriter and put it in the little box that holds the uncompleted manuscript I happen to be working on, and put the cover on the typewriter. It was ten o'clock on a blustery morning; time for me to go to work. I buttoned my vest and shrugged into my jacket. Given the assignment, I was wearing one of my gentleman's disguises. My outfit today was a double-breasted number in blue with a chalk stripe and the new lapel that sweeps to the lower button. The salesman at Rogers Peet was very enthusiastic about it when I bought it, needing a suitable uniform to interview some local tycoons a few months back. Gloria thought it looked elegant; I thought it made me look like either a banker or a gangster: white shirt and dark tie, banker; blue shirt and loud tie, gangster.

Today I wore a white button-down shirt and a regimental tie given to me by Garrett for my birthday. I wasn't sure what regiment, but knowing Garrett I would have bet on something like His Majesty's Eleventh Corps de Balloon or the Ninth Imperial Light Camel.

Into the topcoat, on with the homburg, and out the door. The program was simple in outline, but might be difficult to accomplish. I was to pick up Sandra Lelane and go with her to the apartment building that Pearly Gates was convinced his missing wife had inhabited. We were then to somehow gain entrance to the apartment and see what we could see. It was the "gain entrance" part that might be tricky. Since the staff of the building apparently knew Two-Headed Mary as Phillippa Gates, nee Stern, and was unaware that she had a daughter, we had no handle to use and would have to improvise as the occasion demanded. I hailed a passing Checker cab and got in. "Seventy-seventh and Central Park West," I told the driver, a wiry bald man whose name, according to his license posted by the meter, was Thomas Jefferson Finkle.

He turned to look at me. "It's maybe four blocks. For four blocks it isn't worth dropping the flag. You could walk it easier," he said. "You could use the exercise. You wouldn't even work up a sweat."

"I'm a big tipper," I told him.

"Sure," he said. "You tip what? Maybe twenty percent? On a fifteen-cent ride that's three cents. I'm excited."

"We're going on from there," I told him.

"What, another four blocks?" he growled, unconvinced, slid the panel closed and flipped the meter on.

It was just ten-thirty when we pulled up, and Miss Lelane was waiting outside her building. New York is a blase city, whose citizens are too world-weary and nonchalant to pause and stare at the famous or notorious who pass among them, so only two or three people had paused to stare at Sandra Lelane. But they had an excuse; wearing a camel-hair coat and a felt hat that looked like a sort of flattened-out miniature fedora, she was sedately beautiful and well worth staring at. She made me feel lightheaded and poetic. I opened the door for her. "Small is the worth," I recited,

> *"Of beauty from the light retired*
> *Bid her come forth,*
> *Suffer herself to be desired,*
> *And not blush so to be admired."*

"Well," she said, seating herself and closing the door. "And so early in the morning, too. Is it Andrew Marvell?"

I shook my head. "No, but you've got the right period. Edmund Waller."

She nodded. "Did you enjoy the play?" she asked.

"The—oh, you mean *Fine and Dandy*. I loved it. And I loved you in it." I had conversed with actors and actresses before, and I knew what she wanted to hear. Luckily in this case it was strictly true.

I leaned forward and tapped on the glass panel. "Eightieth and Park, this time. Go through the park."

He twisted around to face us and opened the panel. "And how else would I go?"

"I don't know. You might have decided to go around. For the exercise."

"I got a weak heart," he told me. He slid the panel closed and pulled away from the curb.

I leaned back in my seat and smiled at Sandra to show her it was all in fun.

Sandra looked at me thoughtfully. "Your boss is a strange man," she said.

"You won't get any argument from me," I told her. "But to just which of his strangenesses are you alluding?"

"I had a talk with Vera about him. You know—Vera Dain."

"The actress," I said brightly in a masterly understatement; sort of like referring to Lindbergh as "the pilot" or Dutch Schultz as "the crook."

Sandra smiled. "That's right. That one. She went around with Brass for a couple of years."

"That was before my time," I said.

"According to Vera, he doesn't like publicity."

"True."

"But he's a columnist! Damon Runyon loves publicity. Winchell creates his own!"

"True," I said.

"He wouldn't take her to the Stork or to Twenty-One. He would only take her to places where he wouldn't be recognized. He took her to places that were so obscure that they didn't even recognize *her*."

"When the boss goes to places like the Stork Club, he's working," I told her.

"But, as Vera said, what's the point of going out with a columnist if you can't even get your name in his column?"

"Brass dislikes having his personal life known," I said. "He wants to be known only by and through his writings. I am quoting him in this."

She shook her head. Such behavior was out of her ken. "But I do appreciate what he's doing," she said. "Brass is devoting a lot of his time—and a lot of your time—in helping me find out what happened to my mother. And he probably won't be able to use any of it in his column."

"My time comes cheap," I told her. "The boss is always looking for excuses to get me out of the office. I can't decide whether I'm an employee, a trainee, or a pilot project for the make-work program of the WPA."

She smiled a slight smile. "Whatever his motive," she said, "it's nice of him. And of you."

"My pleasure," I told her sincerely.

Sandra stared out the window at the passing trees and shrubs atop the transverse wall for a minute and then turned back to me. "I had dinner with some of the girls from the show last night," she said. "The other two female principals and a few of the gypsies. We talked about Lydia Laurent most of the evening. We didn't intend to, but there it was. About her and her murder and the way they found her body. I knew the kid. She was sweet. Kind. Not awfully talented, but she tried hard and she worked hard. Who would want to harm her? Who would do a thing like that?"

"You've got me," I told her. "There was a kid in my home town who used to set cats on fire. He said he didn't know why, it just came over him on occasion that it was something he should do. Then one day he drowned. The story went around that the King of the Cats had come and held his head underwater. It was as good a story as any."

"The King of the Cats?" Sandra asked.

I shrugged. "That's what they said."

She sort of smiled, and then shook her head. "It was a dismal dinner," she said. "Dismal."

"I can imagine," I said.

"Someone suggested that there's some connection between Lydia and my mother. Do you know about that?"

"Did this someone say what the connection was?"

"She didn't know. It was just a rumor she heard. Lydia was the roommate of that missing girl, Billie Trask. Did you know that?"

"We had a visit from a police inspector yesterday," I told her. "He told us all about it."

"Is it true she was found in the park naked? That's what the papers said. Was she molested?"

I told Sandra what Inspector Raab had told us about the way the body was found. She shook her head. "It is dismal. It's as if there's a strange epidemic going around. First Billie Trask and my mom disappear, and now this."

"It could all be connected," I agreed. "But we don't know in what way. I guess that's what we should be trying to find out."

"Just what is it we're going to do now?" Sandra asked. "Your boss wasn't very informative on the phone."

"Did he tell you about your mother's putative husband?"

She smiled. "Putative, I like that. It sounds like one of Brass's words."

"I guess it rubs off," I said.

"He told me a little. A Texan. Full of oil."

I relayed what we knew of the tale of Phillippa and the Texan.

"So this is the apartment we're going to? The one Mom was supposedly living in when Pearly Gates came courting?"

"The one," I said.

"How are we going to do this?" Sandra asked as the cab left the transverse through Central Park and headed up 79th Street.

I shook my head. "I have no idea."

"What did Brass say?" she asked.

"That it would be a good idea to go look at this apartment. The method, he said, would be dictated by circumstance. He did suggest that a five-dollar bill might work wonders."

"Well, let us hope so."

"If not you can practice your histrionics. Few men can resist a crying woman."

"Yes," she agreed. "They do what she wants just to shut her up. Is Pearly Gates going to join us?"

"No. Since we don't know what's going on, Brass thought that the less your putative stepfather knew about your mother's past, until and unless she chooses to tell him, the better."

Sandra nodded. "Well then," she said.

"Just so," I agreed.

We pulled up to the corner of 80th Street and Park Avenue, and Thomas Jefferson Finkle turned around and opened the glass panel. "Okay, sport, we're here," he said. "That'll be forty cents."

I handed him two quarters and a dime. "No, no, don't thank me," I told him. "I'm a big fan of Clifford Odets."

"Whatever," he said, pocketing the money.

Nine-ten Park Avenue was a quiet, unassuming twelve-story building on the southwest corner of 80th Street. The doorman's uniform was hardly as ornate as that of a captain in, say, the Italian navy. "Good morning," he said, holding the taxi door for us. "May I help you?"

I paused until the door was closed and the cab had driven off. "I believe Mrs. Phillippa Gates lives here," I said.

He cocked his head thoughtfully. "Mrs. Phillippa—"

"You probably know her as Mrs. Stern," I suggested.

"Oh, yes," he said. "Of course. Mrs. Stern. I'm sorry but Mrs. Stern is not in residence at the moment."

"Are you sure?" I asked.

"Yes, sir," he said, looking offended. "But I can ring her apartment if you like."

"We would appreciate it," Sandra said.

"Of course. Follow me."

We entered the lobby and the doorman went to the house switchboard, which sat in a small alcove between the two elevators. After a few manipulations with the earpiece to his ear, he unplugged it and shook his head. "Sorry," he said, "Mrs. Stern doesn't answer."

"How long has she been away?" I asked.

"Sorry, I couldn't tell you that."

"Did she leave word as to where she was going?"

He shook his head. "Sorry."

I leaned forward. "Are you sure that she is not in the apartment?"

He looked at me with the patient, exasperated look that Parisians reserve for American tourists. "I just rang—"

I palmed a five-spot, preparing to pass it to him. "We'd like to go up and see," I told him.

He shook his head. "That would be irregular. The super wouldn't allow it."

"Have you asked him?"

"As a matter of fact, Mr., ah, Gates, was here on Saturday and, as we haven't formally been advised of the new, ah, relationship, the super didn't let him upstairs."

I put the bill back in my pocket. If he wouldn't take Pearly's money, he wouldn't take mine. "Can't be too careful," I said.

"Yes, sir," he agreed.

"Are you sure there's nobody up there?" Sandra asked, looking concerned and slightly tearful. "Supposing that Mother broke her leg or had an attack or something. I wouldn't be surprised if she had an attack. She may be just laying up there alone!"

"Excuse me, ma'am?"

I stepped closer to him and spoke earnestly. "Have you looked into the apartment, say anytime in the past week?"

He drew back. "Of course not!"

"Are you certain that Mrs. Stern isn't lying on the floor in the living room, or the bedroom, unconscious—in need of medical help?"

"Well, sir, that's highly unlikely. After all—"

I interrupted him. "This lady is her daughter, she's very worried. She hasn't heard from her mother in some time, and we can't get an answer on the phone. We'd like to go upstairs and look around, make sure she's all right."

The doorman looked doubtful. "You can ask the superintendent," he said, "but I'm sure he wouldn't allow it."

"Will you call the superintendent for us?" I asked.

"I'm sorry. He isn't in at the moment."

Sandra's eyes got wide and a note of hysteria crept into her voice. "Mother might be upstairs, lying unconscious," she cried, wringing her hands, which I thought was overdoing it, but she's the actress. "Or worse! I have to get to her! What are we to do?" She dissolved into sobs.

I patted her gently on the back. "Perhaps we should call the police," I suggested. "I imagine a policeman could open the door for us. Just to look around, make sure Mrs. Stern is all right. I just hope it doesn't upset the other tenants, to see policemen in the building. But that can't be helped." I gestured toward the plug board. "Is this the outside line?"

The doorman had taken a step back, as one might retreat from someone carrying the plague. "No, sir, it is not. This is the house phone only. The central switchboard is in the superintendent's apartment."

"But if he isn't here...?"

"His wife and another lady operate the switchboard," the doorman told us. "One of them is always at the board."

"Admirable," I said. "You wait here," I told Sandra. "I'll go out and find a policeman."

"Wait!" the doorman said. "We wouldn't want—It wouldn't be—You just wait here for a minute. Please!" He touched the call button for the elevator on the left, and shifted from foot to foot until it arrived. After a whispered colloquy with the elevator man, they changed places, and the doorman entered the elevator while the elevator man stood by the door and tried not to stare at us. The elevator door closed and it groaned and whined and started up.

Sandra clutched my arm and, bringing her sobbing face close to mine, she whispered, "I need a drink!"

I patted her on the shoulder. "Be brave," I said loudly and firmly.

After a couple of minutes the elevator returned, whining and groaning, and thumped to a stop and the door opened. A tall, slender man emerged. He was dressed in a tweed suit and Ascot and carrying a walking stick of some dark wood with a gold handle in the shape of an owl. His dark hair was graying at the temples, but his carefully trimmed mustache and beard were still jet-black. He was past middle age, but how much past I couldn't say. He was wearing steel-rimmed glasses. If he was introduced as the president of a bank, or a sporting club, or a small European country, I would believe it.

"Now then," he said in a smooth, reasonable voice, looking from Sandra to me and back. "What's all this?"

"We'd like to see Mrs. Stern or Mrs. Gates, whichever you prefer," I told him. "Who are you?"

"My name is Colonel Wills. You've been feeding Bernard here with some cock-and-bull story about poor Mrs. Stern lying unconscious in her apartment. And this young lady claims to be her daughter, when I happen to know she has no daughter. I want an explanation. And, by God, if anyone around here is going to call the police, it shall be I!"

Sandra was looking at Wills with a funny expression on her face. She took a handkerchief from her purse and dried her eyes. "Your name is Colonel Wills?" she asked.

He nodded. "That's right, young lady."

Sandra nervously clutched at the strand of pearls that circled her neck. "Couldn't you help us? I just want to make sure that my mother, Mrs. Stern, is okay."

He peered at her over his glasses. "That's all, eh?"

"Do you live here?" Sandra asked, twisting the pearl strand between her fingers. "Perhaps we should go up to your apartment to talk this over."

"Well," he said. "Well." He looked at me and back at Sandra. She dropped her hands to her side and stared intently at his face. He smiled. "Perhaps we should."

Now if that don't beat all, as my childhood buddies back in Ohio would have said. He had changed his tune quicker than

Kay Kyser, and I was nonplussed at his sudden acquiescence. But Sandra and the colonel seemed to be plussed, so I kept quiet.

He gestured us into the elevator. The doorman and elevator man switched places again, and we went up.

The apartment was large and could have been the stage setting for an elegant drawing-room comedy. The furniture was antique, but not overpowering and, if I'm any judge, cost a bundle. But, of course, I'm no judge. The colonel waved us into the living room, which was mostly shades of white, and we sat down on an el of a couch. The colonel sat on the right-angle section and propped his feet up on the coffee table.

"Well?" he said.

"I could use a drink," Sandra said.

"Silly me," the colonel said, "I'm forgetting my manners." He pushed a small gold button on the end table, and a real-live butler appeared at a side door and stood motionless.

"What will you have?" the colonel asked.

"A martini," Sandra said.

"Scotch and water," I said. It would have been churlish to refuse.

The butler disappeared back through the door.

"Nice place," I said.

"I like it," the colonel replied.

The drinks came. Colonel Wills was drinking something green with club soda. "All right," he said after taking a sip. "You gave me the office, now tell me the tale. What's the pitch? What do you want?"

"You don't recognize me?" Sandra asked.

"No," he said. "Should I?"

"I was smaller the last time you saw me."

"No doubt," he said, unimpressed.

Sandra smiled and put her hand lightly on my arm. "This is Morgan DeWitt," she told the colonel. "He works for Alexander Brass, the columnist. They are helping me find my mother." Twisting in her seat she indicated the colonel with an upturned palm. "Morgan, this is the Grand Duke Feodore Alexandrovitch, or Manderson Kent of the Shropshire Kents, or Leopold van Spottsbergen, or Astor K. Vandermier, or Captain Sander Biddell,

United States Navy, Retired, or..."

The colonel with the many names put his glass on the table with a thump and rose to his feet. "Now look—" he said.

Sandra rose with him. "Better known to those who love him as the Professor," she finished. "Professor, I'm Lucille—Amber's kid."

He stared at her.

"Really," she said.

"No!" he sat down. "Well, I'll be—Little Lucille. Say—remember that time in Sheboygan—"

"We were never in Sheboygan," she told him.

"I guess you're right. Remember the Fisher brothers, Jim and Alec?"

"You mean Peter and his sister Sal?"

"Was that their names? Remember the big score we made running the golden wire on that grain elevator bates from St. Louis? Rented a private railroad car for that one. Had him running around the country and took him for twenty thousand dollars, then we blew him off with a cackle bladder in Buffalo, New York."

"The mark was from Cleveland, he owned a dry-goods store, we took him for closer to thirty thousand, and we blew him off in Jersey City. But you got the cackle bladder right. Mom always said we had more luck that we deserved on that one."

"Well," the Professor said. "I guess it is you."

"I guess it is," she agreed.

"It's nice to see you, kid. The last time you came around you were—what?—thirteen?"

"I think so. Maybe fourteen."

"Then you got high-hat on your mom and moved out, the way she tells it."

"That's pretty close."

"You always had a mind of your own," the Professor said, raising his glass with the green liquid. "To you, my dear, and to your mom."

"Thanks," she said, touching his glass with her own.

I took a sip of my scotch. "So," I said, "you're the Professor. It's good to meet you." I looked from one to the other. "I've heard a lot about you, what with this and that."

The Professor leaned forward and stared at me as though he

wanted to memorize my face, and then he leaned back. "Is he with it?" he asked Sandra.

"His boss is," Sandra said.

"Alexander Brass," the Professor said. "I know him. I could like him if I took the time. He is with it."

"With what?" I demanded.

"The con," Sandra explained. "The grift. The Professor wants to know if you're one of us—of them."

"Boy, you could make a fortune in the grift," the Professor told me, continuing to examine my face. "I haven't seen anybody with such an innocent-looking phiz since Sweet Billy McFine left the business."

"I thought I looked jaded and hard," I said. "I'm disappointed."

"Not much call for jaded and hard," the Professor said. "Innocent will take you far."

Sandra took the Professor's hand and squeezed it in her fist like a small child clinging to her daddy. "Where's my mom?" she asked.

"Honey, I wish I knew," the Professor told her. "She hasn't been around here for more than two weeks."

"Straight?"

"Straight. She was working this cowboy mark, using the apartment right below this one for the convincer. We keep it here for such purposes. Very elegant and posh, it is. We were setting him up for a golden wire store, 'cause he thinks he knows about horses, being from Texas, when she decides she's in love with him and ups and marries him. Well, if it were anyone but Mary I would have thought she was working a con of her own, and been real unhappy. But I know she's on the up and up, and we're not out much sugar, so what the hell. Then she goes away."

"I thought you'd be retired by now, living on that land you own in Florida," Sandra said.

"Ah, my child, I went to visit that portion of Florida to which I have title in fee simple, as it were, and discovered that the fee was not the only thing that was simple. The land is underwater at high tide. Likewise at low tide. It is, to put it concisely, a swamp."

"You were swindled?" Sandra asked incredulously.

"Is there no bottom to the depths of human depravity to which some people will sink? Yes, I was had."

"What did you do?" I asked, picturing a gunfight at ten paces on the streets of Coral Gables.

"I sold the property for three times what I paid for it; but that's not the point. The event taught me a great lesson."

"Which was?"

"When you go up against a real estate salesman wear both belt and braces, and keep your wallet in a buttoned pocket; they make gritting seem honest and respectable by comparison."

"So you're still at the game?" Sandra asked.

"Like Harry Lauder, I'm making my fourth and last farewell performance," the Professor said.

"How'd you rope Mom back into it?"

"It was a sort of mutual lassoing," the Professor said. "We were having dinner together one night and we got to talking over old times. And we decided to give it one more spin, just for the hell of it."

"You mean you talked Mom into it."

"I suppose she missed the thrill of the chase. Like an old fire horse answering the bell one last time—"

"You mean you talked Mom into it."

The Professor sighed. "Yes, I suppose I did."

"Mom is not old," Sandra said.

"It was just a simile. Mary is assuredly not old. It is I for whom the bells of age are tolling."

"You're not old, either, Professor. And you won't be too old when you're a hundred and twenty—dead or alive," Sandra told him.

"Thank you, my dear. But, is that right? You have no idea where your mother is?"

Sandra nodded and looked glum.

"That's right, Professor," I told him. "We've been looking for her for the past week. Didn't you see the mention in 'Brass Tacks'?"

"Brass's newspaper column? I saw it. Doesn't mean I believed it. Unlike Will Rogers, I know nothing whatever that I've read in the papers."

"Weren't you concerned when Mom disappeared?" Sandra asked.

"No, child. You see, I had no idea she had really disappeared. I assumed she was off with her new husband and hadn't bothered informing her pals on the Street."

"But when he came here looking for her?"

"I thought perhaps they had had a spat. I wasn't prepared to discuss with him anything that Mary might not have already told him, and I had no idea of just how much that might be. There are some things, I think, that she wouldn't wish him to know."

"That's so," she agreed.

The Professor looked at me. "May I assume that nothing of what we say here will get printed in Mr. Brass's column?"

"Nothing that we hear from you will get used in a column without your permission unless we hear it from someone else. And even then we probably wouldn't use it. As the boss says, if we couldn't keep secrets, we wouldn't hear any."

"Understand then that you have my blanket non-permission to ever print anything you hear from me. Ever," the Professor repeated. "Any time."

"I understand," I told him.

"You know," the Professor said thoughtfully, turning back to Sandra, "there was another man around asking for your mom a few days ago."

"When?" I asked.

"Who?" Sandra asked.

"Manders, the super, told me about it," the Professor explained. "The man didn't exactly ask for Mary, he said he was here to pick up her bags. He had a note."

I sat up. "Did Manders give him the bags?"

"There were no bags to give, as far as I know. Mary kept very little stuff of her own here. A change of clothes, perhaps; clean underthings. He didn't give the office, and Manders thought it sounded funny, so he told the man to have Mary call the building and explain what she wanted. She never called."

"What office?" I asked.

"The office," Sandra explained, making the gesture at her throat that I had seen her make downstairs. "It's a signal we use. If you're wearing a tie, it's straightening the tie. If you're not, it's coming as close as you can with what you have, making some gesture that won't be noticed by anyone not in the know. Why it's called 'the office' I don't know. Do you know, Professor?"

"Lost in the mists of pre-history, my dear," the Professor said.

"When I gave the Professor the office in the lobby, for example—"

"—I know that she was 'in the know' or 'with it,' as we say," the Professor finished. "So, even though I didn't recognize her, I brought you both up to my apartment for a private chat."

"There are other signs," Sandra said. "Like"—she made a brushing gesture with the fingers of her left hand on her right sleeve—"keep away. Or—"

The Professor smiled broadly. "Now, now," he said. "Mustn't give away all our little secrets at once."

"He's annoyed," Sandra told me. "He always smiles like that when he's annoyed. He used to get annoyed at me a lot when I was a child."

"Nonsense," the Professor said. "You were a natural." He leaned back and started telling stories about life on the con. I think he was trying to make up for having shown that he distrusted me, or perhaps he was just trying to make me feel at home. Sandra broke in occasionally with her reminiscences, grifting as seen through the eyes of a little girl. They were having fun, and I was getting an unexpected education in the art of the swindle.

We talked for another hour or so, and I learned a lot more about the life of a professional con man, but nothing useful about Two-Headed Mary. We did go down to the apartment below to see whether she had left any clue to her whereabouts, but no soap.

Sometime around noon the Professor invited us to stay for lunch: blintzes smothered in last-of-the-season peaches with just a touch of cognac. Sandra accepted; I declined. I'm not sure why. Perhaps I thought they should be alone together for a while to talk over old times and life with Two-Headed Mary before she grew her second head. Mostly I think it was that I was enjoying myself too much. I could see how people could be swept along by the Professor, believe whatever he told them and do whatever he asked. He walked me to the elevator door and told me to come back anytime, but call first. "And bring along Mr. Brass," he added. "I'd like to talk to him." He gave me his card, which, I noticed claimed he was Septimus Vogle, Managing Director of the Continental Aerodrome Consortium. I didn't ask.

12

picked up a ham and Swiss on rye toast, lettuce and mustard, no mayo, half a pickle, and a cardboard container of milk at Danny's and brought them back to the office. After typing a report on our meeting with the Professor and sticking it on Brass's desk, I settled down behind my own desk with a copy of this morning's *World*. Brass's short piece on K. Jeffrey's reward was in today's column, sandwiched between a whimsical description of the tiny performers at Professor Huber's Flea Circus on 42nd Street and an item headed "A Brief Panegyric to the Silent Screen." He tries to use at least one obscure word in every column to enrich his readers' vocabulary. "Brass Tacks" is an educational experience for the reader, will he or nil he.

I draped a napkin about my knees, and mused over the item as I munched my ham on rye.

MATINEE MARY is still among the missing, and her friends on Glitter Boulevard hope nothing evil has happened to her. Jeff Welton, producer of that Broadway boffo *Lucky Lady,* is offering a two-G reward to locate either her or Billie Trask, the box-office wench who disappeared with the weekend's receipts a couple of weeks ago. Word around town is that the two ladies know each other and their disappearances may be connected. "I don't think Billie took the money," Welton told this reporter. "She isn't that kind of girl."

That's two big ones, boys and girls, for distribution among those with word of either of the absent Broadway ladies. First come, first served. Read the Advert elsewhere in the *World* for details.

Brass used Broadway slang in his Broadway items to give the reader a feeling of being in the know. Broadway characters tend to speak with a unique kind of careful illiteracy, and the show business had a language all its own; but I've never heard this newspaper version of the slang spoken on Broadway, or anywhere outside of Brass's and Winchell's columns. As Brass explained it, it was what readers had come to expect so it was what he gave them. I think that Brass and Winchell made it all up between them.

Brass was playing it with a light touch. He could have gone in for dark suppositions: "After the Central Park murder this weekend of chorine Lydia Laurent, friend of the missing pair, fears of foul play have saddened, and perhaps frightened, the close-knit theatrical community…"

Gloria came in around three, carrying two small paper sacks. She went through to Brass's office and placed them on his desk. He stared at them through narrowed eyes. "Any problems?" he asked.

"I had to go ten dollars higher than I expected," she said, sounding disgusted. "I must be losing my touch."

"I doubt that," he said. "Was there anything?"

"Nothing that shouted out," she told him. "Maybe on a closer examination."

He sighed. "Well, let's take a look."

"What are we looking at?" I asked, standing in the doorway.

"I've just been visiting the apartment on East Fifty-fourth that was shared by the dead girl, Lydia Laurent, and Billie Trask," Gloria told me.

"The missing girl," I said brightly.

"Just so," Brass said.

"And from a trip to the Royal Theater, where the chorus girls each have individual lockers. My guess was right," Gloria told Brass. "The police didn't search Lydia's locker at the theater. Either they didn't know it was there, or they didn't think it was worth the trouble. They may have been right. If there's anything worth looking at in either of those bags, I can't see it."

I elbowed past Gloria and dropped onto the couch. "How'd you get in?" I asked her.

"The locker, I popped the lock. The apartment, I gave the super a ten." She turned to Brass. "I'm sorry, it shouldn't have cost a dime, but the super knew he had something, with the police crawling around, and he said some guy from the *Mirror* was there yesterday and gave him a twenty to get in."

Brass leaned back in his chair and put his hands behind his head. "I don't believe it," he said.

"I know," she said. "I didn't believe it myself. I must be losing it."

Brass smiled and shook his head. "Nonsense! Some people's avarice is greater than their concupiscence, no matter what the lure, and there's nothing to be done about it. What I don't believe is that a reporter from the *Mirror* paid the super twenty dollars."

"So, when you said you had to go ten dollars higher than you expected,"I asked her, "you meant that you expected to get in for free?"

She looked at me with the look that froze mercury. "Of course," she said.

Brass leaned forward and picked up one of the bags. "Who was the reporter from the *Mirror*?"

"I asked the super. He didn't know. A little, skinny man with a big nose and bad teeth. That doesn't sound like anyone I've seen at the *Mirror*."

"There wouldn't be anything at the apartment worth taking a picture of," Brass said. "Or am I wrong?"

"No, just an apartment. Cleaner than many, but it didn't have much furniture to get in the way. Those girls lived a frugal life."

"And the case isn't big enough to give that kind of play. Just one more kid buys it in the big city. Nobody from the *Mirror* gave the super a twenty," Brass said. "If there wasn't anything worth shooting, there wasn't anything worth paying more than a finif for."

"That was my thought," Gloria agreed.

"The description sounds like the man that was with the pseudo-Sandra out in Brooklyn," I volunteered.

"It does, doesn't it?" Brass agreed. "Was the apartment turned over?"

Gloria shook her head. "No. Neat and clean. Twenty dollars or no twenty dollars, the super insisted on standing in the doorway and watching while the guy looked over the apartment. Wouldn't let him take anything away."

"He let you take stuff away," I said.

She smiled at me and nodded. It was not worth discussing.

"Well," Brass said, "let's see what you got." He upended the paper sack he was holding, dumping its contents in a pile on the desktop.

"That's what came from the apartment," Gloria told him. "It was pretty well gone over by the police, the super said. I don't know what they took away."

Brass poked at the pile with his finger. There were three or four unpaid bills, a half-dozen envelopes that looked like personal correspondence, a bracelet, a pair of earrings, and a book: *Wine from These Grapes* by Edna St. Vincent Millay. The bracelet was a circle of heavy links of what appeared to be gold with what appeared to be a diamond set atop each link. The earrings were small circles of some green stone. "I hope that whatever the police took away was more inspirational than this batch," he said. "Are they all the belongings of Miss Laurent?"

Gloria separated the collection into two small piles. She pointed to one pile. "Laurent." The other. "Trask." She dumped the other bag onto the Laurent pile: two lipsticks, a compact, a pair of stockings, a tube of Dr. Fogler's Fine Liniment, a box of aspirin powders, and two photographs: one of an older woman and the other of a young boy and a dog of indeterminate age. "I didn't see any point in leaving anything in the locker," she said, "although I doubt if any of this stuff means anything to us."

Brass took the envelopes, which were in the "Trask" pile, and sat on the couch. "Did you read through these?" he asked Gloria.

"No. I just dropped them in the bag. I'd feel funny reading them. They might be very private."

"Were they hidden?"

"Not really. They were in the drawer with her underwear, in a sort of net that she used to keep worn hose. It's the sort of thing girls with roommates do to keep some things private."

"Um," Brass said. "The police didn't find them, but I doubt if they poked too thoroughly through the girl's worn stockings."

"The police should hire some female detectives," Gloria said.

Brass nodded. "That will be a long time coming." He sorted the envelopes into two piles, by return address: three from a Mrs. Jacob Trask of Hagerstown, Maryland, and three from a Jemmy Brookes of Baltimore, Maryland. "I think our interest in what happened to Lydia Laurent and how she died must override any considerations of personal privacy," he said. "And it seems likely that whatever happened to Billie Trask is related to what happened to Miss Laurent. We are voyeurs in a good cause."

"Oh, I know," Gloria said. "And besides, we're newspaper men, and we're paid to be nosy. Other people pay us to be nosy for them."

"Very nicely said," Brass told her. "I may use it in a column." Although Brass felt free to use in his column anything he heard that wasn't being told him in confidence, he was scrupulous about giving credit. Famous, infamous, or unknown, it didn't matter. If you said it, your name got attached to it in the column. I had been mentioned three or four times myself. Gloria must have given up counting some time ago.

Brass looked at one of the envelopes with Mrs. Trask's return address. "Dime store," he said. "Presumably from the girl's mother." He examined one of the other trio, holding it up to the light and rubbing it between his fingers. "Personalized stationery of reasonable quality," he said. "A return address in Baltimore. And the postmark bears that out." He sniffed the envelope. "Faint odor of, ah…"

"Jasmine," Gloria said.

"Very good, thank you. Jasmine. We can assume that 'Jemmy' is female. Well, let's see if we have anything useful."

Brass read the letters slowly and thoughtfully, starting with the ones from Billie Trask's mother, and then passed them along to Gloria, who passed them to me. I read them out of a sense of duty. After all, I was a newspaper man, it was my job.

The mother's letters dated to before Billie had her accident and left the chorus. They were loving and chatty and full of back-home gossip, with a hint of something deeper. Toward the end of that first letter, Mother Trask wrote:

…Your poppa asked me the other day if I was hearing from you, and of course I told him I was cause I don't want to lie to your

poppa. He kind of grunted, you know what I mean, and that was that. But he never even asked before. Maybe if he asks again I'll show him some of your letters. Not the one where you say as how you forgive him, although I'm glad of that, but you know he never can admit he's done anything wrong and never will…

Forgive him for what, I wondered. But then I decided I was glad that I probably would never know.

The letters from Jemmy Brookes of Baltimore, Maryland, placed her as a close friend of Billie Trask. One was possibly interesting, in view of what we knew:

Ma Chere Bil—

C'etait bonne to hear from you enfin. Oui, Doddie told you right, Jule popped the question, and we plan to get hitched just as soon as he can get a job. He doesn't want me to work after we're married, so I'll have to quit the sec pool, which believe you me won't be much of a hardship. He ses that a man should support his woman, which is kind of Victorian, ses I, but sweet with all of that. But with jobs being the way they are—or, say, the way they aren't!!—it may be a while. You'll be my maid of honor on the big day, whenever it may be.

Je do so worry about you all alone in the big city. Although I'm glad that you're not quite so alone anymore-and I don't mean votre roommate, although she sounds like a nice girl.

I'd watch out for this one, tho. I know you're a big girl and can take care of yourself and not do anything you don't want to do. But he sounds like a big boy whos had a lot more practice with girls like you than you have with guys like him. And like you said, sometimes being with a guy can make you want to do what you dont want to do, at least until it's done and it's too late.

I promise to come up to visit some time when I have the bus fare. I'm looking forward to see you on stage, even if it is only in the chorus. After all, Jimmy Cagney started in the chorus, and look at him now—Public Enemy #1. You have a great future ahead of you kiddo.

Love n stuff
Jem

Which shows, I suppose, that it doesn't pay to predict. Billie was not exactly public enemy number one, but she was spending the present hiding out from the cops, and a good part of her future would probably be spent in a home for naughty women somewhere Upstate. Unless Brass was right and she was innocent. But he just said things like that to provoke a reaction. It's like the joke that Pinky told me about the man who went into Ratner's on 2nd Avenue and ordered a bowl of borscht. The waiter tells him, "Don't have the borscht today, it's not so good. Have the schav instead."

"But I don't want schav," the man insists, "I want borscht."

"In good conscience I cannot serve you the borscht today, it just isn't up to our standard."

"I don't care about your standard, I want the borscht!"

"Trust me—"

"You won't bring me the borscht? Then bring me the manager!"

So the manager comes over and listens to the story. "Ordinarily," he tells the man, "the customer is always right. But today I happen to know that the borscht is truly not as good as it should be. Have the schav."

So the man gets up and storms out of the restaurant. The manager turns to the waiter and says, "You think he came in here to eat? No, he just wanted to argue."

That's Brass. You may think he came in to eat, but he just wants to argue. What makes it really irritating is his habit of being right.

Brass poked further into the detritus of a girl's life and took up the bracelet from the Billie Trask pile. He tossed it up and down in his hand a couple of times, and then stared closely at it. "Well!" he said.

Gloria pulled one of the upright wooden chairs closer to the desk and sat down. "You noticed," she said. "The police probably thought it was costume junk, but it's not."

"Not," Brass agreed. He opened one of the lower drawers to his desk and rummaged about in it until he found a jeweler's loupe, which he stuck in his eye. "Very good workmanship," he said, peering at the bracelet. "By the weight I'd say it was gold, and fairly solid, and there's a jeweler's mark inside the catch." He reached over and ran one of the stones along the nearest window pane. It scratched the glass. "Well," he said again.

"If the earrings are real also," Gloria said, "you're looking at at least a thousand dollars."

"That's what I would say," Brass agreed.

"Maybe it was some stage-door Johnny," I suggested.

"If so her girlfriends should know of it, and presumably so should the police," Brass said. "But we'll ask around."

"Her boyfriend?" Gloria asked.

"Which would be a strong indication that the girl is innocent of the theft," Brass said. "If she has a boyfriend who can give her gewgaws like these, then she presumably could have gotten any small sum of money she needed from him—and we have no indication that she was in need of any large sum of money. And the story that they were in it together is unlikely. The boyfriend wouldn't connive at stealing box-office receipts worth less than the jewelry he gave her."

"Unless the jewelry was stolen," I suggested. "Maybe the boyfriend was a burglar."

"What a thought," Brass said. "We'll have to check the stolen jewelry hot sheet."

"My kind of job," Gloria said.

The phone rang at the small switchboard in the outer office—the only place it does ring—and Gloria picked up the receiver on Brass's desk. "Alexander Brass's office," she said. "Who?" she said. "I'll see," she said. She put her hand over the mouthpiece. "It's the desk downstairs," she told Brass. "There's a Madam Florintina wants to see you about the reward."

"Do I know her?" Brass asked.

Gloria shook her head.

Brass pursed his lips. "I suppose I should have expected it," he said, "but I keep forgetting the innate perversity of the human race. Doesn't the item say to get in touch with Welton, not me?"

"Not explicitly," I told him.

"Well, you go downstairs and be explicit," he told me. "Don't bring her back up here, you take care of it."

"Supposing she has something worth listening to?"

"Then listen!"

I shrugged and nodded. He'd teach this woman, whomever she

was, not to come annoying him with information.

Gloria took her hand off the mouthpiece. "Tell Madam Florintina that Monsieur DeWitt will be right down to parlez to her. Okay, thanks." She hung up. "Third-floor reception," she told me.

"Okay."

The *New York World's* city room is on the third floor, the heart, if not the soul, of the paper. An ornate marble interior staircase goes from the ground floor to the third floor, and anyone can climb it and at least get as far as the reception desk on three. The first three floors are where the newspaper deals with its public in person. Mezzanine: classified ads, lost and found, birth and death announcements, contest winners. Second floor: the advertising department and the circulation department. Third floor: city room, sports department, mail room, and the headquarters of the City Wire Service, the teletype service that distributed local news and fed it to the United Press circuit.

The woman standing by the information desk at the head of the stairs was not from the world of Broadway. If anyone hired her to dance it would be to feel the floor tremble. She was short and wide, somewhere between forty and seventy years old, and wore a white peasant blouse and copious layers of varicolored skirts. She was bedecked with necklaces made up of large colorful stones and bedizened with gold bracelets and rings. Her handbag was a red and white straw contraption that could have held two small boys and a goat.

"Madam Florintina?" I asked.

"That's me," she agreed. "Are you DeWitt?"

"I am," I said. "You have something for us?"

She took me by the sleeve and pulled me over to the beat-up leather couch across from the information desk. "I might," she said plopping onto a cushion and tugging on my sleeve until I sat next to her. "But I'll need some facts first."

"What sort of facts?"

She reached into her handbag and groped around for a while until she came up with a large notebook, and then went back in for a search for a pencil. When she had both she dropped the handbag to the floor and tucked it between her knees. "Just the usual," she told me. "Dates of birth for Two-Headed Mary and Jeffrey Welton, time to the nearest hour if possible, and their birthplace, date and time of the girls' disappearance; that sort of thing."

"Is that all?"

"Well, the exact time the curtain went up on the first night of *Lucky Lady,* and the time of the robbery would be helpful."

I suppressed a sigh. "You're an astrologer!"

"We prefer 'astrologist,'" she said. "I thought the person at the desk told you; I am Madam Florintina." She reached again into her handbag, fished around for a minute, and came out with a 5-x-8 card; red and black ink on heavy gray stock. She thrust it into my hand.

The signs of the Zodiac formed a circle around the outer edge of the card. In the center it said "Madam Florintina" over "by appointment" and a phone number. Under that, in small italics, the motto: "The Stars Know All!"

"Very tasteful," I said.

"Yes," she said, "and expensive." She took it back and stuck it deep into the handbag. "Now"—she opened the notebook on her lap, examined the pencil closely, retrieved a small sharpener from her handbag and touched up the pencil point. "Birth dates."

"The police probably have them," I said.

"But the police aren't offering a reward," she said.

"Neither are we," I told her. "The reward is being offered by Mr. Jeffrey Welton and the *Lucky Lady* company. That's what it says in the 'Brass Tacks' column."

"I know," she said. "But I need to check a few things before I go to speak to Mr. Welton. I thought you people could help me." She leaned toward me and her puffy dark eyes stared intently into mine. "We could split the reward," she said. "I'm not greedy." Her breath smelled of nutmeg.

I shook my head. "But, outside of your star charts or whatever, which I'm sure will be of immense value once they're done, you don't have any useful information."

She grinned. The nutmeg, or something, had done a job on her teeth. "I might," she said. "When a Scorpio gets in trouble, she really gets in trouble. Scorpios go through life leaving a trail of the bridges they've burned behind them. It's not as though I didn't warn her."

"Who?"

"When do I get the reward?"

"When you go to Mr. Jeffrey Welton and tell him something useful."

"I'd rather speak to Mr. Brass."

"Mr. Brass isn't paying a reward."

She closed her notebook. "Maybe he should," she said. "Can you give me those natal dates?"

"I don't have them on me," I told her.

"Call someone. If you're not interested in money, then you can have my story first. Right after I get my money."

"You'll have to tell me what the story is," I said.

"Right after I get my money." She pushed herself to her feet and thrust the notebook back in the handbag. "I told them about the Lindbergh baby, but they wouldn't listen to me. And now that poor Mr. Hauptmann is on death row. But I don't want to say anything until I'm sure. I have to do his chart first."

"Whose?" I asked.

"You're a Leo," she said. "It's in your eyes."

"Pisces," I told her.

"What's your rising sign?"

"I have no idea."

"Well then!" She tucked her bag under her arm and headed for the staircase.

She was the first. The second was a cadaverous-looking man in an ill-fitting suit who walked as though his shoes were too tight. His name was Quenton Adelsberg, and he hadn't known he had this power till one day he got hit in the head by a ricochet bullet during the beer baron wars in Yonkers about ten years back. He could sense where missing things—and people—were. All he needed was an article of clothing that had been worn by one of the missing women, preferably an intimate item that had been worn next to the skin.

And for the rest of the day they came, by telephone, telegram, by letter, and in person; those who thought that they deserved the reward and that Brass should give it to them. One was a psychic who could sense the astral vibrations of the missing ladies, one had a spirit guide who was intimate friends with Two-Headed

Mary's spirit guide, but needed to be coaxed to tell where she was. Some of them had overheard someone suspicious speaking at a bar, or on a trolley car. Some had the locations of the missing women revealed to them in a dream. Brass let me handle all of them. I could not think of an appropriate way to thank him.

13

The next morning, a message sitting on my desk requested my presence at the District Attorney's office. It had been delivered, Gloria told me, by a policeman, but he hadn't waited around. This I chose to regard as a good sign. If the policeman had orders to wait for me and escort me in, I would not have been comforted. I went downtown around ten-thirty, and was told to talk to an assistant D.A. named Silberman. Then I was kept waiting on a bench in the corridor for two hours and ten minutes. They treated me nicely, and got me a fried egg sandwich on a kaiser and an egg cream while I was waiting, which they let me pay for.

At quarter to one I was ushered into Silberman's office. A thin, wiry, totally bald man with a narrow, carefully trimmed black mustache and the look of a man who has heard everything and doesn't believe a word of it, he was wearing a double-breasted blue suit with wide lapels that reflected more than the usual amount of light, and an extra-wide dark blue bow tie speckled with little white squares. When I entered he had a napkin tucked under his chin and was just finishing the last bite of a pastrami on rye. He nodded at me and asked me if I wanted the pickle. I said no, thanks. He nodded again and wadded the scraps and waxed-paper wrapping into a ball and tossed them in the trash basket by the side of his desk. He pulled the napkin out of his collar, rolled it carefully, and thrust it into the top left-hand drawer of his desk while looking at me speculatively through his oversized glasses.

After a moment he slammed the drawer closed and smiled the smile of the tiger stalking the kid. "Sit down, kid," he said. "Tell me about it."

I dropped into the chair on the far side of his desk. I'd spent the last two hours sitting on a flat, narrow wooden bench, but his chair was no improvement. I think he cut a couple of inches off the legs so he'd be taller than his guests. "About what?"

He leaned back in his chair and surveyed me for a minute over the expanse of his empty desktop. "You told Inspector Raab that you didn't know Lydia Laurent, but that wasn't exactly true, was it?"

I leaned back in my chair, but it swayed alarmingly so I dropped its front legs back to the ground. I tried to look contrite. "I suppose I'd better tell you the truth."

"Ah!" he said, leaning forward and putting his elbows on the desk. "Yes, I think you'd better."

I leaned forward confidentially. "I never met Lydia Laurent," I told him. "I would not have known her if she walked through the door. What I told Inspector Raab was, and is still, the exact truth. Sorry."

"Hmpf," he said. "And her roommate, Billie Trask?" He pointed a finger at me. "Was it Billie Trask that you had your relationship with?"

"'With whom you had your relationship,'" I corrected.

"What's that?"

"Never mind. I never met Miss Trask either," I told him.

"Hmpf!" he reiterated.

Silberman had a one-track mind, and he wasn't going to be derailed by anything I said. For most of the next two hours he questioned me about my "relationships" with Lydia Laurent and Billie Trask. He had a folder in front of him that he would refer to when he asked the questions, and he would carefully stick it in the center drawer of his desk, which he would lock, the two or three times he was called out of the office. I don't think there was actually anything in the folder, but I might be wrong.

His questions attacked the facts of the case and my story—or rather my lack of a story—from a dozen different angles, some of them I thought fairly clever, and each denial only made him more determined to come up with a better means of entrapment with the next set of questions. He understood my position, he explained; I didn't want to get involved in a murder and grand theft. But now was the time to come clean, before I got myself in any deeper. Which girl's lover had I been? Didn't I realize that it was only a matter of time before they located someone who had seen us together? It would be better if I came clean before that happened, and cooperated with the D.A.'s office. Had I discovered that she had another boyfriend, and killed her in a jealous rage (Laurent) or caused her to run off with the boyfriend (Trask)? What had I done with the money (Trask)?

Why had I undressed the girl when she was dead (Laurent)— was I some kind of pervert, or was I hiding something?

When he ran out of questions he spent some time glaring at me to show me how unsatisfied he was with my answers, and then had me write out a statement detailing my lack of knowledge of the life or death of Lydia Laurent and the disappearance of her roommate. He warned me about perjury before I signed, and pulled two people in from another office to witness my signature. Then he held it in the air in front of him with the thumb and forefinger of each hand. "This is your last chance," he said. "I can rip this up now, and you can tell me the truth, or you can take the consequences when we find out that you're lying. It's up to you."

"I don't care whether you rip it up or not," I told him. "My story isn't going to change, because it's the simple truth. I stand by my constitutional right as an American to tell the truth." I know that doesn't mean anything, I just thought it was time I brought the Constitution into the conversation. Talking about the Constitution always seems to annoy public officials. I had to bite my tongue to keep from telling him about the letters and the jewelry we'd found, just to be able to tell him something, but I didn't. It was Brass's information, and besides the police had had first crack at it. Besides that, if it meant anything useful, I didn't know what it was. And by this time, I didn't like him very much.

It was almost three o'clock when I got back to the office. Brass had his feet up on the desk and was reading the book of Edna St. Vincent Millay's poetry that had been among the possessions rescued from Billie Trask's apartment. He closed the book and listened carefully while I told him of my adventures. When I was done he shook his head. "They're taking an undue interest in what is, for the District Attorney's office, a rather usual murder," he said. "Somebody must be applying pressure. Which means it must be somebody capable of applying pressure; someone with connections in what passes in this city for high places."

"So someone is leaning on the D.A., and the D.A. is leaning on me;" I said. "I'm not sure I like being the low man on this particular human pyramid."

"I'm sure the D.A. is not limiting his attentions to you," Brass said. "Don't let it bother you."

"That's not as reassuring as I'd like it to be," I said. "Silberman called me 'kid.' I don't like being called 'kid.'"

"Ah!" Brass said. "You dislike being pulled off your pedestal."

"What pedestal?"

"Your position as a journalist; sometimes ally and sometimes thorn in the side of the police. Your ability to wander into police stations and hobnob with the officers, to cross police lines, to go backstage at theaters, to interview rooms full of beautiful chorus girls. Your privileged status as a member of the Fourth Estate."

"That's not so," I said hotly. "I just dislike being treated like a suspect when I didn't do anything."

"Now you know how it feels," Brass said. "Think of the people who are in prison as we speak, and who, if the truth were known, didn't do anything."

"Yeah," I said. "But I *really* didn't do anything!"

Brass snorted and picked up his book.

"Poetry," I said. "I didn't know you liked poetry."

"I am one with Terence," Brass replied without looking up from the book. "'*U'Humani nil a me alienum puto.*' Nothing human is alien to me."

"I see," I said.

"This might interest you," Brass said, flipping over to the title page and showing it to me. There was an inscription, written with a broad-point pen:

> to Billie-O Billie-O Billie my dear—
> *One word is too often profaned*
> *For me to profane it;*

One feeling too falsely disdain'd
For thee to disdain it...

It was not signed. "The quote doesn't sound like Edna St. Vincent Millay," I said.

"It's not, it's Percy Shelley," Brass told me. "The boyfriend—we assume it's the boyfriend—quotes Shelley and gives Millay. What does that tell us about him?"

"I don't know," I confessed.

"I don't either," Brass said, "but let's keep it in mind. Incidentally, the rest of the poem indicates that the word that is going unsaid, is 'love.' Was it, perhaps, a word that she wanted to hear from the boyfriend, but he refused to say?"

"You got me, boss," I said.

Brass sighed a long-suffering sigh. "I'll make a deal with you," he said. "Don't call me 'boss,' and I won't call you 'kid.'"

"I'll try," I said. After all, he's the boss.

Gloria came in from the front office escorting *New York World* ace crime reporter Alan Shine. A small man with what we will politely call a prematurely receding hairline, Shine covers the police beat, and does it very well. At every Crime of the Century from the Hall-Mills case to the Lindbergh baby kidnapping, major coverage under Shine's byline has appeared on the front page of the *World*.

"Greetings all," Shine said, tossing his hat onto a corner of Brass's desk.

"Hello, Shine," Brass said. "I thought you'd be in New Orleans talking to the friends and associates of the defunct senator."

"Nah." Shine shook his head. "Nothing in it for me. The paper can get all it wants without sending me."

"So you don't subscribe to the theory that Roosevelt ordered the hit?"

"I think it was a local job. Word's going around that this guy the cops killed, Dr. Weiss, didn't even do the hit, he was set up. It would be a fun one to cover, but I don't speak the local language. I wouldn't know who to grease, who to talk nice to, or who to avoid. A fellow, even a newspaper fellow, can get killed in a place like that."

I grinned at the idea of Shine being afraid of anything. While he was on the job, he was fearless. I'd seen him accost cops, politicians, and mobsters, and even irate husbands and wives, in the pursuit of a story. "So you chose not to go?" I asked.

"The big boys upstairs chose not to send me. The *World* has a deal with the *New Orleans Telegraph-Intelligencer* for all the news they think fit to send along, so they don't need me."

"Poor lad," Brass said. "Restricted to the mundane world of New York City murders. So, what can I do for you?"

"Just a few words for publication, and I'll be off. I must say it's convenient, having my subjects right here in the *World* building. It's getting rougher and rougher to get across town during the daytime. Lucky so much crime happens at night."

"What kind of words? 'I regret the rising incidence of violent crime, and put the blame squarely where it belongs: on the disgraceful disturbance of the flight patterns of migratory water fowl. It's because they have neither ducks nor geese to shoot at that these gunmen are going around shooting each other.' And you can quote me! Anonymously, of course."

"Nah!" Shine said. "When I want a quote from you, I'll just make it up like I usually do. No point in bothering an important columnist when I already know what I want him to say. Besides, this time the words I want are from my old buddy DeWitt here." he turned to me.

"I don't think I like my newfound popularity," I said. "First Inspector Raab, and then the D.A.'s office, and now you."

"They got to you already?" Shine said. "That's impossible. I just found out myself, and nobody else has been told, as far as I know."

"Told what?" Brass asked.

"About the fact that she came to see you before she got killed. I just got it from Clarence at the desk, and he kept it for me."

I took a deep breath. "As I just got finished telling an assistant D.A. named Silberman, I never met Lydia Laurent. Really."

"I got that already," Shine told me. "We're not discussing Miss Laurent. We're discussing the late Madam Florintina."

That stopped me. "Madam—"

Shine looked at me quizzically. "You didn't know?"

Brass rubbed his thumb along the side of his nose. "Well," he said. "She's the astrologer who came by yesterday, isn't she? She's dead? How?"

"The usual way," Shine told him. "Not breathing, heart stopped."

"Very funny," Brass said.

"If you think that's funny," Shine told him, "did you hear the one about the rabbi and the priest going up the express elevator to the top of the Empire State Building?"

Brass held up a silencing palm. "No humor this morning. I'm not in a humorous mood. How did the lady die?"

"So far they think strangled," Shine told him. "I haven't been able to get a look at the autopsy report yet, if there's anything more than that. She was found at about seven this morning in the passenger seat of an Auburn sedan parked on Thirty-eighth Street between Seventh and Eighth."

"The garment district," I said.

"For what that's worth," Shine said. "Is it worth anything? Does it tell you anything helpful?"

I shook my head. "Unfortunately, no."

Shine turned to Brass. "You?"

"Nothing," Brass said. "But I am feeling set upon by circumstance."

"You!" I said. "Imagine what Raab is going to do when he finds out I saw this woman yesterday! And Assistant District Attorney Silberman is going to be dreaming up questions never before uttered by human mouth."

Shine perched on a corner of Brass's desk. "Okay now, give!" he told me. "What did she want to see you about?"

"She didn't want to see me," I told him. "She wanted to see Brass. She settled for me."

Shine looked at Brass and back at me. "What about?"

"Yes," Brass said. "I'd kind of like to hear it myself. You didn't say the lady said anything worthy of note."

"She didn't, as far as I know," I told him.

"What did she say?"

I turned to Shine. "She came to see us about the reward. Did you see the piece in 'Brass Tacks'?"

"K. Jeffrey's reward for the missing ladies? Yes, I read about it. I thought he was picking the winners personally. What did she want with you people?"

"I don't know, but she was one of many. We got over a dozen calls and visitors yesterday."

"And a few today," Brass said. "Gloria fielded them in your absence. Some cannot read very well, some cannot comprehend what they read, and some come to me because I am their friend and 'Brass Tacks' is the friendly letter I write them every day but Sunday."

"Which was she?" Shine asked me.

"I think she distrusted Welton and wanted our support to make sure she got paid." I closed my eyes and concentrated for a minute, and then repeated, as closely as I could, my conversation with Madam Florintina. We reporters get pretty good at recreating what we have heard and seen, so I was sure I got most of it right, or so close as made no difference. Brass and Shine listened intently. When I was done the silence stretched out for a while.

"What the hell was that about?" Shine asked finally. "Did she know anything or didn't she?"

"Yesterday I would have sworn that she didn't," I said, "but today..."

"She wasn't robbed or molested?" Brass asked.

"She wasn't molested, if you mean sexually," Shine said. "As to whether she was robbed, well, we'd have to know what she was carrying with her. She still had her wallet, and there was a dollar and seventy cents in her change purse, and a five-dollar bill hidden in her, ah, delicate undergarments."

"Did she see Welton?"

"I don't know. Nobody has thought to ask him, as we didn't know there was any connection."

Brass thought this over for a moment and then turned to Gloria. "Get Inspector Raab on the phone. Ask him to drop by. Tell him I've got something for him."

She nodded and headed back to her desk.

"Damn!" I said. "I'm going to spend the rest of my life explaining to cops that I know nothing worth explaining."

"Why don't you spend the next half hour typing out a statement detailing your conversation with the madam astrologer," Brass said. "It will save you some time when Raab gets here. Also make a carbon for me."

"Astrologist," I said. "She said she prefers astrologist."

"Interesting," Brass said. "I never heard that before. I wonder whether there's a distinction, or if it's just a preference." He was pleased; a new word to add to his word list.

Shine took the battered fedora that city desk reporters are required to own from where he'd tossed it on the desk and jammed it on his head. "If Raab has anything interesting to contribute, pass it on to me," he said. "I think I'll go talk to Welton before he's interviewed by the homicide boys." He nodded and left.

I went back to my cubicle and made a carbon paper sandwich, rolled it into the typer and began. Having just gone over the events in my mind, it was a snap to set them down in something approaching a logical order. As I typed it out, I remembered more detail. I was able to stretch it to five pages, double-spaced.

Raab stalked into Brass's office just as I finished copyediting my opus. I paper-clipped the two copies and followed meekly behind.

"Well?" Raab demanded, braking to a stop in front of the desk.

Brass nodded and smiled. "Good afternoon, Inspector," he said. "Reasonably well, thank you. And you?"

"Very cute," Raab said. "Why am I here? Miss Adams said you have something for me."

I dropped the copies of my report on the desk and retired to what I hoped would be a neutral corner.

Brass picked up the copies and tapped them on the side of the desk. "I believe you're investigating a new homicide," he said.

"That's a safe bet,' Raab said. "We're running at about three murders a week here in the city. Is this a philosophical discussion about homicide, or did you have a specific case in mind?"

"I believe she called herself Madam Florintina," Brass said.

Raab thought it over for a second. "Yeah," he said. "The stargazer. What about her?"

"I'd like to know how she died, what the autopsy report said, what, if anything, you've found out about her."

"Is that all?" Raab asked. "You sure you wouldn't like to know what the commissioner had for lunch, and who Dewey's planning to indict next?"

Brass rapidly skimmed the pages I'd handed him and then

passed them over to Raab. "I have a legitimate interest," he said. "DeWitt might be the last person to have seen her alive. Except her killer, of course."

"DeWitt again, eh?" Raab said, pausing to glare at me before turning his attention to the report. He slowly backed up to the couch and dropped onto it while he was reading. When he had turned over the last page he flipped forward to review part of it, and then turned to me. "Is this all of it?" he asked.

"All," I said.

"You weren't expecting her to call?"

"I had never heard of her until I met her," I said.

"That's not what I asked, but never mind." He turned to Brass. "You verify this?"

"How can I?" Brass asked. "I wasn't there."

"Did you have any reason to expect her call?"

"Only the innate inability of human beings to understand the written word. As far as expecting Madam Florintina specifically to call, no."

Raab turned to me. "She remained on the third floor for the whole time?"

"As far as I know," I said. "If she went anywhere else in the building, she did it while I wasn't looking. The man at the reception desk could tell you."

"I'll speak with him directly I finish with you," Raab said. "She promised you a story right after she did some chart. What kind of chart? What sort of story?"

"I assume she meant an astrological chart, but I don't know what sort of story she had in mind. She didn't say."

"Did you tell Brass?"

"I gave him a quick rundown on what she said when I came back upstairs. I don't remember whether I told him that she said she had a story for us, because I didn't think it very important."

"You didn't think her having a story for you was very important?" Raab asked incredulously.

"Everybody has a story for us," I explained. "When I go into a nightclub with Mr. Brass, the hat-check girl murmurs 'I could tell your boss some stories if I wanted to.' The shoeshine boy wants to know how much we'll pay him for an exclusive on some hot tip he's heard. When I go to a party, at least five people take me aside and promise me a hot story if I either use their name or promise not to use it, depending. It never comes to anything. And Mr. Brass has it ten times as bad as I do."

"That's true," Brass said. "I don't remember whether DeWitt mentioned that this woman said she had a story for us; but if he did I would have discounted it. We probably would have both chuckled briefly and gone on with the discussion. I remember once in 1931 at a party—July, I think it was—I was introduced to a woman who didn't say either 'What an interesting life you must lead' or 'I could tell you some stories you could use, if I wanted to.'"

"So where do you get your information?"

"Usually from the people involved. Although I do have sources all over the city and scattered throughout the rest of the country. When some stranger whom I meet casually at a party or wherever has something of interest to tell me, he or she invariably just takes me aside and tells it to me right then and there, without much preface. Either that or they make a definite appointment to talk to me later in private, if the information is too sensitive to blab to a crowd."

Raab thought that over, and then turned to me. "So when Madam Florintina said she had a story for you, you paid no attention?"

"Well, I didn't know she was going to get killed."

"You think she went from here to see K. Jeffrey Welton?"

"That's what she seemed intent on doing, so I would think that's what she did. Whether she actually saw him or not, I couldn't tell you."

Brass leaned back and laced his hands together. "Now a couple of facts from you, Inspector. To satisfy my curiosity."

"What sort of facts?"

"What time was she killed?"

"Late evening. Say around midnight."

"Whose car was she in?"

"An attorney named Schipp. It had been stolen from him earlier in the evening. He and his wife went to see a play. *Tobacco Road* at the Forrest Theater on Forty-ninth Street. When they came out, the car was gone. A brand-new Auburn Straight-Eight, he'd only had it for about a week. He thinks he parked on Forty-seventh off Eighth, but you know how those things are. He spent an hour looking for the car, thinking maybe he had forgotten where it was parked. But it was gone. His wife is sure it was parked in front of Bitterman's Costume Shop, and she's probably right. Not that it matters."

"How did Madam Florintina die?"

"Strangled."

"Like the Laurent girl?"

"You putting them together?"

"Do they fit?"

"Lydia Laurent was strangled manually, from the front. Madam Florintina was strangled with some sort of ligature—a rope or a belt or some such. And she struggled, probably scratched her assailant. Her face is bruised, one of her fingernails is broken, and there is someone else's skin under several of the nails on her right hand."

"So the killer got scraped up?"

"It would seem so. If we're lucky enough to get a line on him before the scrapes heal, we might have something."

"No suspects?"

"Presumably whoever she was going to finger for you and Welton would be a suspect, if she actually named a name. I'd better go talk to Welton."

"I guess you had," Brass agreed.

14

Gloria left for the residence hotel on East 24th Street that she calls home around six P.M., and Brass and I went down to Victor's Barber Shop to get a trim shortly thereafter. The bi-weekly excursion to Victor's was a ritual we both observed, although we usually didn't do it in tandem. It just worked out that way today. Victor, a tall, slender man with a bulbous nose and a mane of silver hair, owned the eight-chair barber shop located off the lobby of the *World* building; it was close, convenient, and a ready source for newsroom gossip.

The walls of Victor's shop were plastered with the mementos of Victor's hair management of the famous, the notorious, and the photogenic, as well as visible signs of his pride in being an American. There was a framed photograph of Victor grinning behind his barber chair, with ex-mayor Jimmy Walker beaming up from the chair. It was autographed "To Victor—who really knows how to trim a guy. Your pal, Jimmy." There were similar pictures of Victor with Governor Lehman; with F.D.R., taken when he was governor of New York; with Babe Ruth; with Grouch and Chico Marx (autographed, "To Victor, you're a barrel of laughs, —Groucho / I don't think so, —Chico"); with Dutch Schultz (not autographed); and with a couple dozen other New York notables. Brass's photo was in a position of honor by the door, as was that of Winston Sanders, publisher of the *World*. Along the wall behind the desk with the cash register were a series of plaques commemorating

Victor's assistance in raising money in war bond drives and war relief charity drives during and after the Great War.

The shop was open from six in the morning until eight at night, ten at night on Fridays and Saturdays, and it always had at least three barbers—no waiting. And one of them was always Victor himself. When the man slept, I couldn't tell you.

Brass usually indulged in a manicure while he was being tonsured, but I seldom did. It was the sort of thing that a small-town Ohio boy doesn't learn to do gracefully. I will admit that it would have been worth fifty cents to have Gwen, the manicurist, sit by me and hold my hand for fifteen minutes, but I couldn't yet bring myself to have her file my nails.

"Victor, of course, did Brass's hair himself. My barber was a wizened but dexterous old fellow named Marcello, who had been with Victor since before the Great War, and who flung around hot towels with abandon and wielded the straight razor as though he were a musketeer. He had just pulled the hot towel off my face and I was emerging from the heat-shock-induced stupor when a vague figure scraped a stool across the floor and settled down on it next to my chair. My eyes focused on the face that was peering at mine. It looked familiar. It was familiar. "Junior!" I said.

"Got it in one!" Junior Skulley said. "I didn't know whether you'd recognize me without a drink in my hand."

"It took a second," I told him. "You're entirely out of your setting." I looked him over. He was wearing a tan sports jacket and gray slacks, and a redder-than-red wide tie. "I didn't know that tan and gray went together," I remarked.

He looked down at himself. "They do when the jacket's cashmere," he said.

"Silly me," I said. "Is this a coincidence or enemy action?"

"You mean, what am I doing here? I came looking for you, and the elevator starter in the lobby told me you were probably in here."

"Well, there'll be coal in his stocking this Christmas," I said.

"Now, now, don't be testy. I told him it was important, and so it is."

"What is it, are you collecting for the Boozer's Guild Relief Fund annual picnic already?"

Junior smiled. He was a hard man to insult. "I don't need your help in supporting any Boozer's Fund," he said. "Besides, I'm seriously considering giving up drinking."

"No!" I said in mock horror. I twisted in my seat to get a better look at him, but Marcello twisted my head back in place so he could attack it with his scissors, and I had to be content with staring at Junior in the mirror over the sink. "What is it, bleeding ulcers? Pink elephants? Sudden bouts of remorse, and you don't remember what you're sorry for? Whole evenings wiped from your memory? Or has one of your chorines let you know what she thinks of kissing a man who smells like a distillery?"

He considered seriously, and finally shook his head. "Nah!" he said. "By the time they kiss me, they're usually too drunk to tell what I smell like."

"I can believe that," I said.

He nodded. "It's just that, ah, well, since it's been legal, it isn't as much fun any more."

"Junior, it's been legal for about two years now," I reminded him.

"Really?" He stared at his fingers. "My how time flies when you're swozzled."

"So what did you want to see me about?"

He looked puzzled for a few seconds, and then his face brightened. "I need to consult with you. I need your advice."

"My advice?" I may have heard something more unlikely, but not in recent memory. "What about?"

"Do you remember when we came across each other in the back room of Sardi's?" he asked, staring intently at me, as though he were asking whether I remembered a precious moment from our childhood together in the old one-room schoolhouse. "It wasn't so long ago."

"When you barged in on a private party and made a pest of yourself? Yes, I remember."

"Yes, well, of course you would. Well, you see, it's this way. I was at the Kit Kat with a chorine companion—"

I stuck an arm out from under the sheet that covered me from neck to toe and patted Junior on the knee. "My gosh, Junior, you're reasonably sober! You never could have gotten that last sentence out without stumbling if you were as soused as you usually are. You ought to expand on your triumph! Try 'conspicuously carousing with a crinoline-clad corpulent chorine companion.'"

"She was not!" he said indignantly.

"Just for the alliteration," I explained.

I had taken him off the subject, and he spent a moment mentally stumbling around for it. He might be reasonably sober, but the habits of cognition and ratiocination were not strong in him. "Well," he said, "this girl came into the club and tried to talk my date into going to Sardi's. She gave her this card—your card—and said you wanted to talk to her."

I thought that over for a second. "Goddamn! You were out with Lydia Laurent!"

"I was," he said. "I was indeed."

"And then she was murdered!"

"Subsequent to my leaving her," he said. "I had nothing to do with her death. I know nothing about it. Believe me! I wouldn't have let anyone hurt that little girl." He shook his head. "Why under the sun would anybody want to kill such a lovely creature? The ways of man passeth understanding. Or something."

"What happened that evening? Why didn't she and Viola come in to join the rest of the group?"

"Is that the other girl's name? Well, I suggested that we all go on to Sardi's and have a little supper and she could speak to you. But we didn't see you there in the front room, so we ordered food and drink and waited for you to arrive. I gave Viola five dollars to sort of thank her for her troubles. You know. Hoping she'd take the hint and go away. And so she did."

"What a prince," I said.

He nodded in recognition of his princeliness. "You were already in the back room but I didn't know that. I didn't even know there was a back room. I said to Lydia, I said, 'Well, we've looked for him, now let's finish up and go to my place for a nightcap.' You understand, old man."

"Clearly," I told him.

"Well, our waiter said he thought you were in the back room, so I told Lydia to eat her steak and I'd go look. And I did."

"And of course you told her we were there with a table full of her friends, and she should join us. Of course you did." I was annoyed.

"Well, honestly I thought you had quite enough young ladies all to yourself, so I told Lydia that you were nowhere to be found, and she ate her shell steak and we went off into the night. I feel bad about it, but there it is."

The barber's chair on the other side of Junior swiveled around. "And just where did you go?" Brass asked, as Victor used his little brush to remove the last of the little clipped hairs from where they might have fallen around Brass's neck.

Junior did a double-take worthy of Stan Laurel. "It's the 'Brass Tacks' man himself," he said. "I didn't see you there."

"I wasn't on view," Brass said. "I was getting a haircut. Where did you and Miss Laurent go when you left Sardi's?"

"We could take bets," I said.

"Well, you'd be wrong," Junior said, sounding insulted. "I took her to her apartment and left her at the door."

"She must have been very persuasive," I said.

"Insistent," he agreed. "But, I thought, there's always tomorrow." He paused and shook his head as though clearing some bad thoughts. "But I was wrong, wasn't I? There was no tomorrow, not for Lydia."

"What time did you get her home?" Brass asked.

Junior stared at the floor thoughtfully. "I have no idea," he said after a minute. "I'm lucky I remember what day it was. Another reason I'm going to stop drinking. I'm losing track of the passage of time."

Victor snapped a towel in Brass's direction several times, as a gesture of finality, brushed his shirt and turned the chair to face the front. Brass stood and shrugged into his jacket. Victor gave the jacket a couple of cleansing passes with the brush, stood back to survey his work and nodded. "All done," he said. "Perfecto!"

Brass nodded. "Thank you, Victor. Stick it on my tab." He turned to Junior Skulley. "So you left her at her door and walked away? She didn't invite you in? No nightcap?"

Marcello tilted my head down to do a final bit of snipping at some recalcitrant hairs at the back of my neck.

"She would have," Junior said defensively, "but there was someone there in the apartment."

My head snapped back up and I almost jumped out of the chair. If Marcello hadn't been dextrous with the scissors, he would have stabbed me in the neck. "What?"

"Well, you know, I was ready to come in. Just for a drink, you know. But when she opened the door, there was this man inside."

Brass sat back down on the barber's chair. "Who?"

"I don't know. Is this important?"

"It means that you're no longer the last person to see Lydia Laurent alive."

"Well of course not," Junior said. "Whoever killed her was the last person to see her alive."

"And the police will be glad to discover that it wasn't you."

"The police. The police?" Junior took a deep breath and let it out slowly. "Good God!" he said.

"Perhaps we should go upstairs to continue this conversation," Brass suggested.

"I suppose," Junior Skulley said. "Got any booze upstairs?"

"I thought you were going to give up drinking," I said.

Junior smiled a weak smile. "Not just yet."

"Something can be worked out," Brass said.

I let Marcello remove the sheet and dust me off, and told him to put it on Brass's tab, and we laughed about that, and he put it on my tab, which I would clear up as usual at the end of the month, and then we headed for the elevators. Brass unlocked the door to the office suite and flicked the lights on, and we went through to his office. He turned on the floor lamp by the side of the desk and waved me to the closet, which concealed his bar. I mixed a bourbon and soda for Junior, a Cognac neat for Brass, and a scotch and water for myself. Prohibition has been over for about seven hundred days, but I still get a feeling of doing something illicit and faintly wicked when I pour an alcoholic beverage into a glass. I think that the thrill of it was a large part of why people drank so much, and that the consumption of alcohol is going to go down now that it's legal again. But I could be wrong. Brass says that the bootleggers and the speaks created a sort of countrywide ritual, and that drinking became a great secret that we all shared, like the mystical rites of a church or fraternal order that had the population of the whole country as members. But he could be wrong.

"Now," Brass said when we were all settled; Junior and I on the couch and Brass behind his desk, "tell me about this man."

"I didn't see him," Junior said. "I was standing outside when she opened the door and stepped in. I heard this man's voice saying something like 'It's about time' and 'Where have you been?' Like that. And she said, 'My gosh, what are you doing here?'"

"And you didn't just barge in to see who it was? Didn't you feel jealous?"

"I never feel jealous," Junior said. "It's a ridiculous emotion, like you have the right to control someone else's life. I don't want anyone controlling my life, after all."

"Very noble," Brass said.

Junior shrugged. "I don't have to work at it," he said. "I just don't feel jealousy. Maybe that's no good. Maybe it's because I don't really care about anybody. That's been suggested."

"So you didn't even take a peek at whoever was inside the apartment?"

"Well, to tell you the truth I thought it was her father, someone like that. There was something in the voice—it didn't sound like a lover; it was too bossy."

"So you just went away?"

"I said 'Bye, now,' and turned and walked away. Just so. I don't mess with fathers."

"How would you describe the man's voice?" I asked.

Junior thought about it. "Kind of high, and kind of sharp precise."

"How long had you been going out with Lydia Laurent?"

"As a matter of fact, just that once, that's all. Most of the chorus girls only let me go out with them once or twice. I buy them a couple of dinners, and we dance somewhere if they aren't too tired, and I take them home. Sometimes I take them to my flat, but more often I just take them home. And the third or fourth time I ask them out they pat me on the back and say no, thanks; why don't you ask Susie over there, or whoever. I'm sort of passed from girl to girl like a cold. They think I'm harmless. They think I'm a joke."

I didn't expect such self-knowledge from Junior. "Then why do you do it?" I asked him.

He shrugged. "Why not? I like to go out with beautiful girls. And I can afford it. And sex is overrated anyway, particularly after six or seven drinks."

There was a pause while we stared into our glasses and thought our private thoughts.

"Why are you telling us about this now?" Brass asked.

Junior looked unhappy and stared at his feet. "I've started seeing a girl, Monica, and I think it's serious. I mean, we've only been out maybe half a dozen times, but we talk to each other about— things. Real things. I don't know how to explain it, but this feels different. She wants me to give up drinking. And she suggested that I tell the police about this business. She thinks it's important. I don't want to talk to the police, they make me nervous. So I told her I'd talk to DeWitt here, because he knows about such things and he's my friend and would tell me what to do."

"I'm your friend?" I may have sounded surprised.

"Sure," he said. "Under that, you know, that witty banter that we go back and forth with, we're pals."

"And I'm Marie of Roumania," I told him.

"See!" he said. "Witty banter."

Brass took a deep breath and restrained whatever comment came to mind. "Is that it?" he asked. "Have you any other information to unburden yourself of?"

"I have emptied myself of my burdens," Junior told him, "and am feeling light as a feather."

"Well, you'd better just float over to Homicide North on Seventy-seventh between Lex and Third and ask for Inspector Raab. Tell him I sent you, and tell him your story. He will treat you very gently."

Junior Skulley looked doubtful. "Must I?" he asked.

"Do you want someone else to tell them that they saw you out with Lydia Laurent on the evening she was killed before you have a chance to? You'll spend a long time as a guest of the city explaining that one. Even if the homicide boys don't think you did it, they'll be afraid that some hotshot reporter will pick up on the story and suggest in print that maybe your father's influence bought you a free ride."

Junior nodded dolefully. "That's what Monica said."

"She's right. I'm surprised it hasn't happened already."

"All right." He stood up. "First thing in the morning."

"Now," Brass told him.

He looked at me.

"Now," I told him.

He shrugged. "I'll get a cab."

After Junior left, Brass swiveled around and stared out the window. This was usually a sign that he was hard at work, but I had no idea what he could be working on; so maybe he was just staring out the window. I waited awhile in respectful silence to see whether he was working or staring. After a couple of minutes, I cleared my throat once or twice, but Brass didn't even tell me to shut up, which probably meant that he was working. When he is on the track of an idea, he becomes hard of hearing and unresponsive to those around him.

I was working up to stretching and yawning and announcing that I supposed I would go home now. Going home was no problem; supposing I'd go home, however, was surprisingly difficult. Somehow Brass always made me feel that I was deserting him in his time of need, and that I was about to miss something incredibly fascinating.

Brass turned back to the room before I had a chance to do my supposing. "What time is it?" he asked.

I pulled out the hunter pocket watch I had inherited from my Uncle Matthias—who had been editor of the weekly paper in a small town in Ohio but, as far as I know, had never hunted a day in his life; but it was an elegant watch—and snapped it open. "Quarter past seven," I told him.

"Let's go downstairs and see if we can catch Jonn Sturdevant in his office," Brass said. "I'd like to talk to him."

Sturdevant was the drama critic for the *New York World*. He spelled his first name "Jonn," but whether he was born that way, or had attained greatness, I know not. He had two assistants—who liked to call themselves associates—and a few other journalists might occasionally write reviews or pieces on the condition of modern drama here or elsewhere; but Sturdevant was the voice that mattered. His review alone couldn't make a hit out of a real dog, but praise from him could keep a play afloat long enough to at least break even, and a pan could kill a new production dead in the water. And if Brooks Atkinson of the *Times* or Richard Watts Jr. of the *Herald Tribune* agreed with Sturdevant that the show was good, it could count on a guaranteed six-month run.

He knew everything and everyone and was treated like a conquering general; that is, fawned upon in his presence and despised behind his back. But with all of this he kept his perspective, his sense of humor, and his objectivity. His opinions might not always be right, balanced, or completely fair, but they were his honest opinions. He had even been known to print a retraction or revised estimate when later events showed that he was wrong.

He was also the Queen of Gossip about the show business, although he could use little of it in his reviews, and he was always eager to trade good stories over demitasse cups of the sweet, black Turkish coffee he brewed on a gas ring in his office.

There was no desk in his fifth-floor office, a medium-sized aerie separating the religion editor from the fashion editor; merely a small table against the wall where he wrote out his reviews longhand before passing them to some menial to be typed out. That and piles of books, play scripts, magazines, and notebooks, and a variety of prizes, awards, and mementos scattered about like leaves on the Strand. "Hello, dear boys," he said as we came into view around the corner that shielded his office from the elevator. "You're scant moments too late." He was sitting like Buddha on a small camp stool with a stack of manuscripts on his lap.

"Too late for what?" Brass asked.

"The immortal Yankee Doodle man himself has just skipped off down the stairs."

"George M. Cohan?"

"Indeed. He is in from his place in Connecticut to discuss a new musical with Messieurs Rodgers and Hart. Now won't that be an American classic if it comes off? I ask you."

We arranged ourselves in the doorway of Sturdevant's office, since there was no place to sit unless you cleared a spot on the floor. "I'm sorry I missed him," Brass said. "Anything I can use in my column?"

"Not yet, dear boy," Sturdevant said. "It's all tenuous and gossamer, and the Cohan doesn't want any publicity until it's decided. Except for the merest mention—which I'm going to do myself. The idea is"—he leaned forward conspiratorially—"a musical about Franklin D. And George is going to play the president! How's that for a god-awful notion? Franklin Roosevelt in tap shoes!"

"The best kind," Brass said.

"I said to him, George dear boy, it's all very well, but is the New York theater audience ready for a singing, tap-dancing president? And he said to me that if Gershwin could do it, he could damn well do it, too. Which is a distinct point. So, with much trepidation, I added 'George, you're getting a bit long in the tooth for such strenuous activity night after night, aren't you?' So the immortal Cohan stripped off his top coat, hitched up his pants, and did five minutes of energetic buck and wing for me right in this hall. I tell you, the sound of tapping feet reverberated like thunder. It was thrilling! As he dropped, scarcely sweating, into his seat, I swore never to doubt his terpsichorean vitality and endurance again. And he must be nearing sixty, if he's a day."

I looked around. "What seat?"

"I brought a bentwood chair over from religion for him to sit on while we talked. Would you like one?"

"No thanks, John," Brass told him. "Just a couple of quick questions, if you don't mind if I pick your brain."

"Mind? Not a bit, dear boy. Reciprocal brain-picking is what journalism is all about. What secrets may I lay bare for you?"

"Tell me about *Lucky Lady*."

"The musical?" Sturdevant stared up at the ceiling, which I noticed was covered with some sort of white gauze draping. "At the Monarch Theater, opened March twelfth, which was a Tuesday. Producer: K. Jeffrey Welton, the wonder boy. An epithet he made up for himself, by the way. Directed by Kapofsky, who has a modicum of talent if he sticks to fluff. Music by Jimmy Sillit, lyrics by A.S. Lucas, book by Saddler. From an idea that was already stale when the pyramids were Pharaoh Ramses the Second's WPA project. Boy meets girl. Girl wins Irish sweepstakes, leaves boy to collect money. Girl meets sharper who is only after the money. Everybody knows this but the girl. Boy has taken job as tap-dancing steward on ship girl is also on. Why is never said. Girl thinks she has lost all the money. Fights with sharper, who is about to throw her overboard when boy appears from behind smokestack and saves her. Sharper falls overboard. Girl says, 'I've been such a fool!' And falls into his arms. They dance. Money is recovered."

"That's it?" I asked.

"That's it," Brass agreed. "Boy meets girl. Boy loses girl. Boy gets girl. The universal plot. Love will find a way; put your money on love."

"There are a couple of songs that are hummable," Sturdevant said. "'Keep Your Eyes Where They Belong' and 'Dance Along with Me' are probably the best. Judith Perril does a decent job as the ingenue, although ingenues do seem to be getting older with each passing season, don't they?"

"How's the show doing?"

"Well, it's hard to tell, old boy. It must be doing all right; they haven't posted closing notices. But the management does seem to be papering the house on occasion."

Brass nodded. Papering the house—giving out free or really cheap tickets to make sure the theater had few empty seats—had probably been going on since the days of Shakespeare. It might be done on a night an important critic was coming, or just to make sure the cast plays to a full house. The laughs are always better that way. It was also a way to build an audience in the face of bad reviews if you think word-of-mouth is going to be good. Since it effectively costs the theater nothing extra to play to a full house, many producers thought it was the cheapest, most effective advertising they could do. But if it didn't work, pretty soon the cast would be playing to an all-paper audience; and where would the money for their salaries come from?"

"You think they're not doing as well as they say?" Brass asked.

"Would you be shocked, dear boy? I doubt whether any production has done as well as the producer claims."

"Have you heard anything about Billie Trask and the missing money?"

"Rumors, dear boy; rumors and gossip is all." Sturdevant shifted the pile of scripts off his lap and onto the floor. "My ear is always to the ground, but I've learned not to trust what the groundlings tell me. Some of her compatriots from the chorus say she took the money for her lover, and the two of them have fled to Cuba—or was it British Guyana?—where they can presumably live like king and queen for ever and ever on two days' box-office receipts. Some others say she took the money to get away from her lover, or just to get away from the evil, heartless big city. I have heard that she fled for some other reason entirely, and someone else took advantage of her flight to remove the money. Some say she ran off with your favorite do-gooder, Two-Headed Mary, either with or without the money. What's your bet?"

"If I was a betting man," Brass said, "I'd give this one a pass. None of the guesses really makes sense. And none of them explain what happened to Lydia Laurent."

"The girl who was killed?" Sturdevant peered at Brass, his eyes glittering. "You think there's a connection? I know they were roommates."

"You may choose to believe in coincidence, if you like," Brass said.

"That's good of you, dear boy," Sturdevant replied, "but I learned a long time ago that when anyone says 'You'll never believe what just happened,' I should take him at his word."

"Have you heard anything about Lydia Laurent?" Brass asked.

"Not a thing," Sturdevant said. "Except that she had nary a stitch covering her, and DeWitt's card clutched in her hand when she was found. And she'd been tied up. But then, some people like being tied up." He looked at me. "I understand she missed her appointment with you. Do you suppose she could have been killed to prevent her talking to you in the future?"

"I'd rather not suppose anything of the sort," I told him. "I was asking about Two-Headed Mary. I can't see that there's any information about her that would be worth killing for."

"Ah, dear boy, that's because you don't know what it is that she knew; what tidbit of information she was going to cast upon you. Perhaps Mary is no longer with us, and Lydia Laurent knew the cause of her sudden demise. And perhaps the killer thought that she might, ah, 'spill the beans,' as it were."

"That would mean that she was involved," I said.

"Not necessarily. Perhaps she knew something that she didn't know she knew, if you can follow that."

"If Two-Headed Mary is dead, the killer hid the body very carefully," I said, just to be argumentative. "Why wouldn't he have done the same with Laurent's body?"

Sturdevant waggled an explanatory finger. "It is an unnecessary complication to hide a body," he said. "You should ask rather why he would have gone to the trouble with Two-Headed Mary. What is he trying to conceal?"

"That's a very interesting thought," Brass said. "You may have something there."

Sturdevant beamed. "I knew reading detective stories would come in useful some day."

15

I went home early for me; it was about nine-thirty when I took my hot potato knish and container of milk from the little cafeteria on 72nd and Broadway up to my room and settled down to continue the adventures of "Sindbad the Unconquerable." Or perhaps, "Of Sorcery and the Sea: An Adventure of Sindbad the Sailor." I wrote three more pages and got him up to thirteen years old, and then sat down on the edge of my bed and reread the whole thing. I was overcome with waves of doubt; which usually doesn't happen until I reach page twenty or so, and I was only on page seven.

The plot line I had worked out in my head involved Sindbad commanding a trireme or quinquereme, or one of those remes, on a voyage of mystical discovery, with lots of fighting and mythical monsters and gods and goddesses and treasure and beautiful princesses. The sort of adventure any boy of advanced years would love to read. Then why did I spend the first chapter of the book with him as a child? Why? I think that much of the planning of a piece of fiction is done by the subconscious mind, and the conscious just fills in the nouns and the grammar. I might be writing a piece of brilliant evocative fantasy or a piece of pap for the pulps, and I had no idea which. Or I might be just leading myself further and further into a blind alley from which there was no reasonable escape.

Well, I thought, I might as well let my subconscious do what I'm paying it for and figure out what Sindbad's next move is while I get a good night's sleep. I loosened my tie and hung it carefully with its three mates on the closet door.

The phone rang.

I am the proud possessor of a telephone in my own room, the only private phone, I believe, in the whole building. Even Mrs. Bianchi, the landlady, uses the pay phone on the first-floor landing. Brass had me put in a phone, even paying for the installation, so he could reach me when he needed to. So, as it was after eleven o'clock of a weekday night—

It was Brass. "You awake?" he asked.

"Yes."

"Good. Take a cab and come by and pick me up."

I replaced my tie, combed my hair, shrugged back into my jacket, put on my top coat and hat, and headed downstairs. A chill drizzle had started since I got home. I turned up the collar of my top coat, pulled my hat down firmly, and flagged a Checker cab. I directed the driver to 33 Central Park South, where Brass has his penthouse apartment. He was waiting outside when we pulled up, long black raincoat buttoned to his chin, dark gray felt hat pulled down over his eyes, looking grim.

"Where to?" I asked.

"The Royal Theater," he said, climbing in.

The cab pulled away from the curb. "Has something happened?" I asked.

"Yes," Brass said.

"Another murder?"

"No," Brass said.

"Something about Sandra Lelane?"

"Yes," Brass said.

I took a deep breath. "Are we playing twenty questions?" I asked him. "Animal, vegetable, or mineral?"

Brass scowled. "Miss Lelane got a phone call from her mother. Wait a few minutes and let her tell it."

Well. So Sandra Lelane's mother had resurfaced. So Two-Headed Mary wasn't dead after all, as we had all silently feared. That was good news, but a little confusing. Where had she been? Where was she now? Why didn't I just wait five minutes and find out?

Sandra Lelane was waiting for us in front of the theater, by the large poster advertising her play. Hatless and coatless and clutching a brown scarf around her head for protection from the rain, her skirt whipping in the wind, she looked like she was posing for a *Saturday Evening Post* cover. The only thing missing was a small, rain-soaked dog staring up at her. The story illustrated would be about a young actress trying to decide between taking the lead in a Broadway play or going back to Ogallala to the boy who loves her.

She led us down the alley to the stage door, and we followed. "Thank you for coming," she said. "Let's talk in my dressing room."

"You look tired. Have you eaten?" Brass asked. "We could go to one of the little supper clubs in the area. Maybe Pietro's or Jimmy's Chop House. They're fairly quiet, and we could talk over a steak, or a bowl of soup."

"Maybe after," she said. "I need to know we can't be overheard." She took us backstage and excused herself for a moment to talk to the night doorman. I walked out to the middle of the stage. The work lights were on, and a cleaning crew was at work in the orchestra.

"So this is where the magic happens," I said, that being the tritest thing I could think of on the spur of the moment. "One day you're an unknown in the back of the chorus, and the next day you're a star."

"Don't laugh," Brass said. "Americans have few dreams, and that is one of their favorites."

Lelane came back and led the way to her dressing room. "Everyone from the cast and crew has gone home," she said, "except the wardrobe mistress and she's on the other side of the stage, so we can talk in here."

The star's dressing room was actually a small two-room suite, with a bathroom about the size of an upended shoe box stuck in one corner of the inner room. Both rooms held racks of costumes, presumably all the changes that Sandra needed during the course of the show with a few extras in case of emergencies.

Sandra sat on the wooden chair in front of her makeup table. She took off the scarf and began toweling dry her hair. Brass removed his overcoat and hat, hung them on a hook by the door, and lowered himself into the easy chair that filled one corner of the room. I likewise shed my outer garments and was about to toss them on the daybed, when I saw the look of alarm on Sandra's face and remembered: a hat on the bed or couch in a dressing room is bad, bad luck; almost as bad as saying the name of "The Scottish Play" inside a theater. So I hung them up next to Brass's, straddled a wooden folding chair, turning it so I was facing Sandra, and awaited developments.

"Okay," Brass said. "Tell me about it."

Sandra peered outside just to make sure the corridor was empty, and then closed her door. "I'm scared," she said.

"Your mother called?"

"Yes. I didn't want to tell you any more over the phone. I don't have my own phone in here; I hate getting calls during a show. So I used the stage manager's phone, and it's not very private."

"Is that the one your mother called you on?"

"No. Her call came in on the house phone. I took it in the front office. It was during the second-act intermission. I dialed you right after curtain calls."

"What's the problem?" Brass asked. "Why isn't this the best news in the world? She's okay, isn't she?"

"I guess so. I hope so."

Brass leaned forward in his chair. "What do you—"He paused and shook his head. "No, I apologize. Asking questions just slows things down. Just tell the story your way and we'll listen."

"All right," Sandra said. "One of the ushers came back here to tell me that my mother was on the phone in the office just as intermission began. Of course I threw on a robe and ran to the office as fast as I could."

Brass nodded.

"I thought it might be some sort of joke, but it was Mom."

Brass raised his hand. "One second," he said. "You're sure it was Mary? You're certain you recognized her voice?"

"I am," she said. "But I wouldn't have had to. It was also what she said."

"Again I apologize for interrupting," Brass said. "Go on."

"I'll give you the conversation as closely as I can remember it. Then you'll see—well, let me tell you first."

"Good," Brass said.

"I said, 'Hello?'

"Mom said, 'Is that you, Lucille?' A good sign that it was her, even if I hadn't recognized the voice; because nobody in the business knows my real name."

Brass nodded again and made an encouraging sound. I stared expectantly and tried to guess what was coming, the way you will when someone is telling a story or a joke. Nothing came to mind.

"I said, 'Mom? Are you all right?' or something like that.

"She said, 'Lucille, listen closely, darling, I only have a few minutes. First, I'm perfectly all right. I just have to stay in seclusion for a while longer.'

"I kind of yelled into the phone, 'Mom, we're so worried about you! Where have you been? Where are you?'

"'Now listen and don't interrupt your old mother,' she said. 'There's something you have to do for me, and it's very important. Like in the old days. Okay, honey? Okay?'

"Now that chilled me, because—well, let me tell it all first, then I'll explain."

"Go on," Brass said.

"So I said, 'Sure, Mom, whatever you want.'

"And she said, 'I can't get a hold of your Uncle Andrew. I've been trying for days and days, and I have an important message for him. Could you find him for me?'

"And I said, 'Sure, Mom, I'll find him. Any idea where he is?'

"And she said, 'Now if I knew where he was, I wouldn't have to ask you to find him, now, would I? Ask around. I can't do it myself, or I wouldn't bother you. But it's very important. Very.'

"So I said, 'Okay, Mom. I'll find him. Where can I reach you when I do?'

"And she said, 'Just give him a message. Tell him I'm fine, and I'll be in touch with him soon. Tell him that you talked to me, and that he should hang on. You got that?'

"'Sure. You're okay, and he should hang on. Hang on to what?'

"'Never you mind. Just tell him. He'll know.'

"'Okay,' I said.

"She said, 'I'll call you in a couple of days, make sure you found your uncle. Thanks a lot, honey. I'm sorry I've worried you.'

"'Wait!' I said—I yelled. 'Tell me where you are. When are you coming back?'

"'I don't know exactly,' Mom said. 'Listen, honey—take care of yourself!' And she hung up."

Sandra paused and looked at each of us. "That's it?" I asked.

She nodded. "That was it. I stayed on the line hoping the operator would come on. Then I could say something like 'Operator, I was accidentally cut off. Could you give me the number of the person I was just speaking to so I can call them back?' But the phone went dead, and no operator came on the line."

"A good try," I said.

Brass stirred like a lion waking from its sleep. "So your mother didn't tell you where she was, what she was doing, or how long she was going to be away?" he asked.

"No."

"Who is your Uncle Andrew?" Brass asked.

"I have no idea," she said. "As far as I am aware, I don't have an Uncle Andrew."

"Oh," Brass said into the silence.

"The only Andrew I know is Andrew Ffalkis, the character actor; and Mother doesn't know him."

"Then what on earth was your mother talking about?"

"I have no idea—and I'm scared!"

"Maybe she has some sort of amnesia," I suggested. "The sort of thing that makes her confused about the past. Maybe she's at some sort of rest home where they're taking care of her until she recovers, and she doesn't want to alarm you."

Sandra looked at me. "Do you believe that?"

"No," I admitted. "But it's possible."

"Not likely," Brass said. "What exactly," he asked Sandra, "is it that's frightening you?"

Sandra folded her hands on her lap like a little girl preparing to recite in class. "We used to have signals, Mom and I," she said in a soft voice. "When I was a kid and we were on the con."

"You mean like giving the office," I said, ostentatiously adjusting the knot on my tie.

Brass observed my gesture with a faint smile. " 'A little learning is a dangerous thing," he said.

"Like that," Sandra agreed. "Except the office is a sort of general gesture; everyone in the grift knows it. These were little signals that Mom and I made up between us. I used to think it was a great game."

"What sort of signals?" Brass asked.

"Well, there were the visual cues like the brush-off"—she brushed an imaginary spot off her skirt—"and the 'you don't know me'"—she patted the back of her right hand with her left hand. "And there were verbal cues. 'On Monday' was the signal for 'go home.' If Mom was working a mark and didn't want me around, she'd say, 'We'll go to the store on Monday' or 'I'm going up to see your teacher on Monday', and I'd think of some excuse to leave and go back to wherever we were staying."

"But supposing she actually wanted to do something on Monday?" I asked.

"Then she'd say 'Monday' and not 'on Monday.' She'd leave off the 'on.' 'We're going fishing Monday,' she'd say. The whole point of the signals is that they have to sound as natural as possible."

"I can see that," I said.

"And if she ever says 'okay,'—a natural thing to say, 'okay'— that means that everything that follows is not true."

"And she said 'okay' in the phone call." Brass said.

"That's right, she did."

He took a deep breath. "How long has it been since you and your mom used this code?"

"Maybe ten years. I've been out of the grift for about that long."

"You don't think it could have been a mistake? Could she have forgotten?"

"She said it twice," Sandra said. "She hasn't forgotten. She was warning me that she was about to tell me a story that I shouldn't believe. And that means..." Sandra paused.

"That means," Brass finished, "that someone else was listening."

"Why—" I started to ask, and then stopped. It was obvious: Two-Headed Mary would only have to use the code if a third person were listening. Silly me.

"But I don't get the point," Sandra said. "If she was trying to tell me something, she didn't get it across."

"Well," Brass said thoughtfully. "If you're right, she wasn't trying to convey information to you, beside the happy fact that she is still alive and all right. She was telling the story for someone else's benefit. So what is it she said? You're to find this mythical Uncle Andrew and tell him—tell him what?—that your mother is fine. That he should hang on. Hang on to what?"

"That's what I asked," Sandra said. "She didn't answer."

"It's an interesting puzzle," Brass said. "And is there anything in the conversation to give us a hint as to where she was, or where she has been? Any other coded messages?"

"Unfortunately not," Sandra said. "But there was one other thing—"

"What's that?"

"What she said right before she hung up. 'Take care of yourself,' she said."

Brass nodded. "Yes? Sounds like a motherly sentiment. Is it another code-word?"

"It is," Sandra said. "We've always thought it was rather subtle, since it means exactly what it says."

"Take care of yourself?" I repeated.

"Yes. It means that there is danger and to watch out. It may mean to flee—to get out of the situation, whatever it is."

"What situation?" Brass asked.

Sandra's face flushed and she raised her arms to the sides of her head, her hands balled into tight fists. "How should I know?" she wailed. "I'm only her daughter, why would she tell me anything?" After a second her hands dropped back into her lap and she continued in a very calm, very controlled voice: "I don't know what's happened to her, and I don't know what she is warning me about. I don't like it and I am afraid."

Brass pursed his lips and nodded. "There seems little doubt that it was your mother who called you," he said. "She was trying to get you to do something, or to make someone else think that you were going to do something. And she was trying to warn you; but of what danger, and from where?"

Brass stared off into the middle distance, his eyes focused somewhere beyond the makeup table. After two minutes of silence, he turned to her and asked, "Do you live alone?"

"Yes," she said. "I ditched my roommates as soon as I could afford to. A girl likes to have some privacy."

He rose to his feet. "Come with me!"

"Where?" Sandra asked.

"I want to think this out and I'm hungry," Brass said. "We'll go to Jimmy's and I'll have a steak. If you two aren't hungry, you can watch me eat."

I got up and put my coat on. Eating steak is one of the things I do best.

Jimmy's Chop House was a late-night bistro on 50th west of Seventh that stayed open until two or three in the morning and catered to late-night people: reporters, actors, producers, song writers, cabaret performers; all the people that the rest of the world considers "interesting" until they try to take out a bank loan.

It was quarter past midnight when we settled into the table in the far corner of Jimmy's. Brass excused himself to make a phone call and to say hello to Laverne Taylor, who was singing her usual mix of show tunes and the blues, sweet and low and smoky, and accompanying herself on the piano by the bar. She broke into "Hard-Hearted Hanna," as Brass made his way back to the table, paused for a sip from the glass of bourbon she kept on the piano, and then took up "You're Getting to Be a Habit with Me."

Brass and I both ordered a steak and fries and the house salad; Sandra went for the ris de veau, which are sweetbreads and which are a house specialty. Jimmy has a French chef for everything but the steaks. Brass got into a lengthy discussion with Jimmy about wines, and finally ended up ordering a Château Latour-Pomerol, which turned out to be a red wine from Bordeaux. Which turned out to go well with steak—or, I'm sure, without steak.

The place was nearly empty except for a table of three near the center of the room. Two of the three were fellow writers. One was Dorothy Parker, whose early book, *Enough Rope*, had been one of the reasons why I thought writing might be an honorable and attainable profession. She made it look easy. It wasn't until I tried it that I realized just how hard making it look easy was. The other was Robert Benchley, a man who found the humor in the mundane. It was only after the third or fourth belly laugh at one of his essays that you realized that you were laughing at yourself.

The other man at the table was a stranger to me. Parker seemed unhappy: she was leaning forward with her elbows on the table and her head in her hands. The other man was talking earnestly to her. Benchley was alternating patting her on the back and sipping the highball in front of him. When he happened to look over to our table he waved and then stood up and gingerly walked over; his gait suggesting that the floor was littered with raw eggs and he didn't want to break a single shell. Either that, or the drink in his hand was not his first.

"How do, Alexander Brass," he said as he reached the table and clutched onto the back of my chair for support. "*Come stai?* That's Italian."

"Really?" Brass said.

"Indeed. A noble language. I have been studying it. "*Quei due uomini con I buoi arriveranno domani.*"

"I can see that," Brass agreed.

Benchley nodded. "I am leaving for Italy tomorrow. Today. On a ship."

"For how long?" Sandra asked from across the table.

Benchley refocused. "Oh," he said. "Miss Lelane. How do. You are talented and beautiful, and you can sing, too. I can't sing. I am going to Italy for a month. Would you care to cast aside your worldly cares and accompany me?"

She smiled. "I'd have to give two weeks' notice," she said. "And by then you'd have done everything exciting."

"Highly unlikely," Benchley said. "I've never done anything exciting before. Mine is a dull life, punctuated by moments of sheer ennui."

"That's not what I've heard," she said.

"Rumors spread by my enemies," Benchley told her.

"Are you going to hole up in a villa in Como to write the great American novel?" Brass asked. "More great American novels seem to be written in Italy than anywhere else. Closely followed by Paris, of course."

"I am going to Italy to represent our country, if they don't catch me at it," Benchley explained ponderously. "I am going to give Mussolini what for. Possibly even what five. I am going to Rome to visit the Forum. I am going to Florence to chat with the old masters. I was going to Venice, but they tell me the streets are flooded."

"Have a great trip," Brass said. "I expect to read about it in *The New Yorker*."

"So does Ross," Benchley said, waving at the table behind him. "He expects some clever little travel vignettes. I told him he'd take what I gave him, clever or not, and it was a little late to worry about cleverness now. I told him if he wanted clever, he should have hired Thurber. Of course he *did* hire Thurber, so where does that leave me?"

Which identified the other man at the table: Harold Ross, editor of *The New Yorker*; the man who published Benchley and Parker and Thurber, as well as E. B. White and Clarence Day and William Steig and Peter Arno. The man who had already sent me three rejection slips.

"Ross is trying to talk Dorothy into taking over my job as theater reviewer while I'm abroad," Benchley told Brass, waving a hand at the scene behind him. "She doesn't want to. She says that a reviewer must be honest, and she'll lose the few friends she has left. I told her, nonsense, she hasn't got any friends, and she called me a nasty name. That's what I get for trying to meditate-mediate-between friends. You may put that in your column, if you like."

"Writers aren't news," Brass said.

"Thank God for that!" Benchley said, and he tipped an imaginary hat to Sandra and wandered back to his table.

Our food arrived and we ate silently except for an occasional "Pass the salt." Brass chewed thoughtfully and sipped Château Latour-Pomerol and stared into space. I hoped that he was doing the thinking that he had promised. I tried to do some myself. Two-Headed Mary had called her daughter and told her to give Uncle Andrew an important message. The message was "I'm fine." We were all relieved to hear that she was fine, but why was that of particular importance to Uncle Andrew? And who was Uncle Andrew? And what was it that Two-Headed Mary had warned Sandra to be careful about? And where was she and where had she been and who was listening in to the conversation and why? It was all unsatisfactory.

When I ran out of things to think about I took a healthy swallow of wine and a penultimate bite of steak and leaned toward Sandra. "How are your sweetbreads?" I asked.

"Good," she said. "Want a taste?"

I shook my head. "No thanks," I said. "I don't eat anything unless

I know where it's been, and sweetbreads are a mystery to me."

"It's veal pancreas," she told me. "Occasionally they use the thymus gland, but that's not considered as good. Don't look surprised," she added, seeing my expression. "I used to wait tables at a French restaurant when I was getting started. You learn things like that."

"That pancreas stuff might mean something to you," I told her, "but I am none the wiser for the information."

She filled her fork with the stuff and offered it to me across the table. "Here," she said. "Expand your horizons. Taste it!"

I am not a churl. When a beautiful woman offers me a morsel of food, I take it.

I tasted. The bit of sweetbread was soft but firm, sort of like a mushroom. The sauce was thick and tasted of mushrooms and a generous amount of garlic. It wasn't bad. "Thank you," I said. "I have now learned something new for the day."

"What's that?" she asked.

"That pancreas, or possibly thymus, whatever that is, is edible," I told her, "and that stale bread or pieces of rubber eraser would probably taste good in a thick garlic-flavored sauce."

She smiled. It was an effort, but she did. "It's one of the secrets of French cuisine. That and butter and cream and veal bones."

"Veal bones?"

"If you boil them for hours and hours they make a sauce."

"I'll bet they do," I told her.

Our waiter cleared away the debris and brought three separate little pots of coffee and three dessert plates of Charlotte Malakoff au Chocolat, which is another of the chef's specialties, and which, as Garrett says about his favorite unblended scotch whisky, goes down singing hymns.

"I've been thinking," Brass said.

"We certainly hoped so," I told him.

He ignored me. "A couple of questions," he said to Sandra.

"Tell me about the telephone call. Try to remember what you heard, if anything."

Sandra looked at him thoughtfully. "I don't think I can add anything to what I already told you," she said.

"Not your mother's conversation," he told her, "but any other sounds or noises. Background sounds or sounds on the line. Clicks, buzzes, hums, music, car noises, any cross-talk on the line; anything like that."

She nodded. "I see. Let me think." She stared at the double row of autographed pictures on the wall and her brow furrowed as she tried to remember. "There were clicks," she said. "And a fair amount of the sort of line noise that sounds like somebody is gargling in the distant background. Does that help?"

"Probably not," Brass said. "But the more facts you collect the better the chance of something useful being among the collection. What about when you hung up? You say no operator came on?"

"That's right."

"How long did you wait?"

"At least a couple of minutes."

"Did you get a dial tone?"

"No, I never did. The phone just stayed dead. Does that mean anything?"

"Probably that the circuit didn't go through one of the new automated exchanges. I doubt if we can tell much from that, but it's another item for the list."

"Not a very long list," Sandra said, staring down into her dessert. "I mean, she's still alive, and that's something. But I wish I knew what's going on."

Brass reached over and squeezed her shoulder, which she seemed to consider reassuring. "We'll get there," he told her. "Now let's consider the message itself. Not as you heard it, but as the unknown listener heard it. What was she telling him? What did he learn?"

"That I have an Uncle Andrew," Sandra said. "Kindly old Uncle Andrew."

"More than that. Mary managed to convey that she has been trying to get in touch with Uncle Andrew, but has been unable to."

"Yes," Sandra agreed. "And where does that get us?"

"Patience," Brass said. "I'm sounding this out as I go along."

"Maybe," I suggested, "there's something that she was supposed to do for this person, but it hasn't been done, and when this person found out it wasn't done she invented this Andrew so she could blame it on him."

Brass looked at me thoughtfully. "Very good, Morgan," he said. "But I think you have it backward."

"Just don't ask me to repeat it," I said.

"What do you mean backward?" Sandra asked.

"I think it's fairly clear that your mother is being held against her will," Brass said.

"You mean she's been kidnapped?"

"Something like that. But certainly not for ransom. We would have had the ransom demand long since."

Sandra nodded. "What then?"

"Probably knowledge."

"What," I asked, "are you talking about?"

"I think she knows something that the kidnapper wants to find out, or else she knows something that the kidnapper doesn't want anyone else to find out."

"If this kidnapper is the same person who killed the girl in the park, why doesn't he just kill her?" I asked.

Sandra gasped and brought her napkin to her face.

"Oh, God," I said. "I'm sorry. It's okay. I mean, he hasn't killed her. We know she's alive so far. If she just could have been a little more informative in that phone call…"

Sandra looked at me and her eyes filled with tears. She dropped the napkin and pulled a large handkerchief from her purse and wiped her eyes severely, and then wiped them again. And then she gave up and put her head in her hands and cried.

"Very good, DeWitt," Brass said, glaring at me.

"No, no," Sandra said. "It's not his fault. He just said what I've been thinking. My mother is out there somewhere—out in the world—and she needs my help. And I can't figure out what the hell she's talking about! A hell of a daughter I am!"

Brass patted her on the back tentatively, at which she burst into tears again so he withdrew his hand. Comfort was not what Sandra wanted right now; she wanted her mother.

Brass stared into space. "Every good con man," he said speculatively, "or con woman, always has an ace in the hole. No matter what hand was dealt to Two-Headed Mary, she had that old ace in the hole to fall back on. You know that."

It took about a minute for Sandra to reduce her crying to a bad case of sniffles and raise her head. She wiped her eyes and her nose and took a deep breath. "That's the saying," she said. "Always keep that old ace in the hole. But what ace are we talking about? What's her ace?"

"My guess is that it's 'Uncle Andrew,'" Brass told her. "I know I'm doing a lot of guessing this evening, and that's no way to build a logical case. But one must work with what one has. This makes sense. It may not be right, but I'll bet it's a close approximation."

"What?" I asked. "What makes sense?"

"I was just remembering what we were taught in the war," Brass said. "Once is happenstance, twice is coincidence, three times is enemy action."

I nodded. That was one of Brass's favorite quotes, and he dragged it out at every opportunity. But, in this case what did it mean?

"What do you mean?" I asked.

Brass counted on his fingers. "One, Billie Trask disappears, with or without the company's money. Two, Two-Headed Mary disappears. Three, Billy Trask's roommate, Mary's friend, Lydia Laurent is murdered and her body dumped in Central Park. Now, although the people are all connected, we have no proof that the events are related. But that's where I'm putting my money."

"And four," I added, "Madam Florintina becomes at one with the universe."

"That's right," Brass agreed. "That's part of the pattern."

"Madam who?" Sandra asked.

"An astrologist," Brass told her. "She came to see us. DeWitt talked to her. Then she was killed."

Sandra turned to me. "What did she say?" she asked.

"She wanted to know everybody's birth dates," I told her. "She was after the reward."

"Oh," Sandra said. "I heard about that. All the gypsies are talking about it. K. Jeffrey and *Lucky Lady* offering that reward. There was some talk the show was going to close, but I guess if he can put up two thousand dollars, they must be doing all right."

"Now there's a motive for K. Jeffrey's largesse we never thought of," Brass told me. "Two thousand dollars' worth of publicity for his show. And if nobody comes forward, he might not even have to pay it."

"It's a shock to discover that everybody's got an angle," I said. "I hardly know what to believe in anymore."

Brass explained to Sandra what had happened to the astrologist.

"So you think Madam Florintina's death is a part of this pattern?" she asked. "You think she knew something about... about my mother—and got killed?"

"Something like that," Brass said.

"Oh, God!" Sandra said.

Brass nodded in sympathy. "These things would seem to be all related," he said, "and the fact that your mother is still alive is the only good news we have so far."

"Did Madam Florintina talk to K. Jeffrey?"

"I don't know. The police and our ace crime reporter, Alan Shine, went over to interrogate Welton, but as yet I haven't heard what they found out." Brass gestured across the room. "Ah, good!" he said. "He's here."

I turned. Theodore Garrett had come in and was headed toward our table. This evening he was dressed like a gentleman, and would fit in anywhere, especially if the year were 1895. He was wearing a black Chesterfield overcoat with a velvet collar, black and gray striped pants, a high-collared shirt with an Ascot, and carrying a black top hat. I understand that diplomats still dress like that. Perhaps Garrett was impersonating a diplomat.

"Miss Lelane," Brass said as Garrett reached the table. "You remember Mr. Garrett."

Garrett bowed from the waist. "Delighted," he said.

Sandra clapped her hands. "Very good," she said. "Let me guess: it's not quite right for *Victoria Regina*. Perhaps *The Barretts of Wimpole Street*?"

"My clothing?" Garrett gestured toward himself. "It's not, strictly speaking, a costume. I have my suits and coats made for me by Saddler's of Oxford Street. Unfortunately they haven't cut a new pattern in forty years. Their clientele is very select, and very loyal."

"It must be so," Sandra agreed.

"Mr. Garrett is going to see you home, if you can stand being around such elegance," Brass told her.

"That's all right," Sandra said. "I don't need an escort."

Garrett visibly did his best not to look insulted. The stage lost a great ham when Garrett decided not to tread the boards.

"You may be right," Brass said. "On the other hand, you may be mistaken. Your mother thinks that you may be in danger, and at the moment she knows more about it than we do. That's why I called Mr. Garrett."

"Oh," Sandra said.

"Once you are home, you will pack a bag, perhaps two bags, and Mr. Garrett will bring you back to my apartment, where we have prepared the spare bedroom for you."

"Oh," Sandra said. "What about the show? What about my going to the theater?"

"Mr. Garrett will go with you and bring you back."

"Well won't that be something. I haven't had a chaperone since—come to think of it, I've never had a chaperone. This will be a new experience."

"I shall endeavor to make it a pleasant one, mum," Garrett said, bowing humbly from the waist.

"By the way," Brass added, "it might be a good idea not to mention Two-Headed Mary's phone call to anyone for the time being."

"I agree," Sandra said. She stood up. "Well, Mr. Garrett, let's get going."

Garrett bowed again. "Your servant, mum," he said.

16

Brass arrived at the office a little after eleven. I had been there for about twenty minutes, and was still busy answering the mail. The pile of unanswered letters was getting thicker; pretty soon Brass was going to have to spring for some part-time help to catch up. We usually offer the job to one of the reporters from downstairs. Reporters are always in need of money, and many of them know how to type. A newsy working the evening slot could come in a few hours early and type replies. Most of the letters fell into one of five categories, and the formula we used for replies was easy to learn. Brass paid seventy-five cents an hour, and threw in lunch; and where else in town can you get a deal like that?

At noon, Brass came through the hall and beckoned, and I followed him to the outer office. "Come, Morgan," he said. "We have an appointment. Gloria, you'll have to take care of Mr. Simmonds when and if he arrives."

"The prospect brightens my day," she said. "What should I tell him if he appears?"

"Tell him I'd be glad to come down to Atlanta to speak to his business group if he pays the fare: round-trip, first-class sleeping-car tickets for the three of us; I think you two deserve a paid vacation, particularly if I can get someone else to pay for it. And he should put us up for two nights at a good hotel; something named 'Peachtree' will probably do. Tell him my honorarium will bet at least a thousand dollars; how much more I leave to his good sense. If he thinks that's too much—and why should he?—don't go below seven-fifty.

"Also tell him that all he's buying is my speech to the group. I may or may not mention his organization or the city of Atlanta in my column subsequently, and my mention, if there is one, may or may not be favorable. Tell him that I react very badly to the sight of 'colored only' waiting rooms, bathrooms, or drinking fountains, and that, if I do write about my trip, that might be what I write about. Tell him that the only intelligent Southerners I have ever met have all been persons of color, with the exception of Will Rogers, and he's from Oklahoma."

Gloria smiled a tight smile. The Mona Lisa had nothing on Gloria in the mysterious smile department. "Do I get to tell him that word-for-word, or can I edit it a bit?"

Brass shrugged. "Tell him what you like. Work out the best deal you can with him, if he's still interested after my caveat."

"I've talked to him twice," Gloria said. "I don't think he likes dealing with women."

"The more fool he," Brass said. "If he won't deal with you, then he won't get me. Send him to Winchell. Walter is usually unaware of his surroundings, and if you stick a plate of rubber chicken in front of him, he'll give a speech."

"Okay," she said.

"If he doesn't show up by one, go to lunch."

We were in a cab before I found out where we were going.

"The Monarch Theater, driver," Brass said.

"Are we visiting K. Jeffrey," I asked him as the cab pulled out, "or are we looking over the scene of the crime?"

"We are going to meet Welton's brother, Edward," Brass told me. "At Edward's request."

"What does Edward want with us?"

"We're about to find out."

They were waiting for us at the Monarch's box office; K. Jeffrey and brother Edward and the company manager, a small, skinny man named Foxy Vulpone. Edward Welton was tall and angular and craggy; he looked like a constipated Abraham Lincoln. They took us through to the theater's private offices, a suite of rooms off of the lobby. We settled in the middle room, which could have served as the drawing room in a Civil War melodrama. Brass and I occupied opposite ends of a swayback couch. K. Jeffrey almost disappeared into the swivel chair behind an oak desk top-heavy with scripts, some of them looking as if they may well have dated back to the Civil War, and brother Edward perched on a severe, hardwood chair.

"I know, I know," K. Jeffrey said, seeing my reaction to the room. "Very Belasco. The furniture's a hundred years old, and has been used daily for that whole hundred years. But new furniture for the office is not in the budget, and old man Grice won't spend a dime on upkeep of his theaters."

"Is this a Grice theater?" Brass asked. "I didn't know."

Welton nodded. "Salmon Grice is my landlord. I have the place on a long-term lease, so I'll be putting shows on here in the Monarch Theater until 1950."

"Good luck," I said.

"It's not so bad," Welton told me. "As long as two productions out of three are smash hits, and the building doesn't fall down around my ears, I'll do all right. Listen, it's lunchtime. Would you fellows like sandwiches and coffee before we get started? Hot pastrami okay?"

We murmured our assent, and Welton turned to the company manager. "Foxy, trot over to the Stage Deli and get a halfdozen hot pastrami sandwiches, will you? And coffee all around. Take a couple of dollars out of petty cash. There's a good chap."

Brother Edward leaned forward in his chair as Foxy trotted out of the room. "Mr. Brass," he said. "I am told that you have connections in what they call 'the underworld.' Is that so?"

Brass stared at Edward for a moment, and then shifted in his seat. "Yes," he said.

"I am also given to understand that you are a man who can hold his tongue, despite your deplorable profession. Is that true?"

K. Jeffrey laughed. "Don't believe the stories," he said. "Tact is not Edward's middle name."

Edward gave K. Jeffrey a dirty look, and then turned back to Brass. "Well, sir?"

"If you mean can I keep a secret," Brass said. "Yes, if it's one I want to keep."

"I can make it worth your while," Edward said, tapping his right forefinger on the dark brown suit pants leg covering his right knee. "I am in need of some information, and possibly some assistance. I will pay up to five hundred dollars for this. Cash."

"A princely offer, Edward," K. Jeffrey said, slapping his thigh with the palm of his hand and grinning broadly. "A princely offer. Why for that much, I'd do it myself!"

"My brother thinks this is funny, Mr. Brass," Edward said. "Why this should be I do not know, but he does. There are many things that Kasden thinks funny in which the rest of the family does not see the humor."

"Kasden?" I asked. "So that's what the 'K' is for."

K. Jeffrey grimaced. "It's an old family name," he said. "Now carried by an uncle and myself. I was named after Uncle Kasden in hopes that, being childless and approaching sixty when I was born, he would leave his money to our side of the family. To the great chagrin of the family, and the personal disappointment of my mother, Uncle Kasden married a Swedish acrobat the day after my fifth birthday. They now have four children, and my uncle is trying hard, night after night, to make it five. Or so my mother says. She does not approve. How she managed to have two sons and a daughter is beyond me."

"Kasden!" Edward barked.

K. Jeffrey raised his hand. "I know, I know," he said. "It's shocking and horrifying to discuss S-E-X in public."

"Sex is one thing," Edward said firmly, "vulgarity is quite another. But you've always been a vulgar little monster."

"That's me," K. Jeffrey agreed. "Vulgar as dirt. I must have been a changeling. Somewhere there is a little goblin child with exquisite manners."

Edward raised his chin and glared at his brother. "In your rush to shock," he said, clipping his syllables sharply at the end, "you show little regard for your family name. My God! You got kicked out of Yale—"

"Suspended for one semester," K. Jeffrey amended.

"You almost married a showgirl, which would have gotten you kicked out of the family—"

This was too much, even for the unflappable K. Jeffrey. He

jumped to his feet, knocking a pile of scripts from his desk to the floor. "The family!" he bellowed, thrusting his face toward his brother. "You talk like they're goddamn royalty! We make shoes! Cheap shoes! We made our money mass-producing cheap shoes! What is so goddamn royal about that?"

Edward looked at him with a stony-faced calm. "Working is no disgrace, brother; you should try it some time," he said with measured deliberation.

"I'll be glad to hammer the nails into your coffin, brother," K. Jeffrey spat out. Then, as suddenly as it had come, his anger evaporated, and he turned and smiled at us. "This is just a little family dispute," he said. "You should see us when we really get going. It's a custom in our family. We enjoy it."

"I don't," Edward said. "Your manners and morals would antagonize a saint."

"Ah!" K. Jeffrey said. "It's the honest, hard-working laborer against the sinners of the theater, and other morality plays." He turned to Brass. "Edward believes in the value of honest toil. Why he can go down to the factory and watch the workers honestly toiling for hours and hours, can't you, brother?"

"You know very well I worked in the Fall River factory when I was seventeen!" Edward said. "You, as I remember, turned down your chance."

"Yes, I did. And yes, you did. For a whole summer. In the mail room, wasn't it? And you took the executives their mail. And they all patted you on the back and told you how clever you were, and how you would go far even if you weren't the boss's son. And the money you earned barely bought gas for your Stutz; you actually lived on your allowance. Tell me, brother Edward: did you ever wonder who they fired to give you that job? Did you wonder how he fed his wife and children? That's what I wondered when it was my turn to take the job. And I asked. They told me not to worry about it. But I couldn't help it, so I politely declined." K. Jeffrey leaned back and glared at his brother, who returned the glare with interest.

Brass rose from his corner of the couch. "If you two would like to put this drama of social significance on the stage, you could probably get an audience," he told them. "But until that happy day, would you please tell me what I'm doing here."

K. Jeffrey took a deep breath and looked away from his brother. Edward glanced at the ceiling and shifted his gaze to Brass.

"I apologize, Mr. Brass," Edward said. "Family matters should be kept in the family. Please sit back down. I do need your assistance."

Foxy came through the outer door, whistling "Blue Moon" as he came down the hall. I wondered if he made a habit of it since Edward arrived, so the brothers would have a chance to conceal their weapons before he appeared. He put a large paper bag down on the desk and distributed its burden of sandwiches and coffee.

"Are you a dancing man, Mr. Vulpone?" Brass asked, accepting his sandwich.

Foxy stared at Brass for a second, and then did a quick minute of soft-shoe, stretched his hands out for the applause, and froze in place. Two seconds later he thawed and resumed dealing sandwiches. "How could you tell, Mr. Brass?" he asked. "Don't tell me you recognized me from the act?"

"Sorry," Brass said. "But it's the way you carry yourself. And your shoes"—He pointed—"black patent leather like your boss, but they're dancing pumps with reinforced heel and sole."

Foxy looked down at his shoes as though seeing them for the first time. "A gift from Mr. Welton," he said. "Patent leather's expensive. I got in the dancing habit years ago, and I practice in them three times a day. For the exercise, you know. Me and Ruth, we used to work the Keith circuit. In 1931 we headlined for a season. Lane and Vulpone, Plain and Fancy."

"You must have been good," Brass said.

"Yes, we were," Foxy said. He shrugged and muttered, "I gotta check out the ticket stock," and left the room.

"Vaudeville's loss is my gain. That man is my good right arm," K. Jeffrey said, indicating the door closing behind Foxy's retreating form. "He takes care of all the little details without which I would have no idea what the hell I'm doing."

"Tell me," Brass asked K. Jeffrey, amid the unwrapping of butcher paper and the uncapping of cardboard cups, "did the police come by and speak to you yesterday?"

K. Jeffrey nodded. "About that soothsayer woman—Madam whoever? Yes, they did."

"Did you see her?"

"Yes." K. Jeffrey took a healthy bite of pastrami and rye and chewed. After he swallowed he went on: "She wanted the reward. Said that if I gave her all the birth dates of everyone involved, she could tell me what happened to Two-Headed Mary, and to Billie Trask, and to my money."

"Did she?" Edward asked, sounding interested. "You didn't tell me that."

"You didn't ask."

"Did you?" Brass asked.

"Did I what? Give her the birth dates? I don't know them. Why should I?"

"What happened then?"

"She said that she might still have something to tell me, but she had to check on something first." He held up his hand. "Before you ask, she didn't say what. She asked to speak to me alone— Liebowitz, the stage manager, was with me at the time—but I declined the honor. Then she went away. The whole meeting took—what?—five minutes. The police wanted to know where she went, but I haven't the faintest."

"And you'd never seen this woman before?"

"You sound like Inspector Raab. No, I never had. I don't go in for astrology."

"Did any of the girls as far as you know?"

"What, go in for astrology? Probably. Actors and actresses are a superstitious lot. But none specifically that I know of. Say—are you interested in this woman's death?"

"Interested?"

"You know, professionally."

Brass considered. "Yes, I guess I am. My readers seem to be interested in the fate of Two-Headed Mary. We've already gotten quite a few letters asking about her, haven't we, Morgan?"

"A couple of dozen at least," I replied.

"And it all seems to be related, doesn't it? The disappearance of Two-Headed Mary, and Billie Trask and your money, and the death of Lydia Laurent? There must be something that ties them together, but I have no idea what it might be."

"That's what I want to consult with you about," Edward said.

"With the understanding, of course, that none of this will get into your newspaper."

Brass leaned forward and opened his mouth to speak, but then closed his mouth again. My guess is that he was going to correct Edward's statement from "newspaper" to "several hundred newspapers," but then thought better of it. You're never too old to learn self-control.

"Do I have that assurance, Mr. Brass?"

"If you are not confessing to murder or high treason, I can promise that I will not use anything that I hear from you unless I hear it separately and independently from another source," Brass said, reciting our usual formula.

Edward didn't look happy.

"Oh, come on, brother dear," K. Jeffrey said. He turned to Brass. "The trouble with my brother is that he regards life as a painful duty. He also believes that everyone has his price, and in that I must report that he has so far been proven right." He spread his arms apart in an elaborate shrug. "So, are you going to tell him, brother dear, or am I?"

Edward sighed. "I am not as rigid as Kasden would have you think. I wrote poetry in college. I was seriously considering becoming a novelist, but then it became necessary for me to take my place in the family business."

"We all have our secret sorrows, brother," K. Jeffrey said with a twisted grin. "I was going to marry a chorus girl."

Brass took a bite from his sandwich, which reduced it to a right-angle length of crust, and put it aside. "So far," he said, "I have heard no secrets worth keeping." He drained his coffee cup.

Edward turned in his chair until he was facing Brass head-on. "Is this man sober and trustworthy?" he asked, indicating me with a flip of his thumb.

"Completely," Brass said. "My secrets are his secrets."

Well! I would have to remember that the next time I ask for a raise. I nodded to Edward, arranging my face to look as sober and trustworthy as I could. He looked at me doubtfully, but then switched his gaze back to Brass.

"Making shoes," Edward said, "is a difficult way to amass a fortune. Great-grandfather Welton also made leather shackles and restraints." He paused, and the silence grew.

"For prisoners?" Brass asked.

"For slaves. For the slavers, which sailed from New England ports. Eventually he owned a part interest in a slaver. The *Sojourner*, out of New Bedford. A sleek, beautiful craft. We have a painting of her under full sail in the moonlight, done by Carter Biddell. With the profits great-grandfather bought land. When the Civil War started, his son, our grandfather, sold boots to both sides. And rifle slings, and harnesses and pack saddles. With the profits he bought more land."

"Your secret is safe with me," Brass told Edward.

"That was seventy years ago," Edward said. "One of the great truths that we all live by is that what one's grandparents did, no matter how reprehensible, is washed clean by the passage of time. Particularly if it made a lot of money."

Edward perched farther forward on his chair. "Oh, I have no pretensions as to how our family got where it is, Mr. Brass, but, having arrived at a pinnacle, not as lofty as some, but a pinnacle nonetheless, we have dug in and set up our trench work, and will answer the call of blood-to-blood, come what may."

"A neat job, brother," K. Jeffrey commented. "You haven't so much mixed your metaphors as stirred them up."

"I have just explained to Mr. Brass why it is that the family just doesn't disown you and let you marry some little tramp or produce shows full of dancing girls on your own hook."

"I used the money from grandfather's trust fund," K. Jeffrey said, with the sort of weariness in his voice that showed that he had gone over this many times before, and didn't enjoy it any more this time.

"It shouldn't be necessary to remind you that the fund is discretionary and can be cut off," Edward commented.

"It is a pleasure to remind you," K. Jeffrey said, leaning across his desk and stabbing a finger in Edward's shoulder, "that *Lucky Lady* is doing smashing box-office business, and I have a cluster of happy angels, ready to back my next show, whatever that might be."

Edward backed away as far as he could without leaving the chair. "By damn, you're even starting to speak like them," he said. I smiled, but my heart wasn't in it. If they had asked me, I would have told them how tired I was of these riches-to-riches stories of the lads who had taken the million dollars their grandfather had left them and run it up into a real fortune. There were too many working stiffs out there who, every time they paid their rent, wondered how they were going to eat for the next week. And too many stiffs who were not working and wondered that every day. But they didn't ask me, which was probably just as well.

"Is this taking us anywhere useful?" Brass asked.

"Yes, brother," K. Jeffrey said. "Back to the matter at hand. Tell Mr. Brass your long and sad tale."

Edward, who was rubbing his shoulder where his brother had poked him and glaring across the desk, turned back to Brass. "Again I apologize," he said. "I need your assistance on a delicate matter. It seems I..." His voice trailed off and he stared desperately around the room, as though searching for a script hidden in a lamp or vase that would tell him what to say. "I hardly know how to begin," he said.

"You want me to do something for you," Brass said, "obviously as a result of something that happened. What happened, when and where did it happen, and what do you want me to do? Let's start with what happened."

Edward took a deep breath and let it out slowly. "The safe in the inner office"—he pointed—"was emptied. Probably by the Trask girl when she left, else why should she have gone? But we doubt whether she acted alone. Regardless, whoever did it took the weekend receipts from *Lucky Lady* and a thick manila envelope that belonged to me. I need to get certain of the contents of that envelope back."

Brass shook his head. "That's a job for the police," he told Edward, "and they won't charge you."

"In the envelope," Edward continued, "is, or was, ten thousand dollars in cash and another ten thousand in United States Treasury Bonds, twenty-year maturity, issued in 1918."

I whistled. It was involuntary. "That's a heavy manila envelope," I said when Edward turned to look at me.

He nodded impatiently and went on. "There is a reason why it is important to get those bonds back. It would be pleasant to get back the money—the cash—but I realize that it is probably irreparably gone. But the bonds may be obtainable. That's what I want you to do, to get the bonds back for me."

"What's special about the bonds, aside from their value?" Brass asked.

K. Jeffrey slapped his hand on the desk and intoned, with feeling:

> "Some for the glories of this world; and some
> Sigh for the Prophet's paradise to come;
> Ah, take the cash, and let the credit go,
> Nor heed the rumble of a distant drum!"

"Is that your advice?" Edward asked in a tight voice.

"No," K. Jeffrey said. "That's Omar Khayyam. Just a random thought. Feel free to ignore it."

"I shall," Edward said. He turned back to Brass. "I would not be telling you this, except that it has become expedient," he said. "If you print it in your newspaper, I shall deny it and sue you for slander."

"Libel," Brass told him.

"Excuse me?"

"You'll sue me for libel. If it's written or printed, it's libel; if it's spoken, it's slander."

"Very well then. I shall sue you for libel."

Brass sighed a heavy sigh. "Mr. Welton, I don't understand you, really I don't. I was invited here because I understood that you needed a favor from me. Then, after informing me that my profession is deplorable, you tell me that you want me to retrieve ten, or possibly twenty thousand dollars; for which you offer me five hundred dollars; then you threaten to sue me.

"Mr. Welton, I don't need your money or your threats. I came here because two women are dead and two more are missing, and I have an interest in finding out what happened to them. Now, if I can help you retrieve your bonds, I will, but I won't take your money—you can donate it to charity; I suggest the Barbara Ellen Home for Unwed Mothers on Fifty-third. Just leave a check through the mail slot."

Edward stared at Brass, his mouth agape. I don't know whether it was that nobody had ever spoken it to him that way before, or that nobody had ever turned down his money before. K. Jeffrey also looked shocked. It took Edward a minute before new words could struggle out of his mouth. "Mr. Brass," he said finally, "it could be that you are indeed high-minded and principled, and would not take advantage when there is advantage it to be taken. But, I ask you sir: how was I to know that? The twenty thousand dollars in that manila envelope was intended as a bribe for a city official. If a man entrusted by the city of New York to conduct its official business will take a twenty-thousand-dollar bribe, who shall I excuse from the sin of venality, and how shall I recognize him?

"I asked you to come here because I was told by my brother that you were the best person for what has to be done, but. I know nothing about you. I have never read your column. I am told you have a radio show; I have never listened to it. I do not know you."

Now it was Brass's turn to have his mouth drop open, but he fought it. He knew that, since he had a readership of two and a half million, that there must be 125,021,000 people in the United States, as of the last census, that didn't read "Brass Tacks." But to know that intellectually was one thing; to actually meet one of them face-to-face, and be civil to the man, that was hard.

Brass smiled, but it was a tight-lipped smile. "Who were you trying to bribe, and what did you expect to get for your money?" he asked.

"I don't think that knowledge would be of any use to you," Edward said. "The bribe hasn't happened, and now it certainly will not, even if we get the bonds back. The, ah, person in question says that he thinks that Mayor LaGuardia is watching over his shoulder, and he doesn't dare do anything suspicious."

"What favors were you trying to get?" Brass asked. "I do have an interest in what's for sale in this town."

"It's a question of land," Edward said. "Due to the Depression, land prices are low throughout this great country, but they are particularly depressed in New York City. The building boom that ended in twenty-nine has left a surplus of apartments and office space."

"You want to buy land?" Brass asked. "For that you'll pay a twenty-thousand-dollar bribe?"

"We want to build a skyscraper," Edward said. His face became animated as he spoke of it, and he made large gestures with his hands. "The Welton Towers. Eighty-seven stories high, with a dirigible mooring mast on top. Not as high as the Empire State Building, but respectable. We'd put our corporate offices on the top floor."

"Quite a grandiose goal," Brass said.

"But building anything in this city is complicated and expensive. Some of the owners of buildings on the site we want won't sell, even though we offer more than fair market value for their homes. The land must be condemned. And then we must get zoning variants and all sorts of special permits. We want the facing of the first five floors to be in Vermont marble, and we have to bring in workers experienced in setting marble. The local building contractors have to be paid off to allow us to do that. And we have to get all the land secured and the permits in place before we can complete the financing."

"You're not paying for it all yourselves?" I asked.

"Oh, no," Edward told me. "You're talking millions of dollars. We'll have the largest chunk of it, of course, but that will only be about fifteen percent."

"So the twenty thousand dollars does not represent a large amount of money to you?" Brass asked.

Edward smiled. "To me, it represents a small fortune," he said, "but to the family, no. We were prepared to spend it anyway."

"Then why is it so important for you to get it back? Why not just forget about it and go on?"

"Because the bonds were ready to be handed over to—ah—the person in question. Because we had already signed them over to him. Because his name is on all ten bonds, and that could put him in prison."

"And you?" Brass asked.

"Possibly, but that is doubtful," Edward said. "We can pay for very good attorneys."

"A Welton in prison?" K. Jeffrey said in mock horror. "Impossible!"

"But it would effectively kill our plans for the Welton Towers," Edward said, ignoring his brother.

"I still don't understand what you want me to do," Brass said.

"I can't go to my contacts in what you call the 'underworld' and ask them if they have any stolen bonds."

"That won't be necessary," Edward said. "A note arrived today, with instructions."

"A note?"

"That's right." He turned to his brother. "Kasden, have you the note?"

K. Jeffrey took an envelope out of his desk drawer and flipped it to his brother. It was a regular plain white business envelope, with nothing to distinguish it from a million others. Edward carefully took the message from within and unfolded and passed it to Brass.

Brass took it gingerly in both hands, one at each corner, and examined it closely. I peered over his shoulder.

It was a regular sheet of white bond paper, which had been folded in three to put in the envelope. The message on it was made up of individual words that appeared to have been cut out of a newspaper and pasted onto the paper. It said:

I HAVE YOUR BONDS,
GIVE $10,000 TO ALEXANDER BRASS
USED MONEY
HE WILL BE TOLD WHERE TO GO.

CRIMINAL AT LARGE

The dollar sign, the ten and the three zeros were cut out separately. "Criminal at Large," which I assumed was meant to be the signature, had been cut out as one piece. The "Alexander Brass" was also one piece, and was in a different typeface.

"My name is from my byline on 'Brass Tacks' in the *New York World*," Brass said. "But the other words are from a different newspaper."

K. Jeffrey leaned over to stare at the note, looking interested. "Which one, do you suppose?"

"*Variety*, I think," Brass said. "Yes, *Variety*, the type style is unmistakable. And besides, 'Criminal at Large' is that Edgar Wallace show that ran a couple of years ago. *Variety* did a piece this week on the box-office gross of different sorts of shows since the stock market crash." Brass continued to stare thoughtfully at the paper. "Symmetrical, isn't it? Ten thousand out, ten thousand in."

K. Jeffrey nodded. "Does that mean anything?"

"Probably not."

"Something else?" Edward asked.

"Doesn't the wording strike you as being a bit odd?" Brass replied.

"I don't know," Edward said. "How do blackmailers usually write?"

"Odd in what way?" K. Jeffrey asked.

Brass folded up the paper and handed it to K. Jeffrey. "I'm not sure," he said. "Maybe it's my imagination. Besides, as your brother says, who knows how blackmailers usually write?"

"Will you do it?" Edward asked.

Brass nodded. "I'll go as far as listening to whatever the person who wrote the note has to say. If it doesn't involve any undue danger, or too outlandish a rigmarole, I'll do the exchange for you."

"Good," Edward said. He took a thick envelope from an inside pocket. "Here is ten thousand dollars in hundred-dollar bills," he said, handing it to Brass. "You'd better count it so there is no room for error. If you can get the bonds back for less, I'll pay you ten percent of what you save. And don't let them cozen you. I won't go a penny higher."

"I'll try not to be cozened," Brass told him.

17

We took a cab back to the office. It wouldn't do to get mugged on the street with ten thousand dollars of someone else's money in your pocket. It was a couple of minutes shy of three-thirty when the elevator deposited us on the sixteenth floor. Brass walked through to his office to put the envelope stuffed with hundreds in the new and improved wall safe that had recently been installed near his desk. He called, "How did it go?" to Gloria at her desk as he passed.

"You're on for a thousand, and you have the wrong idea about the South," she said. "The coloreds don't want to associate with the whites, and that's why they have their own drinking fountains and waiting rooms. This is the gospel according to Mr. Simmonds. And you have a visitor."

After a moment of twirling knobs and slamming of a safe door, Brass returned to the outer office. "Who?" he asked. "And where is he?"

"Mr. 'Just call me Pearly' Gates. There are, apparently, a few names he wants to call you. He's out having a bowl of soup at Danny's. He hasn't eaten all day, he's so upset, so I sent him over there. He'll be back any time now."

"Upset about what?"

"I'll let him tell you. You'll be amused."

"Hmph," Brass said, and retreated to his office.

I gave Gloria a rundown of our day so far, and she was properly impressed. "Goodness," she said, "Mr. B. has pulled all kinds of stunts since I've been here, but that's a new one; an intermediary in a blackmail payoff to conceal the attempted bribery of a city official."

"I hadn't thought of it that way," I said.

"That has long been one of my functions," Gloria told me. "To make sure that the boss is aware of just what it is that he's doing when he gets involved in some of his little projects. He tends to get overenthusiastic."

The office door opened and an angry and determined Pearly Gates bulled his way through, swinging his ten-gallon hat belligerently in front of him to sweep any resisting molecules of air out of the way. He stopped in front of me and clamped the hat back on his head. "You're back!" he bellowed. "And it's about goddamn time!"

"Sorry," I said. "Did you have an appointment?"

"Don't fuss around with me, son, I'm not in the mood. Where's your boss?"

"I'll tell him you're here," I said. "Have a seat."

He glared at me. "Don't you tell me what to do!"

I left him standing there glaring at the space I had occupied, and went back to Brass's office. "Pearly's here," I said, "and he's pawing at the ground and breathing fire."

Brass took a deep breath and shook his head. "I wonder what this is about," he said. "Here—" He fished in the bottom right-hand drawer of his desk and tossed me a leather sack that looked like an oversized sausage. "It's a homemade blackjack I took away from a fellow once. Come back in with Pearly and stand somewhere close to him. If he looks like he's about to draw his six-shooter, let him have it on the back of his head: once, not too hard."

I turned to go retrieve Pearly, but there he was, stomping down the hall on his own. I barely had time to stick the cosh in my belt under my jacket as he stormed into the room. "You didn't want me to hire a private detective, did you, Mr. Brass?" he thundered, making it sound like a hanging offense. He advanced to the desk and set his hands on it, palms down, the better to lean across the desk and glare at Brass. "You were afraid of what I'd find out, weren't you, Mr. Brass? You didn't tell me the truth, did you, Mr. Brass?" Each time he said "Mr." he spat it out as though he couldn't stand the taste in his mouth.

Brass moved back in his chair to put a little distance between himself and the angry Texan. "Sit down, Mr. Gates," he said, speaking calmly, clearly, and precisely, spacing his words so that each hung separately in the air; a sign that he was getting pretty annoyed himself. "I don't know what you're talking about, and I'd like to. Sit down, calm down, slow down, and elucidate."

Gates breathed hard for a minute, like a bull waiting for the right moment to charge, and then he abruptly dropped into the chair beside the desk. "I do not like being gulled and hoodwinked, Mr. Brass," he said, panting to catch his breath.

"Nor do I, Mr. Gates," Brass told him. "Now, what's the story? Who is gulling you, how, and why?"

"You trying to pretend you don't know? You must think I'm pretty damn dumb!" Gates snapped.

Brass stared at the beefy, angular Texan. "Just what is it that you are accusing me of?" he asked flatly. "Assume, for the sake of argument, that I don't know."

"You advised me not to hire myself a private detective to look for Phillippa. Now don't say you didn't!"

"I did so advise you," Brass said.

"You admit it!"

"I declare it. So what?"

"Well, then, you're part of the goddamn scheme, aren't you? You didn't think I'd hire myself a private eye, but I did, and now I know everything, and you might think you're going to get away with this but you're not." He was talking along there pretty fast for a Texan; just a little more acceleration and he'd be about where a New Yorker is when he's talking normally. But Pearly made up in intensity what he lacked in speed. He leaned forward on the desk, his elbows jutting out to the sides. "I ought to just call the police, or maybe I ought to just whale the daylights out of you myself!" He reached under his jacket, and I sidled closer with the cosh; but he was just going for a wad of folded-up papers in his inside pocket. He picked one stapled together set out of the wad and unfolded it and sort of hurled it the six inches over to Brass.

"There's the report from that there private detective agency that you didn't want me to hire," Pearly said. "It's their preliminary report. You hear that? *Pre-lim-in-ary.* That means there's more stuff coming."

Brass took the report and smoothed it out on his desk blotter. I leaned over to get a look at it. J. J. WINTERBOTHAM DETECTIVE AGENCY, read the letterhead, WE NEVER SLEEP. OFFICES IN MOST MAJOR CITIES & MIAMI.

Pearly continued to glare at Brass, as Brass read the document. There were three pages. I was reading it upside-down and at an angle, so I couldn't make out much of the typewritten text. Finally Brass looked up. "I hope you didn't pay much for this document," he said.

Gates scowled. "Why? What's the matter with it?"

"It's superficial, biased, and inaccurate."

"It's wrong? Is that what you claim?" Pearly grabbed the report and held it above his head as though it was a football and he was contemplating a forward pass. "Well, it ain't!"

"Not entirely," Brass admitted.

"My Filly is a confidence trickster-and her name ain't even Phillippa!"

"That's true," Brass said.

"So, you admit it!" Gates plopped the report back down on the desk.

"It's not a question of admitting anything," Brass replied. "I thought it was Mary's job to tell you, not mine. If she preferred to give you a—ah—gentler version of what 'Two-Headed Mary' stood for, why should I have interfered? The question between us, you and I, was what happened to her and where she was, not what her past had been."

"It says here on this paper, which I paid fifty dollars for if you want to know," Gates said, thumping his index finger on the report, "that the woman known as Two-Headed Mary—and the Winterbotham people couldn't find out her real name but that it's not Phillippa—stands in front of theaters and bilks people of their money. That she really lives in Greenwich Village, not on Park Avenue at all. That she has a daughter who's most probably in jail." With each "that" he prodded the document again with his finger.

"And it says here," he added, picking the report up and shaking it in Brass's face and then slamming it down again, "right here in black and white, that she has told so many versions of her past history that it's impossible to find out which is the true one." Gates picked the report up between thumb and forefinger and turned it over so he would no longer have to look at its hateful message.

"Is that all?" Brass asked calmly.

"All? All?" Pearly Gates collapsed in his chair, beyond words.

"So Two-Headed Mary runs a small scam," Brass said. "I can't see what you're so upset about. So she didn't tell you. Did you tell her about the Ten Spot Oil Exploration Syndicate? Or the Grand Lacey Oil Company? Or the Mount Feather Oil Well Company?"

There was an extended silence, and then Gates lifted his head. "Where'd you get that guff?" he asked, a slight growl in his voice.

"Reporters love to tell stories," Brass said. "Especially stories they can't use in their paper. Sid Moscowitz of the *Dallas Morning News* knows all about you. He's just hoping he can prove enough of it to use it some day."

"That sonabitch!"

"The only difference between you and Mary, as I see it," Brass told him, "is that you've made a great deal more money at cheating people out of their nickels and dimes than she has."

Pearly sat up, his face red. "I ain't never done nothing illegal," he growled, losing his grammar. "And anybody what says I did is a lying sonabitch."

"You mean you've never been caught," Brass said. "Well, neither has Mary."

"Each of them companies was perfectly legal and above-board."

"And the fact that they all came up with dry holes, and the producing wells were somehow all assigned to the Mariposa Oil Company, which you own all by yourself—"

"Goddamn bad luck."

Brass shook his head sadly. "Listen, Pearly, I have no interest in showing your less-than-honorable side to the world. Why can't you give Mary a little slack—at least until she shows up and is able to tell it her way?"

Gates slammed his open hand down on the desk. "Cause she's trying to con me, is why! And I ain't gonna sit here and be conned! And as far as I can see, you're part of it!"

"What are you talking about?"

Pearly fished back in his pocket for more papers and drew one out. "You don't know nothing about this?" he asked in an inquisitorial growl, attempting to fling it across the desk. It fluttered to the floor and Pearly had to bend down to retrieve it, which ruined a fine dramatic moment for him.

Brass took the paper and stared at it for a long moment. Then, without a word, he passed it to me.

It was typewritten. Three lines:

```
If you want to see your wife again
Get together $10,000 in small bills
We will inform you where to deliver the money
```

"When did you get this?" Brass asked.

Gates set his face in an angry grimace. "You going to sit there and pretend that you don't know?"

Brass stood up behind his desk. "It sounds like you're accusing me of something, Mr. Gates. Be precise. Exactly what is it that you think I've done?" he asked in the calm, measured voice he used when he was exceptionally furious. "Kidnapping or extortion?"

"You don't think that I think this is a real kidnapping, do you?" Gates asked. "You can't continue to pretend that this note is real now that I know?"

"What do you know?"

Pearly started to blurt out something, but then he paused and took a deep breath. "Two-Headed Mary, the woman I knew as Philippa, is a confidence trickster," he began.

"That might be so," Brass acknowledged.

"And you knew it when I came up here last week."

"That is so."

Pearly thrust his chin forward. "So this whole thing is a confidence trick, and you two are in it together!"

"Really? And just what would my part in it be?"

"For one thing you told me not to go to a private detective, that's what."

Brass leaned on his desk, his face inches away from Gates's. "And how did we cleverly plan that you were going to come see me?"

"You know, that piece in the paper—"

"That piece in two hundred and six papers in the United States and Canada? I must have wanted to con you pretty badly. And all that for a cut of ten thousand dollars? What do you suppose my share will be? How many people do you figure are in on this con, Mr. Gates? All of Greater New York, or is it merely Manhattan? Or perhaps just the theater district? They all know Two-Headed Mary's story, and delight in telling it to passersby. Or so I am told."

Brass sat back down, and Pearly stared at him for a long time. Or at least he stared in his direction, what he was seeing, I don't know. "What about the money?" he said finally.

"What money?"

"The ten thousand. What about that?"

"Someone's attempting to extort money from you. Mary is missing. Possibly she has been kidnapped. If so, the note may be from the kidnapper, or it may be from someone who knows she's missing and is trying to pull a fast one. But I'm reasonably sure that it's not from Mary, which is what you obviously suspect."

"And you're not involved?"

"My word of honor."

Gates leaned forward. "Then why did they tell me to deliver the money to you?"

This time the silence was palpable. You could have touched it, molded it, cut it with a knife. I looked at Brass; Brass looked at me. "There's a certain pattern developing here," Brass said, "that I'm not sure I like."

"How's that?" I asked.

"Crooks using me as a go-between. Once that gets started, no telling where it will end. Winchell seems to enjoy that sort of thing, but I don't." He turned to Pearly. "You said 'they.' Who are 'they'?"

"The kidnappers or whatever. They called me at the hotel. Said if I wanted to get my Filly back I should give you the ten thousand dollars in small bills."

"You keep saying 'they.' Was there more than one?"

"Well, there was just one fellow on the phone, but the note says 'we,' don't it?"

"Whoever it is just wants you to think there's a gang. That last line, 'we will inform you where to deliver the money,' that was cribbed from the Lindbergh baby kidnap note."

Pearly thought that over for a moment. "You think it was the same guy that did that one? But Bruno Hauptmann is in prison."

"Whoever else it is that sent this note, it's not the kidnapper of the Lindbergh baby, whoever that really was," Brass said. "There's an outside chance the Lindbergh kidnapper really was Hauptmann, but they never proved it. But this isn't related. I think it's someone with a strange sense of humor."

"This whole deal is pretty strange," Pearly said. "I guess I really never thought it was you, but I ain't never come across nothing like this before."

"Tell me about it," Brass said.

"Tell you what?"

"Everything you can think of that might relate. How you got the note, how they got in touch with you, everything."

"The message you're looking at came this morning," Pearly said. "Stuck in my mailbox in the hotel. No envelope or nothing, just the paper folded up. It was there when I came down for breakfast. I don't like eating in my room, so I always come down to the dining room for breakfast. Then after breakfast, when I went to my room, the phone rang. A man's voice said, 'Have you got the money?' I said not yet but I can get it real quick, and some stuff about is my Filly all right and can I talk to her and like that. And he said, 'Get the ten thousand and give it to Alexander Brass. We'll tell him how to deliver it. Then you'll get your Filly back.'"

"That's it?" Brass asked.

"Then he hung up. It was right then that the Winterbotham man came to my room with the report. I tell you, that floored me. I thought the whole thing was a con. Then I thought maybe it was serious. I had all kind of thoughts. Maybe her meeting me and everything was a con from the beginning. Maybe she just married me for my money, you know. People do that. But she had this great apartment and everything. I didn't know what to think. I still don't."

"What are you going to do?" Brass asked.

"Hell, I don't know. What should I do?"

"I can tell you this," Brass said. "She married you because she cared about you. It wasn't a con."

Pearly looked at him intently. "You sure about that?"

"That's the way I hear it." Brass said. "Morgan, you heard the Professor. What do you think?"

"Who's this Professor?" Pearly asked.

"A man she used to work with," I told him. "Lives in the same building she does on Park Avenue."

"Oh,"he said. "Were they—"

"Just business partners, no more," I said.

"Oh," he said.

"She told him she loves you," I said.

"Oh," he said.

"I guess I should tell you," Brass said to Pearly. "Her daughter heard from her recently."

"Daughter?" Pearly repeated.

"Yes. She's not in prison, she's never been in prison. She's an actress currently in a Broadway show, and a damn good one."

"Oh." Pearly thought that over for a second. "What did my Filly have to say?"

"It was over the telephone. She sounded like she was being held captive. I think she may be in great danger."

"So her daughter's an actress," Pearly said. "Must be a cute little thing." He dug into his jacket pocket and came out with two thickly stuffed envelopes held together with rubber bands. "Here," he said.

"What's this?"

"It's ten thousand dollars in small bills."

Brass took the envelopes and held them in both hands as though he were weighing them. "I should tell you that I'm not sure paying this will do any good."

"It couldn't hurt," Pearly said.

18

Pearly was now convinced that we were fighting on the side of truth and justice, and he wanted to stay and back us up, "with fists or guns, as the occasion warrants," but Brass convinced him to go back to the hotel and await developments. After Pearly left, I went back to the cubicle that I call an office and pretended to work, but I was waiting for the phone to ring. Gloria was at her desk, copyediting tomorrow's column, but I warrant she also was waiting for the phone to ring. Brass pretended to read some of the out-of-town newspapers he had delivered every day, but if you ask me he, too, was waiting for the phone to ring. It did ring several times, but none of the calls was from a strange man telling us where to bring twenty thousand dollars. Once I went into Brass's office to suggest to him that it might be two separate sets of crooks, and he snorted. "Always glad to amuse you," I said, and stalked back to my hovel.

About six o'clock he called Gloria and me into his office. There was a pad of lined yellow paper on the desk by his side, and the desk top was littered with sheets of the yellow paper on which he had drawn intricate designs along with clusters of indecipherable words. He had been thinking.

"I've been pulled into the middle of this," he told us. "And I don't like it. If it wasn't that, if I'm right, Two-Headed Mary is alive only at the sufferance of a man who has lost all sense of reason and who is going around killing women, I'd turn the whole thing over to Inspector Raab right now. The next move is his, we have to wait for his call, but there are some loose ends we can clear up while we're waiting."

"You know what's behind all this?" I asked.

"I have a good idea of who, and I believe I know some of the why, but not all—not enough. And I don't yet know what to do about it."

"Who is it?" I asked.

"That will await events," Brass told me. "You'll know soon enough."

"I don't even know what I don't know," I said. "Two women disappear, two other women are murdered, and three of them know each other, sort of, and the fourth is a fortune-teller."

"Astrologist," Brass corrected.

"Yeah, whatever," I said. "If she could tell the future, how come she didn't know enough to stay away from whoever killed her?"

Brass shrugged. "If astrology worked," he said, "we could cut the police department down to four strong men and an astrologer to tell them who to arrest. If the occult forces were reliably available to anyone, the world would wear a different face. But, unfortunately, spiritualism, astrology, palmistry, tarot card reading, and all the other myriad forms of necromancy must be lumped together as, at best, unproven, and their practitioners as nans, poseurs, charlatans, or bunco artists."

"You must admit," Gloria said, "that the notion that someone with the Talent-with-a-capital-T can stare at your palm or read your tea leaves and tell your past, present, and future has a certain appeal."

"True," Brass admitted. "But if they know not whereof they speak, they can do a deal of harm. Remember when Glendower proclaims 'I can call spirits from the vasty deep,' Hotspur replies 'Why so can I, or so can any man; but will they come when you do call for them?'"

Gloria nodded. *"Henry the Fourth."*

"Will they come when you call them? That's the question people forget to ask," I said.

"People believe what they need to believe," Brass said. "There'll always be someone out there pitching an easy way to solve all your problems, and a growing crowd of people to listen to the pitch."

The phone rang. I won't say that Brass leaped to answer it, but it was picked up well before the first ring had ceased. "Brass," he said.

"What?" he said.

"Right now?" he asked.

"Oh, all right, come on over," he said. He hung up.

"Company?" I asked brightly.

"Inspector Raab," he said. "He wants to compare notes. He'll be here in fifteen minutes. Why he thinks I have any notes worthy of comparison, I don't know. Let me get you two started while I decide what to tell him." Brass turned to Gloria. "I have a trip in mind for you."

"That's why I love this job," Gloria said. "To what strange and exotic port of call are you sending me?"

"Baltimore," Brass told her.

"My dreams are answered!"

"You're going to talk to Jemmy Brookes."

"The letter writer."

"That's right. Tell her you're a sob sister for the *World* and you're doing a story on Billie Trask, and you're interviewing people back home who know her. You want to know what kind of a girl Billie is, and whether Jemmy thinks she could have stolen the money. Of course she won't think so. See if you can get a look at the letters Billie wrote her. Find out all you can about the boyfriend."

"Right," Gloria said.

"Can you go this evening?"

"I'll go home and pack a bag."

Brass swiveled his chair to look at me. "Your journey is shorter." He pulled his yellow pad over and wrote "Lane & Vulpone" on it, ripped the bit with the writing off, and handed it to me. "Go see Schiff in the morgue and see if he has anything on them or their act. I want a picture if possible. Also see if Schiff has a file on Dr. Pangell, recently of Quogue, Long Island, and check the bunco files for the past history of Madam Florintina." The morgue Brass referred to was the *New York World*'s research department, a vast file room taking up most of the sixth floor, repository of carefully indexed dead stories.

"Okay," I said. "If I draw a blank on Lane and Vulpone, you

want me to try theatrical agents?"

"Good idea," Brass told me.

I went down to the sixth floor and explained my needs to Michael Fredric Schiff, the man who, along with his banks of file cabinets, was the memory of the *New York World*. Schiff disappeared among his files for about fifteen minutes and came back with a photograph and a folder.

The photograph was an 8-x-10 glossy of Foxy Vulpone and a tall, brassy blond. They were posed side by side in mid-step of what seemed to be a shuffle off to the right. He wore top hat and tails, and was holding a cane in both hands. She wore not much of anything, decorated with feathers, and black net stockings and very high-heeled shoes, and had her hands over her head to express the sheer excitement of being alive. In the white margin under the picture it said LANE & VULPONE. On the back were two rubber stamps:

LIBERTY MANAGEMENT
SUITE 1010—810 BROADWAY
CHICKERING 4-6793

and

OPTRA PHOTO STUDIOS
SERVING THE PROFESSION
SINCE 1914
268 TENTH AVENUE—PE6-3926

"Very pretty," I said.

"I have nothing on the doctor," Schiff said. "At least, not under that name." In Schiff's world, people were constantly changing names, just to thwart his filing system. Schiff had a grudge against marriage, because the woman disappeared behind her husband's last name.

"Madam Florintina?" I asked.

"The story on her murder hasn't been filed yet," he said. "There's only one item." He opened the folder. The clipping was dated Monday, July 9, 1928. The headline was STARS RUSH TO

DEFENSE OF FAVORITE FORTUNE-TELLER. The text explained that Madam Florintina had been arrested on Saturday in her apartment on East fifty-fifth Street for bunco fortune-telling, and by Sunday morning she'd been bailed out by Ruth Etting, Eddie Cantor, and much of the cast of the *Ziegfeld Follies* who had shown up en masse at the jail. "I am not a fortune-teller, I am an astrologist," Madam avowed. "Fortune-tellers foretell the future; I give advice based on what the stars tell me." And the stars told the police to let Madam go. "I don't really go for this astrology stuff," Eddie Cantor explained, "but I don't see why she should be locked up for it."

And that was Madam Florintina's only appearance in the pages of the *New York World* until her body was found in a parked car. I copied the date and names into my notebook and thanked Schiff.

"What I'm here for," he said. "One to eleven every day but Monday."

When I got back upstairs Brass was gone. He had left me a note, tucked neatly into my typewriter roller: "If you have anything, leave it on my desk. I have a date. See you tomorrow."

I quickly typed my notes on Madam Florintina's brush with the law and put the typed page and the photo of Lane & Vulpone neatly centered on Brass's desk. Then I shrugged into my topcoat, grabbed my hat, and headed for the elevator.

It was still early, as such things are figured by we denizens of the night, so I thought I would head down to the Village, grab a bite of dinner perhaps at the White Horse, and hang out with my fellow writers and artists for a few hours.

I headed east toward the Eighth Avenue subway. As I reached the corner of Eighth Avenue and was turning downtown, I heard footsteps quicken behind me, and something hard and cold pushed into the small of my back.

"Stop walking. Stand where you are. Don't turn around," came the harsh whisper.

There were a couple of people in sight, about half a block away in various directions, but that was no help; none of them was paying attention to what was happening on the corner. I could yell. I could kick the guy behind me in the shins and run. I could drop and use a sweeping scissor kick to bring the man to the ground. Sure I could.

I had the impression that the voice was coming from below my ears, so my assailant was smaller than I. But a small man with a gun is still a man with a gun. I stopped where I was. I didn't turn around.

A gloved hand holding an envelope reached around me. "Take this!" the voice ordered. "Give it to your boss."

I took the envelope. It was a plain white business envelope with ALEXANDER BRASS printed on the front.

The man behind me suddenly hooked his leg around mine and pushed me violently forward from the shoulders. I flung my arms out and landed on the sidewalk on my palms and forearms and my left knee. My left elbow also seemed to be somehow involved in the landing.

I rolled to the side and sprang to my feet to chase the man, but two things interfered. First, he was a good half block away and sprinting like a champion, his raincoat flapping behind him. Second, my left leg didn't want to work and brought me back to the pavement.

I rose, slowly and painfully, retrieved the envelope from where it had fallen, and limped out into the street to hail a cab.

19

Brass's apartment was unoccupied when I got there, but the elevator man let me in. Sandra Lelane was presumably dancing across the stage at the Royal Theater, and Garrett was there guarding her from somewhere in the wings. Brass was out on what he said in the note was a date. I wondered whether he meant date as in appointment, or date as in young lady, flowers, dinner and dancing, and home for a nightcap. If so, I might not see him until very late. I checked over my bruises, and found myself basically undamaged, although my left knee was refusing to work properly and protested strongly when I made it do anything at all. I still hadn't had dinner, so I raided Brass's ice box and scrambled a couple of eggs and sliced some ham, and ate them at the kitchen table with a bagel and cream cheese and a glass of milk.

It's funny about letters. I had just been given what was certainly a note from our kidnapper-extortionist telling us what to do next and I wanted to open it and read it, but it was addressed to Brass, and so I didn't. I didn't think Brass would mind, and suppose there was something that had a time limit? But still, it was addressed to Brass, his name neatly printed on the front with what looked like a thick-lead pencil, and so I didn't open it.

I was asleep on the couch in the living room when the light was switched on and I heard Brass's voice. "What happened, DeWitt? Did your landlady finally find out your true profession and kick you out?"

"No," I said, struggling to open my eyes, "she doesn't know I work for a columnist, she still thinks I play piano in a whore house."

The three of them were standing together in the doorway, their overcoats still on. So Brass's date had been with Sandra Lelane. Well, I couldn't fault his taste, although it must have been a somber evening, what with Sandra still having no idea how her mother was or what was happening to her. And having Theodore Garrett as a chaperone would be enough to keep one sober in the best of times.

I swung my legs around and sat up. "We have a letter," I told Brass.

"What sort of letter?"

"Hand delivered," I said. I told him briefly how I had acquired the letter and handed it to him.

"You didn't get a good look at your assailant?" Brass asked.

"I got hardly any look at all," I told him. "By the time I got up he was halfway down the block and moving fast. I saw a flapping raincoat. I think it was black, but it might have been dark blue or brown or whatever."

Brass ripped open the envelope and removed a folded sheet of paper. "Typewritten," he said, unfolding it.

Sandra grabbed his arm. "What does it say?"

Brass read: "'Central Park Menagerie at noon. By the bison. You will be called.'"

"Many are called," Garrett intoned, "but few are chosen."

We ignored him. "Is that where you bring the money?" Sandra asked.

"I presume so," Brass said. "Notice the economy of language. It doesn't say 'Don't bring the police,' because he knows I can't do that anyway. It doesn't say 'Come alone,' probably because he doesn't care who comes along. It doesn't even say 'Bring the money,' that being taken for granted."

"I'm coming with you," Sandra said.

Brass thought it over for a second. "Why not?" he said.

"I'll go an hour ahead of time and scout in the bushes," Garrett said. "Find a place overlooking the location. See what's waiting for you. Watch whoever comes."

"Thank you, but I think not," Brass said. "It says 'You will be called.' And I believe there's a public phone booth on the path right by the bison enclosure, which is probably what our miscreant is referring to. Skulking in the bushes won't accomplish anything."

Garrett drew himself up, shoulders back. "I never skulk," he announced. "I scout, I explore, I investigate, I observe; I do not skulk."

"My apologies," Brass told him. "An ill-chosen word."

"Shall we make a plan?" I asked.

"We shall go to sleep," Brass said. "It's two-thirty in the morning. Plenty of time tomorrow, or make that later today, to make a plan. DeWitt, you might as well stay here, if you don't mind the couch. Clean garments can be supplied in the morning."

"Fine with me," I said. I lay back down. In ten minutes I was fast asleep. Sometime during the night someone, probably Garrett, covered me with a quilt.

At eight o'clock, Garrett shook me awake. "Here's a towel and a set of fresh underwear and socks," he said. "They ought to fit. Use the bathroom at the end of the hall. I'll have a shirt for you when you emerge. Breakfast in half an hour."

I followed instructions. The clothes fit reasonably well, although the shirt had one of those collars that fastens with a bar passing under the tie; much too fussy a style for me. I don't know where it came from, neither Brass nor Garrett ever wore such a thing. But borrowers can't be choosers. When I appeared in the dining room for breakfast Brass and Sandra had already arrived, Brass in a dark brown suit sans jacket, and Sandra well wrapped in what appeared to be one of Brass's more elegant bathrobes: a maroon job with scarlet satin collar and cuffs. We discussed possibilities over buckwheat pancakes and maple syrup.

It could be a trick, Brass noted, but it probably wasn't. Our kidnapper could be planning to hijack the money and give nothing in return, but it would take a gang to get the money away from all of us, and Brass said he doubted whether the malefactor we were dealing with had a gang on hand.

"We have to make sure that Mom is okay," Sandra said. "Don't just give him the money without making sure that Mom is okay, and that he's going to let her go!"

Brass looked at her thoughtfully, and then put his hand over hers. "He isn't," he said quietly.

Sandra stared at him. I stared at the two of them. "You must know something we don't," I said, breaking the silence.

"I could be wrong," Brass admitted, "but I don't think so."

"Tell me," Sandra said.

Brass paused to pick his words. "This attempt at ransom is a late development," he said. "Mary was not taken for a ransom, but because of something she knows, or something her abductor thinks she knows. And now it's clear that this is connected with the absence of Billie Trask. I refuse to believe that two separate bands of criminals have picked me to be the go-between in delivering payments for two distinct and unrelated events. But it is clear that the ransom demand for Mary is an afterthought. I might think it was an attempt at extortion by someone not actually involved in the abduction were it not for the evident connection with the missing bonds."

Sandra nodded. Brass must have filled her in on all that during their date.

"Therefore it would seem that the abductor has a strong reason for keeping Mary hidden, and I don't think he'll let her go if we pay him the money. If you hadn't heard from her, I would have thought she was already dead."

Sandra stood up and paced around the dining-room table, her fists clenched, and the lines in her face showing the tightness of the underlying muscles. Walking instead of crying, I thought. Holding in the tears.

"I'm sorry," Brass said. "I shouldn't have been so direct."

"No, no," Sandra said. "I'm glad you're telling me the truth. You think it's possible that Mom may have been killed since the phone call?"

"My God!" Brass said. "No! I am sorry. I should have realized. No, I'm sure she's still alive. The reasons her abductor had for keeping her alive in the first place, whatever they are, must still be good. But we're going to have to work to keep her that way, and to spring her from wherever she's being kept."

"How are we going to do that?" Sandra asked.

Yes, I thought. How?

"By being nimble and quick-thinking and fast on our feet," Brass said. "Our advantage is that he doesn't know how much we know."

"Just how much do we know?" I asked.

The phone rang.

We paused, and I could feel my heart pounding, while Garrett answered the instrument by the kitchen door. After a few seconds of conversation, Garrett waved the handpiece at Brass. "It's for you. Alan Shine."

"Shine? At quarter past nine in the morning?" Brass went over and took the phone. Sandra sat back down. I finished my pancakes and sipped at my coffee.

Brass returned to the table. "Shine's a crime reporter for the *World*," he told Sandra. "A man's body was found last night," he went on, emphasizing the word "man" so Sandra wouldn't have a chance to think what she would otherwise think. "News of it came in on the A.P. wire about half an hour ago. When Shine went up to the research department to see if there was anything in the files about the victim, there was nothing there. But Schiff, the man who runs the department, thought to remark that DeWitt was asking for information on the same man only yesterday. Shine wanted to know if we were going in for clairvoyance, asking for information on a dead man before the body was found."

"Doctor Pangell!" I said. "How did he die? Where was he found?"

"He was in a steamer trunk in the basement of his house in Quogue. He'd been dead for a while; they're not sure how long, but at least a week. A real estate salesman who was preparing the house for sale found him. There hasn't been an autopsy yet, but it looks like he was hit on the head with one of those blunt objects you hear so much about. The Quogue police say they've been watching the good doctor for some time. They suspect him of being one of those friends of the single girl that we hear so much about."

"An abortionist?" I asked.

"Or so they think. I think they're probably right."

"Who is—was—Doctor Pangell?" Sandra asked.

"He's the man who lived at Four-sixty-four Fenton Road. The address, we believe, that your mother wrote on that little note hidden in your stuffed animal."

"This is getting stranger and stranger," Sandra said.

"You've got my vote," I told her.

Brass was staring at the wall. "It gets easier, you know."

"What does?"

"Killing. It gets easier. You kill your first person and your heart is in your mouth. You've just murdered a fellow human being and surely God will punish you, and surely it will be written on your forehead for all to see and how can you get away with it for more than a few hours? And then the police don't arrest you as you step out of your car or off the bus, and there is no official knock on the door in the middle of the night, and your courage gathers.

"You've never killed before because you're afraid of the consequences, but the taking of a life doesn't bother you morally. You're one of those people who doesn't see other people as human beings but only as objects to be manipulated. Now that you see you can get away with it, it gets easier. People are stupid, anyway. You're so bright that they'll never catch you, never even suspect you. It's hard not to laugh in their faces as the police go around investigating these crimes. And, after all, each killing is a necessity. These people have to be eliminated to keep your secret."

"What secret?" I asked.

"Ah," Brass said, wiggling a finger at me, "that would be telling." He turned to Sandra. "The Professor," he said, "do you have his phone number?"

She nodded. "I do."

"Call him. Ask him to come join us."

"Now?"

"If possible."

"All right. I don't know whether he'll be up yet, but I'll give it a shot." Sandra went to the phone.

"He'll be right over," she said, coming back to the table. "And he didn't even ask why."

"Good," Brass said.

"But I will." She came over to Brass's chair and stared down at him. "Why?"

"Because I've decided that you need an Uncle Andrew."

"Oh," she said. "Why?"

"I have a theory," he told her. "And a sort of a plan."

"Let's hear it."

"Wait until the Professor gets here. Then we can all go over it together."

The Professor walked into the dining room twenty minutes after he was called. Sandra had retired to her bedroom to get dressed, and she rejoined us when the Professor came in.

"What's the pitch?" the Professor asked, settling into the chair across from Brass by the head of the table and accepting a cup of coffee from Garrett. "Lucille tells me you need me to get her mom out of a jam. I figure I owe Amber a little something over the years, so here I am."

"Let's stick to one set of names," Brass suggested, "it's less confusing."

"I like 'Lucille' better than 'Sandra,' the Professor said. "But then I've always been something of a traditionalist. So 'Mary' and 'Sandra' it is then. Hello, Sandra. Now, what's the pitch?"

"Mary has been kidnapped," Brass told him. "We need the help of someone bright and quick-witted to help try to keep her alive until we can find her. So here you are."

"You want some buckwheat pancakes?" Garrett asked. "I still have some batter left."

"I never eat before lunch," the Professor told him. "But a jigger of cognac in this coffee would be welcome."

Garrett produced a bottle of Martell and the professor held out his cup. Then he turned back to Brass. "Just what is it you want me to do?"

"You are to be Sandra's Uncle Andrew."

"Mary's brother?"

"Presumably."

"Fine. Why?"

Brass poured himself another cup of coffee and told the Professor what had happened, and what was about to happen by the bison enclosure in the Menagerie.

The Professor listened closely, and nodded thoughtfully when Brass finished the tale. "Do you have any idea of who's doing this?" he asked.

"A very good idea."

"Who?" the Professor asked. "And why?"

Brass thought for a second and then sort of nodded to himself. "It's time," he said. "Mind you, I have no proof to take to a jury, or even to the police, but I'm certain I'm right."

"One person is doing all of this?" Sandra asked. "Killing people and holding my mother and demanding money and everything?"

"Even so," Brass told her.

Sandra took a deep breath. "Who?"

"Our kidnapper and killer is almost certainly K. Jeffrey Welton." Brass paused for a second and looked at each of us. "As to why, that's complicated, but I think I have most of it figured out."

Sandra started to say something, but then closed her mouth and just stared. Garrett and I just tried to look impassively wise.

"The kid producer?" the Professor asked.

"Himself."

"You pretty sure of this? What makes you think so?"

"As I said, I don't have enough to have him arrested. At the moment if I were to accuse him of anything in print, he could sue me for libel. But with your help, we're going to fix that."

"Yes, but why him?"

"You don't have to convince a jury," I told Brass. "Just convince us."

"I wondered about him from the day he came to the office to tell us about the reward," Brass said. "He was just too interested. But that didn't prove anything. If curiosity were a sin, then the ferry across the Styx would carry boatloads of journalists. Which it may anyway, if you consider—"

"No digressions," Sandra told him. "On with the story."

"Right. I became convinced it was him when we went to his office to talk to him and his brother, Edward. It was two things: Foxy and the note."

"Yes?"

"Foxy fit the description of the man who accompanied the woman when Mary's apartment in Brooklyn was searched." Brass turned to me. "Did you find a photograph of the team?"

"Yes," I told him. "It's on your desk at the office."

"Is his partner a tall blond?"

"That's right."

"What about the note?" Sandra asked.

Brass closed his eyes. "'I have your bonds,'" he recited. "'Give ten thousand dollars to Alexander Brass—used money—he will be told where to go.'"

"Signed 'Criminal at Large'," I added.

Brass nodded. "He didn't think it through," he said. "There's no backup allowed for."

"What sort of backup?" Sandra asked.

The Professor nodded. "I see what you mean. Suppose you had turned it down?" he asked. "Refused to play? There's no provision for that."

"Anyone who didn't know he was going to be there when the offer was made to me would have wanted to make sure that I'd take the job, or that he'd know right away if I turned it down," Brass said. "The note would have said 'Have Brass mention Mary's name in his column if he accepts' or 'Put red stripe across poster outside theater' or something. K. Jeffrey didn't think of that because he'd be there when the offer was made. He was confident of his own persuasive ability, and besides, he would know immediately if I turned it down anyway, and he could make other plans. Someone who wasn't there couldn't."

"Why did he want to use you in the first place?" Sandra asked.

"I can't be sure, but probably because he was stealing from his own brother. He wanted somebody in the middle, between them."

"So if he was the thief, what happened to Billie Trask, and why the reward?" I asked.

"Why not offer a reward that he knew he'd never have to pay?" Brass asked. "I'm afraid that Billie Trask is dead."

"He killed that sweet girl?" Sandra asked.

"Probably not," Brass said. "My guess is that a botched abortion killed Billie."

"Doctor Pangell!" I said.

"Right. The scenario, as I see it, is that K. Jeffrey was Billie's secret lover. Remember the way that letter from her friend Jemmy was phrased? 'He sounds like a big boy who's had a lot more practice with girls like you than you have with guys like him.' That sounds like an older man. If it was a stage-door romance the other girls would know about it. But K. Jeffrey could insist that the affair be kept quiet for all sorts of seemingly logical reasons. My guess is that he got her pregnant, which is why she left the chorus and was moved to the front office. He couldn't possibly marry her. What would the family think? He'd be disowned.

So he arranged with Doctor Pangell for an abortion. Whether the doctor performed that service regularly or whether he was obliging Welton is something we'll have to find out. The abortion went bad, and the girl died. I wouldn't be surprised if we find her body somewhere on the grounds around Pangell's house."

"And Welton killed Pangell in a fit of rage," I suggested.

"Probably Pangell tried to blackmail Welton. That's the problem with being thought to be rich, people see you as a source of large sums of money."

"How could Pangell blackmail Welton if he performed an abortion? He couldn't tell anyone?"

"Well, one possibility is that he would claim that Welton brought the girl to him after Welton tried and botched the abortion himself. That may even be what happened."

"And ever since then," Sandra suggested, "he's been killing people to cover up that first murder."

"That's it. Lydia, the roommate, must have known who Billie was dating; may even have known she was pregnant. Whether she threatened to tell, or made the mistake of assuring K. Jeffrey that she wouldn't tell, she was a threat. And one of the girls must have consulted Madam Florintina the astrologist."

"But what about the robbery?"

"Ah!" Brass said. "The robbery gave Welton an alibi: Billie Trask isn't dead, she has run off with the box-office receipts."

"But what about his brother's bonds?"

"It was too good an opportunity to miss. A chance to score on his brother and to pick up a little extra cash to keep his show running."

"I thought it was a hit," Sandra said.

"That's what he wants you to think. Welton's been papering the house. If he can keep the show running for, oh, say two hundred performances, it'll look enough like a hit to convince his family that he's a success and, coincidentally, to convince future backers that he's a producer who can make hits."

"Why did he kidnap Mom?" Sandra asked.

"Because she knows, or he thinks she knows, the truth."

"Then why not just kill her?"

"I think I have that figured out. She has him convinced that your 'Uncle Andrew' shares that knowledge with her, or possibly has a letter from her to open if she disappears. Something like that. He has to keep her alive until he can deal with 'Uncle Andrew.'"

We thought this over. "You're doing a lot of guessing in there," the Professor said.

"True," Brass admitted. "But it all hangs together."

"It sounds to me like you have a gut feeling that this guy did it, and you're pulling in all these reasons to show why you might be right."

Brass considered that. "You might be right," he said. "It did start with what you call a gut feeling."

"Well," the Professor said. "I've learned to trust gut feelings. What do we do now?"

"We go to the Central Park Menagerie and visit the bison," Brass told him. "If I'm right, we'll find out soon enough. If I'm wrong, well, we'll find that out, too. Either way we have a good shot at catching a killer."

"How?"

"I can't give you an exact plan, that will have to await the event. But here's what we have to do…"

20

The day was bleak and dreary, with a dark sky overcast with hints of impending drizzle. The gray of the apartment buildings blended into the gray of the horizon, until it all seemed equally distant and equally dismal. We entered Central Park at 59th and Sixth and walked the curved pathways east to the Menagerie. It was a few minutes before noon when we reached the path that fronted the bison enclosure.

Brass and Sandra and the Professor and I walked in a tight group, presenting a solid front against the unknown. Garrett was about a hundred paces behind, so that he could keep us all in view and see whether anyone we passed was taking an undue interest in us. What he intended to do to such a person, I have no idea, but it was somehow comforting to know there was someone guarding our backs.

The path fronting the bison enclosure ran north-south. The phone booth was on the right side of the enclosure, where a second path forked off to the east. We stood around the booth for less than a minute before the phone rang.

Brass answered with a cautious "Hello?"

"Yes, this is he… I have the money with me… Wait a second, there is one thing… Yes I can make terms, if you want the money… Mary's daughter is with me, and her brother, Andrew. They need proof that Mary is alive and well before we pay you… Hold on, Andrew wants to talk to you."

Brass passed the phone to the Professor, who took a deep breath and began: "Hello?... This is Andrew Cuttingham. I won't ask who you are... Yes I am... Amber Bain, the woman you know as Mary, is my sister... Well, if you want the money I need to know that she is all right... I'm not going to mention any names, sir, but I know who you are and what you have done... Yes, I read the letter. I read it and burned it, so it is all in my head now. I have not told anyone of its contents. I will endeavor to keep your secret if and when you release my sister... You have my word that neither of us will reveal what we know if you release her... If you can prove to me that she is all right, and can guarantee that you will release her, I will personally double the payment... That's right... I am Andrew Cuttingham of Cuttingham Basil and Brand, Two-twenty-six Broad Street. Everyone knows that my word is my bond, sir."

The Professor stood silent for a long moment, and then hung up the phone. "He disconnected," he said.

"Well?" Brass said.

"You were right, Mary evidently told him she had given me— Uncle Andrew—some kind of letter. He said he'll think it over and get in touch with us. He sounded annoyed."

"Did he say anything about my mother?" Sandra asked.

"He said he wasn't prepared to bring her to a phone, but he'd have her with him next time."

"Do you think she's still all right?" Sandra asked.

The Professor patted Sandra on the shoulder. "I'm sure she's okay."

"The question is," Brass said, "did he take the bait? Is he going to believe that you burned the letter?"

"Let's hope so," the Professor said. "In his arrogance, and his belief that no one else is as smart as he is, I think he'll buy it. Is he going to try to kill me? I'd bet on it."

"I thought you were going to give him your home address," Brass said, "so we could stake it out."

"This is better," the Professor told him. "An active brokerage office with me sitting there in plain view. He won't be able to resist."

"Is that a real office address?" I asked.

"Well, not exactly," the Professor told me, "but it sure looks like one."

* * *

We left the park and took a taxi downtown. Two-twenty-six Broad Street was one of the imposing buildings built when it looked like the good times were going to go on forever, and there would never be any such thing as too much office space. It was probably much less than fully rented now, but in the ground-floor corner offices—which now called themselves Cuttingham Basil & Brand, Institutional Brokerage—there was no sign that there had ever been a crash.

"Well," Brass said as we got out of the cab and admired the gold-on-black sign over the doorway. "So this is the big store."

"The latest," the Professor told him. "Let me show you around." As we went through the door we were aware of a buzz of activity all around us. Telephones were ringing, teletype machines were typing, ticker-tape machines were ticking, a large black tote board across the back wall was registering constantly changing stock names and prices, and busy, well-trained people were engaged in their employment. The joint radiated competence, honesty, purposefulness, and a feeling of realized wealth. There were several well-dressed men and women who were certainly customers, a man in a chauffeur's uniform patiently waiting for his boss on a bench along the wall, and a Western Union delivery boy obviously waiting to pick up a return message.

"Like it?" the Professor asked.

"Where do I sign?" I asked.

Sandra did a slow pirouette. "It's perfect!" she breathed. "However did you manage?"

"The previous tenant left all the fixtures and equipment when he jumped out the window," the Professor said. "We just turned them back on and changed a few nameplates."

"He couldn't have jumped very far," I said. "We're on the ground floor."

The Professor smiled a weary smile. "I spoke metaphorically."

"Let's get on with it," Brass said. "No telling when he'll show up."

"Right." The Professor strode to the middle of the floor and clapped his hands. "Ladies and gents," he said. "Listen up! Here's the pitch."

The "office staff" and "customers," a group of about thirty people, gathered in a cluster around the Professor. He explained to them what we were doing, told them it was for Two-Headed Mary, and that it might be dangerous. He said that he'd pay them the day rate if they stayed, but there'd be no score today, and that if anyone wanted to leave he wouldn't blame them.

"What about the gent from Omaha?" someone asked.

"He probably won't be in until tomorrow. If he does come in today, we'll stall him. Percy can take him to dinner."

Everyone laughed. I guess every profession has its in jokes.

Nobody left. They all went back to their assumed jobs and took up where they'd left off, and if anyone could tell that the place wasn't a real, active brokerage office, he was sharper than I.

The Professor's big office desk was pulled out to an executive location in the main office, and a man with a little printing machine in a suitcase made a desk plaque that said

ANDREW CUTTINGHAM
PRESIDENT

in a thin line, modern script.

We weren't sure what Welton—if it was Welton—would attempt, except that his aim would be the demise of Uncle Andrew. We made sure the desk was out of view of the window, in case Welton was a marksman. Perhaps he'd come in to talk and bring a poisoned bottle of scotch. Perhaps he'd invite Uncle Andrew outside, where he could strangle him in privacy. Perhaps he'd stalk in and shoot and merely walk out in the confusion—a favorite of Mafia hit men.

We tried to plan for the various possibilities. We couldn't stop the action too soon; unless the killer actually made an attempt, we would have no proof to give the police. The desk was solid oak and had a well that the Professor could quickly dive into. Several brawny men were positioned nearby; one behind a strategically placed screen. And it would help that there were no real customers; anyone that came in that the crew didn't recognize was probably an enemy.

Brass and Sandra and I went to hide in a little office in the wall to the side of the Professor's desk. It was the original director's office of the defunct firm, and had a one-way glass window. As long as we kept the lights low, we could look out but no one could see in.

It was two hours before he showed up, and then we almost missed him until it was too late. Perhaps we were so cocky in knowing that it was all a stage setting, that we forgot that other people can play parts. He was dressed like a Western Union delivery boy, with freckles and black horn-rim glasses and a shock of red hair sticking out from under his Western Union cap. He sauntered in and sauntered toward Andrew Cuttingham's desk, and we thought nothing of it because we did have a phony Western Union boy in the crew. Our Western Union boy was out getting coffee, but we didn't realize that.

It was Brass who spotted him. "The shoes!" Brass yelled, "Patent leather!" And he was out of his seat and at the door in one dive. I scrambled behind, not sure where I was going or why, as Brass leaped for the desk.

The Western Union boy was pulling a revolver—one of those great big old long-barreled .44s—out of his belt as everything turned to slow motion, and I felt like I was charging through molasses, unable to move fast enough to grab him before he fired.

The Professor was under strict orders to dive under his desk, but he dove across it instead, his hands grabbing for the gun. There was a deafening *boom*, and a spurt of flame, and the Western Union boy was down, with Brass and two other, larger men on him, and the Professor was holding his hand to his chest and looking surprised, and the blood was spurting out from between his fingers.

The Western Union cap was pulled off, and the red wig, and the glasses, and lying there, under a coat of stage makeup and artfully applied freckles, was a quiescent K. Jeffrey Welton.

The Professor sat and said, "Goddamn!" Sandra was at his side, opening his vest, pulling off his bow tie, unbuttoning his shirt.

"You'll live," she told him, "you old idiot. But I'd better get a bandage around that."

21

I went into the men's room and pulled the roller towel from the wall and cut off the part that had been used. Sandra used the clean part to wrap the Professor's chest. The bullet had grazed the right side of his chest, but hadn't penetrated, and once he was wrapped and the blood had stopped flowing, the Professor insisted that he was fine. But Brass and Sandra both insisted that he go to the hospital by ambulance just in case, so he acquiesced. Two burly policemen appeared from somewhere and took charge of Welton. Brass stuck the revolver in a paper bag, and suggested that we take it and Welton right Uptown to Inspector Raab, and the cops agreed. Since they were without a squad car, we used the Professor's large black Lincoln Town Car, which was parked at the curb. Welton was completely silent for most of the ride, but as we pulled in front of the station house he broke out laughing.

"What's so damn funny?" one of the cops barked, and if he hadn't I would have, although I don't think I would have had as effective a bark.

"I was just picturing my brother Edward's face when he hears about this," K. Jeffrey said, and then he clammed up again.

Inspector Raab looked surprised for the first time since I've known him when we came through the squad room door with a handcuffed Welton in tow. "What's this?" he asked.

Brass explained, and handed Raab the revolver-filled paper bag.

"Very good, very good," Raab said. "It's okay, boys," he told the two precinct cops, "we'll take it from here." They saluted and left, and one of Raab's detectives escorted K. Jeffrey over to the holding cell.

"Where is Mary?" Brass demanded.

Welton smiled through the bars. "I have no idea what you're talking about," he said.

"You might as well tell us where she is," Raab said, "Make it easy on yourself."

Welton laughed. "Oh, come on, Inspector," he said. "What possible interest could I have in making it easy for you? In the fullness of time, I might have a few things to tell you about my brother, Edward, but about myself, nothing."

Raab growled.

"Foxy will know," Brass said. "And he might be interested in escaping an accessory to kidnapping and murder rap."

We left Welton smiling in his cell and headed to the theater. Foxy was behind the ticket window in the lobby. "Well, gentlemen?" he said as we approached. "Mr. Welton is not here yet."

"And he won't be," Raab said, reaching through the bars in the ticket window and grabbing Foxy by the collar, "but we can arrange for you to join him if you like!"

"What the hell—" Foxy reached up and tried to pry Raab's fingers loose. "What do you think you're doing?"

Raab let go. "You just stay there," he said. "We're coming around."

We entered the office and loomed over Foxy. When he understood what had happened, he gulped and sat down. "Murder?" he said. "The boss has been killing people? I didn't know, honest to God!"

"You and your wife searched an apartment in Brooklyn for him," Brass said. "And you tried to get into a Park Avenue apartment."

"Sure we did. They were addresses Welton found in Mary's handbag. So what? We didn't kill nobody."

"What the hell did you think was going on?"

"I thought he was manipulating things. K. Jeffrey is always manipulating things. Hell, the whole family is always manipulating things. Like when he got that girl pregnant, he moved her out of the chorus smooth as a greased rabbit."

"And then?" Brass asked.

"And then she ran off with his money. Serves him right, I told him, for leading the poor girl on when he had no intention of marrying her."

"You'd better stick to that story," Brass told him. "What about Two-Headed Mary?"

Foxy stayed belligerently silent.

"Talk!" Raab said. "You're looking at at least a decade in Sing Sing right now, you want to try for two?"

"Aw come on, Inspector," Foxy said. "I didn't do nothing. Whatever Welton did, he didn't ask for my help."

"Two-Headed Mary," Brass repeated.

Foxy considered. "Maybe I did hear some strange noises coming from downstairs," he said.

"Downstairs?"

"This place has three cellars, one below the other, that I know of. I've never been past the first cellar, but there might be something down there."

Raab took Foxy by the collar and pulled him out into the hall. "Let's go see!"

Foxy led the way, his patent leather shoes thumping the way down the wooden steps, insisting with each step that he'd never been down this far before, and that he had nothing to do with whatever we found down here, and that he hoped Two-Headed Mary was all right because, personally, he'd always liked the doll.

The first cellar was full of stored costumes and equipment and flats from shows that were long since defunct. The second cellar had a collection of empty booze bottles of various types and sizes that someone had collected during Prohibition, along with rolls of rubber tubing and coils of copper tubing and two big copper kettles.

The trapdoor to the third cellar was hidden under a couple of large boxes piled innocently near the far wall. When we moved the boxes we saw that the door had a bright and shiny new padlock on it. "I ain't got the key," Foxy whined. Brass found a length of iron pipe and snapped the hasp. We lifted the trap and clambered down the stairs. There was another door, a steel door this time, with a Yale lock. A spill of light showed from under the door.

"Mary!" Brass yelled. "Mary, are you in there? It's Alexander Brass!"

"It's about goddamn time!" Came a muffled soprano bellow from inside.

"Stand aside!" Raab ordered. "I'm going to shoot the locks."

"Wait a minute," Brass said. "That's a steel door. If you just smash the lock it might take a battering ram to open."

Raab paused. "Well then."

"Welton wouldn't want to carry the keys around with him," Brass said. "I'll bet they're around here somewhere."

We fished around the area for about a minute, getting our hands dirty, but didn't find a key.

"Don't hurry or anything," came the call from the other side of the door.

"We can't find the key," Brass called.

"Where's that son of a bitch Welton?" Mary called.

"He's under arrest."

"I've never in my life thought that I'd be pleased to hear those words about anyone," Mary called. "But by God it's good to hear that!"

Brass kept up his thumping and prodding at the wall, and finally one of the bricks jiggled slightly at his thump. He worked it back and forth until he could pull it out, and he peered into the space. "There's a cavity, but it's too dark to see anything," he said. He reached into the cavity. With a satisfied "Hah!" he pulled his hand out and brandished his find. "A key!" He fit it into the lock and, after a twist, the door swung open on well-oiled hinges.

The room inside was fitted out as a Spartan bedroom, with a bunk bed and beat-up wooden chair and table, an aged tin sink in one corner and a toilet behind a curtain in the other corner. There was also a small bookcase half-full of books and a reading lamp. Two-Headed Mary was standing to the left side of the door with a white terrycloth bathrobe clutched around her. "I warn you, I'm going to kiss everyone in sight when I come out," she said. "And then I'm going to have a good cry."

* * *

Two weeks later the excitement had died down, except in the New York papers, which were happily running stories like:

CHORINE REVEALS LOVE TRYST WITH KILLER PRODUCER

Startling Details of Love Nest Revealed

JEANETTE WINTERS, a dancer in *Fine and Dandy*, the long-running Broadway show starring Sandra Lelane, is the third girl to come forward and reveal that she has had a long-time relationship with producer K. Jeffrey Welton. The attractive, long-legged blonde described for this reporter the secret trysting place that...

We were gathered for breakfast that Monday morning in the Professor's Park Avenue apartment. The Professor had a bruised rib and had lost a fair amount of blood, but he was healing well, and as long as the wound didn't get infected, he'd recover with no problems. Mary and her Texan were sitting next to each other on the couch and holding hands, and it was a lovely sight to see.

Gloria had returned from Baltimore with a letter Billie Trask had written to her friend Jemmy that pretty much told the whole story. Men who are plotting evil should remember that most girls have one real close friend from whom they have few secrets. The facts, as related in Billie's letter, were pretty much what Brass had deduced. She had written it right before going with K. Jeffrey to visit Dr. Pangell and have her "condition" seen to. K. Jeffrey had promised to marry her in six months, but he told her that he couldn't do it now because his family would cut him off. When the show was running in the black, and he didn't need his family's money, they'd tie the knot and do it right. And Jemmy, Billie promised, would be maid of honor.

But Billie had been found a week ago under three feet of earth in Dr. Pangell's backyard; dead, as far as the post-mortem could tell, from exsanguination—Pangell had punctured something he shouldn't have, and they couldn't stop the bleeding.

Two-Headed Mary had been Billie's other confidant. She had gone to Mary for advice when K. Jeffrey insisted on the abortion. "I told her to have the kid and leave the creep," Mary told us. "I told her when she got involved with the creep that she was making a mistake, but she didn't listen. Girls in love don't listen to good advice; that's why there are so many little bastards running around." Mary had taken Pangell's name so she could look him up and make sure that at least he was a real doctor. "He was real," she said, "but he wasn't very good." She had stuck the scrap of paper with the doctor's address on it in her special hiding place so she wouldn't forget it. She didn't bother writing the name down—she already knew the name.

The operation had been scheduled for a Sunday. On Monday, Welton had announced that Billie had disappeared, along with the weekend's box-office receipts. Mary went to see Welton on Thesday to tell him that she knew something was wrong with his story, and he'd better produce Billie alive and well. And don't try anything silly, she had added, because she had deposited a tell-all letter with a friend, to be opened if anything happened to her.

K. Jeffrey's idea of not trying anything silly was to grab Mary and thrust her into a dungeon in the depths of his theater. He told her he wasn't going to kill her, just keep her imprisoned until he could figure out a safe way to let her go. What he was really trying to figure out was to whom she had given the incriminating letter. She kept herself alive by allowing him to slowly drag more and more information out of her about what she knew—which was very little, but she was a past master at instant improvisation—and who the friend with the letter was.

"He told me everything," Mary said, refilling her coffee cup from the large silver urn. "As it happened. He told me about killing Lydia, Billie's roommate. She knew about the abortion, which was a great shock to him, but she wasn't sure who Billie's seducer was. Her words: she called him 'Billie's seducer.' She told him that she knew that Billie couldn't have taken the money, and she was going to go to the police to clear Billie's name. So he waited for her in her room, and when she came home from a date he spent the rest of the night trying to talk her out of telling anybody. She wouldn't listen, so he killed her."

"And left her naked in the park?" I asked.

Mary nodded. "You should have seen him when he told me about it," she said. "He was so pleased with himself that he could hardly hold it in. It was about then I decided that he was probably going mad."

"At least he was getting used to killing," Brass said. "He must have killed the doctor already."

"I guess so," Mary said. "He carried the girl's body into the park about three o'clock in the morning, talking to it all the way so that if anybody overheard he would think they were lovers. Then he took her clothes off and left her there all neatly arranged, or so he said. When he got back to the theater he had the bright idea of taking a set of women's clothes from wardrobe and some identification from a purse that had been around for a couple of years and go back and plant it by the body."

"That's sick!" Pearly said.

"Was he trying to make it hard to identify her?" Brass asked.

"I think he was trying to be funny. He laughed a lot when he told me about it. I think that was another reason he kept me alive: he had to tell someone about his cleverness, and what better than the woman he was eventually going to leave entombed in the sub-subbasement of his theater. If he closed the trapdoor, nobody would even know that there was anything down there."

Gloria nodded. "Like that French story—*Phantom of the Opera*," she commented.

"Except that I wouldn't be sneaking around behind the scenes," Mary said. "I'd be starving to death thirty feet below ground."

"What about Madam Florintina?" Brass asked.

"She knew," Mary said. "Or, at least, K. Jeffrey became convinced that she knew. She came at him with a lot of crap about birth dates and sun signs and then said something about having done a chart for Billie, and that the child would have been born in Ares, and she could really use the reward money, and he figured he'd better kill her. So he did." Mary took a deep breath. "Which was when I realized that I had to do something more constructive than sit on my duff and wait to be rescued, or he'd kill off half of Broadway before he got stopped. So I called my lovely daughter."

"Isn't my little Filly something?" Pearly Gates asked proudly, squeezing her hand. "She just goes and upsets this maverick's whole scheme from that little tiny room, and she wasn't even scared."

"I was scared to death," Mary said. "But I wasn't going to let that son of a bitch see it."

"How'd you get him to let you make that phone call?" Sandra asked. "I was so damned relieved to hear your voice, and then so damned scared when you wouldn't tell me where you were and you hung up on me..."

"Well, I finally let him work the name of my 'friend' with the letter out of me. I told him it was my brother, Andrew, and that if I didn't call him once every two weeks—I would have made it once a week, but it was already more than a week since he had grabbed me—he was supposed to open the envelope and read the letter and take it to the police. I was going to call the Professor, who I knew would pick up on the tale I was telling and do something—I had no idea what—to get me out of there." She reached over and patted the professor's hand. "And so you did, my dear."

The Professor smiled. "We've been in tighter spots than that, old pal. Why I remember once in Cleveland—but that story will wait."

"But Welton thought he was wise, and he wouldn't let me call anyone but my daughter. Who, luckily, went to Alexander Brass for help." She turned to Brass, "That was a nice mention you gave me in your column, by the way. And thanks for not blowing the gaff."

"My pleasure," Brass told her.

"My little Filly ain't going to spend her time standing in front of theaters collecting for no war orphans no more," Pearly said. "I'm going to teach her the oil business. And I think she's probably going to teach me a thing or two while we're at it."

"I wouldn't be surprised," Brass said. He put his coffee cup down and leaned back in his chair. "You know, Professor," he said, "I'm sorry we queered your play with the big store operation, but I guess you'll find another location."

"What's wrong with the one I have?" the Professor asked. "I imagine the police have a lot more to ask Welton about besides the location of the place he was apprehended."

"But won't the two cops who took him into custody say something?" I asked.

The Professor smiled. "I doubt it," he told me. "They weren't exactly real cops. They sort of worked for me."

"Oh," I said. I refilled my coffee cup. Maybe I should write a book about a confidence man.

Or, then again, maybe not.

ACKNOWLEDGEMENTS

I would like to acknowledge the assistance of Bill Pronzini, Marcia Muller, Richard A. Lupoff, and Keith Kahla, who each in their own way contributed to the completion of this book.

ABOUT THE AUTHOR

Michael Kurland is the author of more than thirty books, but is perhaps best known for his series of novels starring Professor Moriarty. The first volume, *The Infernal Device*, was nominated for an Edgar Award and the American Book Award, and received stellar reviews, including this from Isaac Asimov: "Michael Kurland has made Moriarty more interesting than Doyle ever made Holmes." It was followed by *Death By Gaslight*, *The Great Game*, *The Empress of India* and *Who Thinks Evil*, published over a period of more than thirty years.

Kurland is also well known as a science fiction writer, and is the author of *The Unicorn Girl*, as well as the bestselling T*en Little Wizards* and *A Study in Sorcery*, fair-play detective stories set in a world where magic works. He has edited several Sherlock Holmes anthologies and written non-fiction titles such as *How to Solve a Murder: The Forensic Handbook*. He lives in California.

THE ANGEL OF HIGHGATE
VAUGHN ENTWISTLE

Lord Geoffrey Thraxton is notorious in Victorian society—a Byronesque rake with a reputation as the "wickedest man in London." After surviving a pistol duel, Thraxton boasts his contempt for death and insults the attending physician. It is a mistake he will regret, for Silas Garrette is a deranged sociopath and chloroform-addict whose mind was broken on the battlefields of Crimea. When Thraxton falls in love with a mysterious woman who haunts Highgate Cemetery by night, he unwittingly provides the murderous doctor with the perfect means to punish a man with no fear of death.

"Entwistle's prose is eloquent and evocative without sacrificing concision. His staging of Victorian London—its memorial parks, stately homes, fog-shrouded streets is cloaked in suspense, shown through an extensive use of detail and sensory imagery... A magnificently written, provocative novel." *Kirkus Reviews*

"Daringly original... Entwistle's cheerfully confident prose sparkles and unsettles by turns." *Historical Novel Society*

DUST AND DESIRE
A JOEL SORRELL NOVEL
CONRAD WILLIAMS

The Four-Year-Old, an extraordinary killer, has arrived in London, hell-bent on destruction... PI Joel Sorrell is approached by the mysterious Kara Geenan, who is desperate to find her missing brother. Joel takes on the case but almost immediately, an attempt his made on his life. The body count increases. And then Kara vanishes too... as those close to Joel are sucked into his nightmare, he realizes he must track down the killer if he is to halt a grisly masterplan – even if it means sacrificing his own life.

"A gritty and compelling story of the damned and the damaged; crackling with dark energy and razor-sharp dialogue. Conrad Williams is an exciting new voice in crime fiction." **Mark Billingham**

"Top quality crime writing from one of the best."
Paul Finch, bestselling author of *Stalkers*

"A beautifully written, pitch-black slice of London noir."
Steve Mosby, author of *The Nightmare Place*

"Dashed with humour and sly one-liners."
Stav Sherez, author of *The Devil's Playground*

SONATA FOR THE DEAD
A JOEL SORRELL NOVEL
CONRAD WILLIAMS

It's four months on from the events of *Dust and Desire*. Joel Sorrell has recovered from the injuries he sustained in his fight with The Four-Year-Old. A body has been found, sealed into the dead space behind a false wall in a flat in Muswell Hill. Beheaded and surrounded by bloodstained pages of typewritten text, it is the third such murder committed by a killer known as The Hack. And it may be linked to his daughter's disappearance.

PRAISE FOR THE AUTHOR

"Williams is so good at what he does that he probably shouldn't be allowed to do it anymore, for the sake of everyone's sanity." *Publishers Weekly* (starred review)

"Conrad Williams writes dark and powerful prose balancing the poetic and elegant with needle-sharp incision." *Guardian*

AVAILABLE JULY 2016

HACK
AN F.X. SHEPHERD NOVEL
KIERAN CROWLEY

It's a dog-eat-dog world at the infamous tabloid the *New York Mail*, where brand new pet columnist F.X. Shepherd finds himself on the trail of The Hacker, a serial killer who is targeting unpleasant celebrities. Bodies and suspects accumulate as Shepherd runs afoul of cutthroat office politics and Ginny Mac, a sexy reporter for a competing newspaper. But when Shepherd is contacted by the Hacker, he realizes he may be next on the list.

"*Hack* is a witty and incisive mystery set in the raucous world of tabloid journalism. Laugh out loud funny and suspenseful—it's like Jack Reacher meets Jack Black."
Rebecca Cantrell, *New York Times* bestselling author of *The Blood Gospel*

"A rollicking, sharp-witted crime novel." ***Kirkus Reviews***

"The man is a legend, a master of his craft, and *Hack* is a seamlessly flowing, imaginative translation of these realms, blended together in exciting, suspenseful and oftentimes hilariously moving prose that reads like a conversation while serving as engrossing fiction, compelling insight and eye-opening commentary. It's a joy to read and captures the imagination from the start." ***Long Island Press***

SHOOT

AN F.X. SHEPHERD NOVEL

KIERAN CROWLEY

F.X. Shepherd is juggling a new job as a PI, while keeping up with his strangely popular pet column. He is hired by a congressman who has received death threats, part of the escalating war between the Republican Party and Tea Party extremists. A series of murders of gun rights politicos at a presidential convention ratchets up the stakes, and Shepherd must fight off his liberal parents, do-anything-for-a-story reporter Jeannie Mac, and a gang of mysterious gunmen.

PRAISE FOR THE AUTHOR

"An in-depth investigation… truly appalling all around: a story seemingly without goodness, except in the telling." *Kirkus Reviews*

"A fast-paced account of the sordid circumstances surrounding the brutal October 2001 bludgeon murder of multimillionaire Ted Ammon." *Publishers Weekly*

AVAILABLE OCTOBER 2016